Suspicion of Murder

G.K. Parks

Copyright © 2014 G.K. Parks

A Modus Operandi imprint

All rights reserved.

ISBN: 0989195848
ISBN-13: 978-0-9891958-4-3

For my loyal readers, this one's for you.

BOOKS IN THE LIV DEMARCO SERIES:

Dangerous Stakes
Operation Stakeout
Unforeseen Danger
Deadly Dealings

BOOKS IN THE ALEXIS PARKER SERIES:

Outcomes and Perspective
Likely Suspects
The Warhol Incident
Mimicry of Banshees
Suspicion of Murder
Racing Through Darkness
Camels and Corpses
Lack of Jurisdiction
Dying for a Fix
Intended Target
Muffled Echoes
Crisis of Conscience
Misplaced Trust
Whitewashed Lies
On Tilt
Purview of Flashbulbs
The Long Game
Burning Embers
Thick Fog

BOOKS IN THE JULIAN MERCER SERIES:

Condemned
Betrayal
Subversion
Reparation
Retaliation

ONE

Tonight, even the steady patter of the rain couldn't lull me to sleep. I rolled over on my side and sighed deeply. Sleep was being elusive yet again as ghosts from the past continued to haunt me. Giving up, I focused on the ceiling and ran through the list of things I had to do in the morning. Martin's slow breathing shifted, and he opened his eyes and squinted through the darkness.

"You're still awake?" he asked.

"It's raining." It wasn't the rain keeping me up, but he didn't have to be a genius to realize it. He reached out and brushed his fingers against my arm, hoping I would welcome his affection. Instead, I turned away from him, beating my pillow into a preferable shape before settling down on the mattress. "Go back to sleep, we both have work in the morning."

"Alexis, what's wrong this time?" He flipped on the lamp and sat up in bed. Sometimes, the darkness was suffocating, but it wasn't the dark causing my insomnia. "We're at your place, the last few cases you've worked have been non-violent, and last time I checked, no one was gunning for either of us. Obviously, it isn't one of the usual suspects."

I had no idea how Martin could be this talkative at five a.m., but had I known, I would have just snuggled against him for the next hour, instead of being annoyed by the conversation.

"Turn off the light." Pulling the blankets to my chin, I waited for the click of the switch. Once the lamp was off, I searched for his arm, wrapping it around my waist. "I'm thinking about Paris, dead models, and hired mercenaries. All the people I've killed," my voice hitched in my throat, "all the people who have tried to kill me and you."

"I'm okay. We're both okay," he whispered in my ear. "You're just anxious about meeting with your new client. It's pre-job jitters, but you are a damn fine consultant. Mark still thinks you're one of the best agents he's ever seen at the OIO."

My career began at the Office of International Operations, the FBI's version of Interpol, but after spending four years training and tracking thieves and smugglers, I relinquished my badge after a mission went south and hoped to get a cushy job in the private sector. My first foray led to James Martin, and after a couple of near-death experiences, the two of us were alive, breathing, and somehow managing to juggle a private life and a professional relationship.

"How'd you get to be so smart?" I teased, slowly relaxing as the minutes ticked by and sleep became a possibility.

"Well, I am infuriatingly brilliant, or so I've been told." Martin had a healthy self-image, probably too healthy. Rolling over, I rested my head against his chest, signifying my newfound intention. "Good night, Alex."

When I woke up, he was gone. Too many sleepless nights had taken their toll, and I didn't hear his alarm go off, or the shower running full blast, or my front door opening and closing. Being dead to the world was never a good thing in my line of work because it could easily turn into more than just a euphemism for being a sound sleeper.

After I completed my morning routine, I found a note on the counter next to the coffeemaker. *I'll see you this weekend. Call if you need anything or just want to talk. – J.M.*

What was I doing spending my weekends with a millionaire CEO? The entire situation was absurd. No one ever ends up in a relationship with the person they're originally hired to protect, but somehow, fate didn't get the memo when it came to the two of us. I probably didn't need to look the proverbial gift-horse in the mouth, not after everything we endured just to get to this comfortable place.

Deciding I needed to stop the pointless musing and get to work, I turned on my computer and began researching the news articles related to the recent string of heists. Last week, a fourth robbery had occurred at one of the most popular clubs in the city. The report provided only vague details. The police had no suspects, but all four of the crimes were thought to involve an inside man. I picked up my phone and dialed Detective Nick O'Connell's personal line to see if he could shed any additional light on the situation.

O'Connell and I had worked together numerous times, and despite his cynical attitude and penchant for merciless teasing, he was a good friend and, more importantly, a good cop. My consulting work for the major crimes division had resulted in a few friendships at the local precinct, and it was reassuring to know there were some guys with badges willing to watch my back or trade favors.

"Alexis Parker, as I live and breathe." O'Connell was in a good mood. "What pray tell are you calling about on this fine morning?"

"Did your wife make you watch *Gone with the Wind* again? Your impression needs some work."

"Fine, what's going on?"

"Taylor from vice called the other day. She knows the guy who runs Club Infinity. He's spooked about the recent string of robberies and thinks some of his employees might be planning something. Can you tell me anything that wasn't in the papers?"

O'Connell chuckled. "You never call just to see how I am. Some friend you are." I ignored the comment, waiting for actual information. "In case you haven't realized this yet, I don't work burglary, but I can pull the case files if you want to read them yourself."

"Thank god. I was afraid you were going to read them to me while trying to perfect your Rhett Butler." We agreed on a time to meet before hanging up.

On the way to the precinct, I stopped by my office to check the mail and answering machine. Nothing but flyers and telemarketers, but it was a nice change of pace from the hectic month I had. Business had picked up lately. Besides my usual security consulting work for Martin Technologies, which was James Martin's company, I had been asked to investigate a few insurance scams and follow a couple of cheating husbands. Nothing intricate or earth-shattering, but a paycheck was a paycheck.

Even though I hoped for humdrum private sector work, the federal agent in me wasn't satisfied unless I was investigating a serious crime. Damn you, Mark Jablonsky, and all the training you shoved down my throat for four years at the OIO. At least I could get my fix by consulting every once in a while for the local authorities.

Upon entering the precinct, I took a deep breath. Sweat, coffee, and frustration permeated the stale air. It smelled just like a police station should. I sauntered into the bullpen and, as usual, found Lt. Moretti's office door closed. Most of the desks in the squad room were empty as the police personnel bustled about. O'Connell's chair was vacant, but his partner, Det. Thompson, looked up and smiled.

"Parker, he's conducting an interview. He should be back in ten."

I sat down in O'Connell's chair and fished a notebook and pen out of my purse. While I waited, another familiar face surfaced at a nearby desk.

"Are you sure you aren't Fed turned cop?" Det. Heathcliff quipped. We had been partnered together two months ago on a murder case. "Are you working for us again?"

"Not this time. I'm here to call in some favors since you guys still owe me. I don't put on heels and a fancy dress for just anyone." I had gone undercover as a model in order to help identify a killer.

Heathcliff shook his head and returned to work. Stoic didn't even begin to describe his ingrained no-nonsense, always a cop demeanor, but at least he didn't hold a grudge when I turned him down for a date.

A few minutes later, O'Connell emerged, carrying a stack of file folders. He placed them at an empty desk and waited for me to surrender his chair.

"It took you long enough," I teased.

"Some of us have actual work to do." O'Connell sat down and clicked away at his keyboard. "Not everyone can spend their nights clubbing and call it a job." He caught my eye and winked.

After sorting through the files and reading each one carefully, I was convinced the heists must have been conducted by a ghost. There were no obvious signs of a break-in and no evidence of tampering. Not even a single tool mark was identified. Whoever was behind this must be a long lost relative of Harry Houdini.

"Any leads?" I asked, shutting the last folder.

"I talked to a couple of the detectives working this. They got nothing. Security cameras were always disabled. The alarms weren't tripped. The owners showed up the next morning and found everything cleaned out. Initially, it looked like a scam, but it keeps happening."

I glanced at the dates on the folders. Just like clockwork, every two weeks another place was hit. "Why doesn't Moretti make this string of robberies a major crime?"

"Don't even," he warned. "We have more than enough going on right now." Nick gave me a pointed look.

I narrowed my eyes, trying to figure out what he meant to convey, but he shook his head and went back to studying his computer monitor. "Thanks for this." I stood up, hoping I wouldn't be late to meet my client. "In case I have to spend my nights working in a club, can I count on you for a quick course in bartending?"

"Sure. No problem."

"See you boys around." I smiled at O'Connell and Thompson and threw a quick head nod to Heathcliff before leaving the precinct.

* * *

It took almost an hour to maneuver the afternoon traffic from the precinct to the upscale club my new client, Ernesto "Ernie" Papadakis, owned. Ernie was half-Greek and half-Cuban and embraced both sides of his heritage. I found him sitting at the bar, eating arroz con pollo and a piece of baklava.

"Mr. Papadakis, I'm Alexis Parker." I remained standing, unsure how to act in this unfamiliar setting. "Alexis," Papadakis wiped his palms on a napkin before extending his hand, "call me Ernie. Has Officer Taylor told you what's been going on? Please, please, take a seat." He brushed off the barstool with his dirty napkin, and I fought the urge to cringe as I sat next to him.

"I'd prefer to hear things firsthand from you."

"So you know about the string of burglaries. They've all happened on the main strip, and I think I'm next." Ernie had a strange accent, but then again, everything about him seemed a little strange. He was pudgy with dark features offset by a bright Hawaiian shirt and light-colored chinos. His watch spoke expensive taste, and a pair of stylish sunglasses hung from his collar. "Where are my manners?" he chided. "Would you care for some baklava?"

"No, thank you." After watching him eat, I might not have an appetite for a few weeks. "Why do you think Infinity is the next target?"

"The other night," he reconsidered the facts, "no, it was Tuesday, I came down the steps from my office, and I heard the staff talking. They're plotting together. All those other burglaries were inside jobs, and they're on the inside."

"Ernie, have you hired anyone new? If the heists have all been inside jobs, then I'm sure your old, trusted employees aren't planning anything."

"Turnover around here happens quickly. I'm one of the premiere hotspots, and I can't keep anyone who has grown complacent. Most are just kids looking for a quick buck or finding a hook-up. Hey, whaddya know, I'm a poet." I wasn't amused, but he didn't notice. "I hired two new waitresses and a bartender last Monday. That was after the fourth heist hit the news. I didn't even think about it until I heard them talking the next day."

"What exactly did you hear?" I glanced around the room, spotting a couple of security cameras and wondering what the rest of the place looked like.

"I can't remember precisely, but it was something like 'uh, we could make bank here in one night. Check out the till at the bar.' Y'know, something like that."

"Did you notify the police?" Overstepping my boundaries wasn't something I wanted to do. If the police wanted to work this angle, I'd be happy letting them do just that.

"They didn't think it sounded solid. That's when I went to Officer Taylor. She removed a few unsavory girls from my club a few months ago. Hookers," he cringed, "don't want the likes of them in here. I'm trying to be uptown not downtown, if you know what I mean. She said I should call a private dick...er, detective, and she gave me your name."

"Mr. Papadakis, how can I help?"

TWO

Ernie's worries ran on the dramatic side. After all, some people talking about making bank or cleaning up didn't necessarily translate into casing the joint. If Infinity was as upscale as Ernie insisted, then the running commentary among his employees could be legitimate. However, for everyone's sake, I agreed to check it out. After my meeting with Mr. Papadakis, I returned to the precinct and convinced Heathcliff to introduce me to the detective in charge of investigating the string of burglaries, Carl Hoskins.

Hoskins had been working burglary for a decade and seemed to know the business well, but he found this case particularly daunting and had no solid leads. Four robberies should result in enough commonalities to profile a potential suspect, but he insisted there weren't any. Following some coaxing and shooting the shit, I convinced Hoskins to provide photocopies of the four open case files in exchange for being kept in the loop.

After ordering a pizza, I stood in my office and

stared at the blank whiteboard with the files opened and scattered at my feet as I tried to list the similarities. They all occurred in nightclubs after close. The video feeds were disconnected, and prior to that, no one suspicious was identified on screen. The cash registers were emptied, as were the safes. No prints were left, and no alarms were triggered during the commission of the crimes.

To further complicate matters, each of the club owners had an alibi for the night in question. The burglaries read like a team effort since it didn't seem possible one person could break into the club, disable the security systems and cameras, rob the safe, open the cash drawer at the bar, and escape undetected. No single person was that good.

Nibbling on a slice of pizza, I checked the employee manifests. A couple of names overlapped, but according to Hoskins' notes, they alibied out. It didn't seem likely an employee was responsible for the burglaries. Who else had access to the inner workings of nightclubs? Maintenance, liquor delivery, frequenters, the list could go on and on. I scribbled the possibilities on my board. Logically, the police were already working these angles, but it never hurt to double-check. Possible suspects were plentiful at this point in the game.

I pulled out the blueprints for the burglarized venues. Each location was set up differently, and there was no way of determining what the interior would look like from the schematics alone. Tonight, a field trip was in order. Folding the pizza box in half, I shoved it inside my office mini-fridge before locking the files in my drawer and heading home to change.

In skintight jeans, killer heels, and a halter top, I wanted to see what I could discover on my own. When I arrived at the first club, it was early enough in the evening to get in without having to wait in line. I noted the location of the bar, the dance floor, any obvious security measures in place, and the private offices. According to the files, different types of safes and locks were at each venue. Two of the clubs used key code technology. One had a regular lock and key, and the last utilized a key card mechanism on the office door. The guilty party had to be technologically savvy and skilled in old school B&E methodology. After finding nothing particularly helpful, I left the first club and ventured to the next.

After repeating the process and bribing the bouncers at the last two locations, I still had no idea what was going on. Each place was completely different from the last, including the skills needed to conduct the heists. Just because the tactics were the same didn't mean the burglars were since every security aspect was unique for each club. Maybe each heist was executed by a different group of thieves working for one mastermind. It was an overwhelming feeling to be thrown into a myriad of dissimilarities that all ended with the same result. No wonder the police were stumped; I was downright baffled.

Concluding my reconnaissance, I ended up back at Infinity. Ambling my way to the bouncer, I bypassed dozens of people waiting in line. Ernie wasn't joking when he said his place was happening.

"Hi, ya," I flirted.

My first test was to see how gullible the doorman might be. A few linemen walked around, checking IDs and questioning those who appeared to be less savory. It was crazy to think a club owner actually wanted to keep drugs and hookers on the outside.

"Miss, the line's back there." He didn't even bother to glance up.

"Do you think there might be a way to move things

along?" I purred.

"Sorry."

"I can make it worth your while." Reaching into my wallet, I produced a fifty. The man looked offended. What was the going rate on bribery these days? "You don't want money?" He motioned to one of the linemen to escort me away. "Fine, get Ernie on the line. He asked to see me." I dropped the flirtation and the act. At least the bouncer couldn't be bought, unless I just wasn't his type.

"Name?"

"Alexis Parker."

He hit a button on his earpiece and spoke my name over the radio. "Sorry, Ms. Parker." He unhooked the velvet rope. "Go on in. The boss is upstairs."

"Thanks."

Inside, I couldn't help but be impressed by the lavish feel Infinity exuded. My impression from this afternoon left me with nary a basis for what I witnessed now. It wasn't the normal bump and grind of hundreds of sweaty, drunk young adults searching for brief companionship while some DJ pumped pounding techno rhythms into the over-processed air. This place was something else entirely. The couches were soft leather with large cushioned square ottomans serving as both tables and extra seats. The music was mellow, and the dancing didn't resemble a writhing, dying beast. Upscale at its finest.

"Alexis?" Ernie had transformed just like his club. He slicked back his hair and wore a black tailored suit with a deep blue dress shirt open at the neck. His watch from before was around his wrist, and a single diamond stud was stuck in his ear. I would have expected to run into nighttime Mr. Papadakis at a board meeting at MT with the elegance and sophistication he conveyed; whereas, daytime Ernie would have been found bumming around on the beach. "Why don't you come upstairs?"

Climbing the spiral staircase in the middle of the room, I noted as much of the club as possible. The upper level was comprised of private, secluded rooms where VIPs could party or conduct business away from prying eyes and the noise of downstairs. Ernie escorted me into his office and shut the door behind us. The room must have been soundproofed because, had I not just walked through the club, I would have never realized we were in a club.

"You have a lovely establishment." I performed a quick sweep of the room and guessed the safe was mounted behind the large painting on the wall.

"Thank you. I'm glad you decided to stop by tonight." He took a seat in his plush leather chair. "You didn't mention when you were starting your surveillance, so I didn't have the doorman put you on the list."

"No worries. I just wanted to look around before reviewing the information you provided on your security measures so I would have some idea of what to picture. Going in blind makes it easier to determine how I would choreograph the break-in and then see how feasible it is." This might have sounded like blabbering to an untrained civilian, but he excitedly grinned.

"How would you do it?"

"Off the top of my head, I'd block the lock on the side door that exits into the alley, hoping the security system couldn't engage with the door ajar. Then I'd stay in the blind spot of the camera near the bar and front door until I could cut the feed and head up the hidden back staircase inside the storeroom behind the bar. Next, I'd go to your office, pick the lock on the door, remove the painting from the wall, open the safe, head back downstairs, hit the cash drawer, and leave the way I came in."

He paled, and his jaw dropped. "How'd you know about the back staircase or the safe?" His skin flushed, rapidly replacing his ashen visage.

"I saw the top of the second staircase before coming in here, and really, why else would you have a painting hanging there?" Ernie was flabbergasted. "Plus, I am a trained investigator. Detecting is what I do," I added, hoping to make him feel better.

"What do I do? Clearly, it wouldn't be difficult to rob this place blind."

I stifled my chuckle at his melodrama. "First of all, it's all talk. I haven't looked at your security schematics yet, so getting into the side door might be a lot harder than it sounded. Next, I'm not a safecracker, and disconnecting your cameras would either require a hands-on approach or some method of remotely shorting them out. Assuming everything is backed up on a hard disk, I'd have to figure out where the system is housed and wipe the footage of my interference." Something pinged in my brain, and I knew where to focus my efforts when assessing the previous four heists.

"I think I should hire you for head of security."

"Wouldn't that be too on the nose?" I retorted. "Now, if you don't mind, I'm going downstairs to act like a club-goer since I didn't dress like this for a second business meeting. Are there any employees in particular you think might be involved?"

"The newest hires are Sam, Gretchen, and Mindy. He's our new bartender, and the two ladies are waitresses. I can point them out before you go downstairs."

We stood outside his office and leaned against the railing, surveying the club below. Ernie pointed to a redhead in a black miniskirt, silver tank top, and apron and a tall, leggy blonde in a matching outfit. Needless to say, I wasn't a fan of the uniform. Sam was the dirty blond with the python tattoo wrapped around his arm. He didn't seem classy enough for this joint, but given the flock of ladies standing at the bar, calling to him, he was a sound hire.

"Just so you know, my bar tab is being added to billable expenses," I warned before going down the steps.

Having never been a club-goer, I found blending in was an arduous task. Deciding to stick with what I knew, I slowly scoped out the dance floor, managing to bounce enough to appear to be dancing while making my way through the crowd. I kept an eye on the waitresses as they served the patrons on the couches. The couch was more my speed, but unless I had a group of my five best friends with me, I'd look even more suspicious sitting there alone. That left only one option, the bar.

Crowded didn't even begin to describe the throng of people surrounding the stools and shouting orders to the three bartenders. Finding the perfect vantage point, I hoped the guy and girl playing tonsil hockey in the corner would decide to vacate, but things didn't look to be in my favor. I would just have to do something to improve my odds.

Bumping into the man seated next to the couple, I jostled his beer right into the lap of the lovely young woman. She immediately jumped out of her chair and screamed. Fortunately, her hockey partner took this turn of events as a cosmic sign. After threatening to force me to pay for her ruined dress, he led her out of the club and back to his place, so he could throw her clothes into the washing machine or onto the floor. Thank god chivalry wasn't dead.

Taking the far seat in the corner, I apologized to the man whose beer I spilled. "Anytime, doll," he replied. "I'm just glad I don't have to intentionally ignore them for a minute longer." Finally, one of the bartenders came over, and I ordered another round for my new friend and a lemon drop martini for myself. "Come here often?" My beer buddy didn't understand I wasn't looking for a man.

"All the time. My boyfriend's the DJ," I lied.

The man nodded and turned away. I was glad that was over with.

Unwilling to risk losing the seat I had so expertly stolen, I didn't move from the barstool the rest of the night. After a couple of hours and turning down half a dozen guys who asked to dance or offered to buy me a drink, Sam came to my end of the bar to clean up.

"Another?" He jerked his chin at my glass.

"Why not?" It was my third, but I had no intention of drinking it. "Can I persuade you to join me?"

"Can't. I'm working. Club policy." He poured the ingredients into a shaker. "You've been sitting here all night. Did someone break your heart?"

"You, for making me drink alone." He adopted a sexy grin and placed a fresh martini on the bar. "Hey, how's the pay here?" I asked.

"Pretty fucking fantastic, just like the women." Men must all read the same book on clichéd pick-up lines. "Looking for a sugar daddy?"

"No, I'm looking for a job."

THREE

After an hour of conversing with Sam, he insisted on putting in a good word with the boss and introduced me to a couple of the waitresses. Tina and Mary had worked at Infinity for the last few months and slipped off my radar quickly. Tina worked nights in order to help pay for her husband's medical degree, and Mary took this job to support herself through grad school. While money was tight for everyone, I didn't think they would risk future careers on illegal endeavors. Mindy and Gretchen, on the other hand, were the suspicious new hires, but I wasn't sure what capabilities either possessed in order to conduct a heist, especially since Mindy appeared to be a complete airhead. But at least it was a start.

It was almost four a.m. by the time I trudged up the steps to my apartment and unlocked the door. My alarm clock was set for nine, and I planned to call Ernie in the morning to give him the heads up that Sam intended to vouch for me. There was no real guarantee Sam would mention it. But Ernie didn't need to be blindsided, or my job would end before it even began.

The next morning, I spoke with Ernie, and we decided I would start training as a waitress on Thursday. This allowed enough time to review his security weaknesses and run backgrounds on his employees. With any luck, he was overreacting, and business would be concluded in a week or two. In the meantime, I went to my office to run the pertinent background checks and finish reviewing the case files.

Sam Harrigan, bartender extraordinaire, had a record for assault. He had been arrested for fighting in a bar. I dismissed his rap sheet as a side effect of his job and continued on. No one else had any known convictions or arrests, which spoke well for Infinity's hiring practices. Since the employees were all upstanding citizens, I might as well focus my time on security. There was a mid-level safe, five security cameras placed strategically throughout the two levels, and key code locks on the interior doors. The windows were barred, and the only exterior exits were the front, side, and a set of double doors in the back for deliveries.

I mulled over the exits. Something gnawed at my subconscious when it came to the deliveries and the back doors. I just couldn't figure out what it was. Changing gears, I unlocked my drawer and pulled out copies of the police reports. The four other break-ins, which I had labeled A to D based on the order of occurrence, all had similar double doors for deliveries. The doors themselves weren't irksome; it was the deliveryman.

Running through the list of vendors, I realized the clubs used the same liquor supplier. Would the deliveryman be the same too? Typing in the information, I came up with a telephone number and phoned the company.

Stoltz Bros. Liquor Emporium was a local liquor store that provided the clubs with a great discount on high-end alcohol. It might also be a front for some illegal activities, but then again, I was trained to be leery. When a woman answered, I asked for information on the delivery driver and his schedule. She told me to go screw myself unless I had a warrant. What a kind and helpful lady. I made a note to call Hoskins about the liquor company.

My whiteboard stared blankly from across the room. "Don't just stand there, tell me something." Talking to inanimate objects might be a sign of mental illness. Then again, I did it all the time, and I passed my psych evals. I picked up a marker and the file folder for Club A and diagrammed the crime.

Two hours later, the front of the board was divided into quarters, and each contained the relevant information on the break-ins, the possible suspects, and the security systems and weaknesses. The video tampering still bothered me, but I lacked the resources to determine how it was altered. Chewing on the lid of the marker, I waited for inspiration to strike. Instead, the bell above my door dinged.

"It's nice to see you aren't inhaling permanent marker fumes," Agent Mark Jablonsky said, taking a seat in my client chair.

"What brings you down here? Shouldn't you be sitting at your desk at the OIO, kissing Director Kendall's ass?"

"Parker, play nice. The Bureau's been called in on a local matter, and I wondered how busy you were." He wasn't normally this vague, so something must be up.

"What's going on?"

"Sorry, I can't say unless you agree to consult. In this instance, you might have some particularly relevant feedback to offer."

I scrutinized his expression, but he wouldn't budge. "Did you hear about the four club robberies?" I raised an eyebrow, and he nodded absently as he reviewed my board and notes. "I'm trying to reassure a client his club is secure."

"When you finish, give me a call. We'll talk then." He took the extra marker off my desk, went to the board, circled four words, and handed back the marker. I stared at the circled words, awestruck.

Saturday night after close. It wasn't rocket science, and I felt like a complete moron. Losing sight of the forest for the trees was a hazard of the job, but I had completely neglected the apparent timetable. Like clockwork, every two weeks a club was hit after closing Saturday night. It was the most opportune time to strike, after the largest number of partiers had been out drinking away their weekend and spending without a care. The money the bars raked in would stay locked in the safe until Monday when the banks reopened. Regardless of my role, if Infinity was targeted, we would know soon enough.

It was time to get down to business. Sticking the police reports on top of my desk, I pulled out my notes on Infinity and flipped my whiteboard over so I could use the space on the back. Even though I was no artist, I diagrammed the layout of the two floors of the building, marked the exits, labeled the cameras and estimated their ranges, tagged the offices and points of interest, and stepped back to admire my handiwork.

How would I conduct the perfect heist? Pulling out the schematics on the security system, I spent the rest of the day reading and reviewing. By the time I came up with a perfect plan, it was dark. I made a list of equipment needed and figured I'd ask Hoskins to check into recent purchase histories at the local hardware and electronic stores. It was labor intensive legwork, but he was a cop. They specialized in grunt work. I left a message on his voicemail, but there was no assurance he would call back with the information. Either way, I agreed to pass along anything I had, and this was it.

I didn't want to go clubbing tonight, but I was on the clock. Stopping at home, I microwaved some leftovers and changed into something club-worthy. After eating, I planned to spend another evening familiarizing myself with Infinity.

The bouncer from last night recognized me and removed the velvet rope without a word. Sam remained behind the bar, and the four waitresses catered to the couch crowd. Ernie was in the storeroom having a discussion with a gentleman who was dressed a little too nicely, even for this swanky club.

Luckily, Tuesday wasn't a popular day, so I managed to find an empty seat at the bar without having to spill any drinks. I tried to keep my glances moving so as not to draw undue attention to Ernie and the mystery man. Something about the backroom meeting didn't sit well with me, and I fiddled with the zipper on my purse, taking comfort in knowing my nine millimeter had a full clip inside.

"What can I get you?" Sam leaned forward so he could be heard over the music.

"The usual." It was nice to have some stability. Plus, he started pouring before I even ordered. Was I really that predictable to a complete stranger?

"Thought so." He put the drink down. "You look the elegant, no-nonsense type." Was this flirtation? I cocked an eyebrow at him. "I talked to the boss, Mr. Papadakis. Did you get a call for an interview?"

"Something like that." I hadn't heard from Ernie since this morning, so I didn't know what to say. "Is that him?" Jerking my chin toward the storeroom, I waited for Sam to follow my gaze.

"Yep. He's talking to one of the backers. When he's done, I'll introduce you."

"Thanks."

A half hour later, the well-dressed man left the storeroom and headed straight for the exit, keeping his head down. It looked like Ernie and I might be having another insightful chat in the immediate future.

"Yo, Mr. Paps," Sam called, "the woman from last night's here. Alexis, right?" He turned around to double-check, and I nodded.

"Why don't you come to my office." Ernie looked flustered. "It'll be quieter and easier to interview you."

I thanked Sam again before taking a sip of my drink and placing a twenty on the bar. It was easy to be generous with someone else's money.

Once Ernie and I got upstairs, he scratched his nose and avoided eye contact. "I didn't expect to see you tonight."

"Did I catch you at a bad time?"

"No, I was just dealing with some business. How may I help your investigation, Alexis?"

"Why do I get the feeling you're in bed with people you shouldn't be involved with?" I took a seat, waiting for him to spill the beans.

"I can promise you I'm not involved in any illegal activities." He was agitated, maybe even afraid.

Assessing him silently, I ran through the few things I actually knew. First, Ernie made sure to keep drugs and hookers out. Second, there was something fishy with the liquor supplier, and lastly, Mr. Well-Dressed looked like a heavy-hitter for one of the crime families. That would explain why Ernie needed to keep the cops outside of his club. Personally, I hadn't witnessed any illegal activities, but that didn't mean this place wasn't a front for money laundering.

When the silence became too thick to take and I feared Ernie might have a coronary, I spoke. "Should I worry about getting my kneecaps busted?" He blanched but shook his head enthusiastically. "Good, and before you open your mouth, I need to instill upon you a very important fact. I do not want to know who you were talking to downstairs. The less I know, the better. Got it?"

"Sure, no problem." He looked relieved.

"I dropped by tonight to get another look around and check on your people. Furthermore, I'm guessing a club's getting hit Saturday night. If it's not Infinity, I'd say you're in the clear, and our business will conclude. Understand?" Now that more complications were added to the mix, I didn't want to stick around any longer than necessary.

"Alexis, I have a question. What are you planning on doing Saturday night to stop it?"

"I'm still working on it. Will your silent partners present any additional problems or issues I need to be aware of? And remember, the less I know, the better."

"No problems. It's my club, and I run it how I see fit. My financial backers like to see returns on their investment and offer constructive criticism, but it's my show." Poor delusional Ernie, the bastard really had no clue, or he liked to pretend he was in charge. Either way, there was a potential shitstorm in his future. "I don't want to see this place get robbed blind, and I'm sure they don't either. It's not good for any business."

"Okay, here's what we're going to do." I went to the wall and examined the painting before removing it and exposing the safe. "If I were to try to open this, how many alarms would I set off?"

"None. But after five tries the system locks, and no one can open it without a reset code." The schematics hadn't been as explicit, but I studied the keypad for a few moments, noticing the slightly worn two and seven keys.

"First off, change the code on the safe. I can guess two of the numbers off the top of my head." He looked skeptical, so I gave him what I had. "Then on Saturday night, before you head home, empty the safe. I don't know how much cash you keep in there, and I don't need to know. But unless you want to explain to your partners and the police how much was stolen, I'd suggest it not be there. Make sure you move it out in a normal bag. Maybe start carrying a duffel with you to work between now and then. Say you're going to the gym or whatever."

He smiled happily and opened the cabinet under the wet bar to show me his bag. "I already do since I get changed in my office every night."

"Great. And make sure you deposit the money at the bank drop on Saturday night because if you think you're going to create your own version of a heist to pull something over on me or the police, I'll know and my friends will know."

"I would never," he said, aghast.

"Think of it as a friendly warning or a reminder, if you will."

FOUR

The next day, Hoskins called to thank me for telling him how to do his job. Apparently, he didn't think I was as brilliant and insightful as I thought I was. The police were already working the angles and checking into leads and suspects, and I was reminded not to step on any toes because, even though I had friends in major crimes, burglary thought I was a pain in the ass. You win some, and you lose some.

Giving up on solving the previous four burglaries, I left my theories concerning the heists on the flipside of my whiteboard and examined Infinity's weaknesses on the front. After determining the most efficient and likely way to rob the place, I shifted back into research mode. I had no real basis to believe Infinity would get robbed late Saturday evening, but in the unlikely event it did, what was I going to do? Based on the heist model I created, I worked on devising my own game plan.

Having no current law enforcement credentials, I couldn't stop the culprits in the act. All I could do was keep an eye out, identify them, and if I felt particularly adventurous or suicidal, depending on my mood, I might try to delay them while waiting for the shining black and white cavalry to roll in and save the day.

Picking up the phone, I dialed Mark to ask for advice. He suggested staying away from the mess and letting the real cops do their jobs, unless of course I wanted to be reinstated at the OIO. After I reminded him this wasn't a federal matter, he hung up.

"Nick," I called O'Connell hoping for his sage wisdom, "I'm between a rock and a hard place."

"How big is the rock?"

"I have a client who's hired me to thwart any attempts at a robbery, but I don't believe the place is going to get robbed."

"Then tell him you did a great job and ask for a bonus." He didn't understand my dilemma.

"What if I'm wrong? Do I stake out the place and apprehend the burglars or run from the scene screaming fire and hope someone calls the cops?"

"Ah." He finally understood. "You want to play sleuth with the burglary boys, and they don't want you on their team."

"Maybe," I grudgingly admitted, and he laughed at the absurdity.

"Do the work you were hired to do and stop there. You don't need to snoop around where you're not wanted. I don't have any friends upstairs who I can coerce to let you play with them. If you're hard-pressed, the Bureau has something cooking that might be up your alley." Whatever was going on, both Nick and Mark were investigating. It had to be something big. Maybe I would check it out after I finished my waitressing gig.

*   *   *

Thursday morning, the ringing phone woke me. It was Martin Technologies, which never bode well. When I answered, vice president Luc Guillot requested my presence to discuss the standardized security protocols. Being a security consultant for MT and previous personal bodyguard to the CEO had afforded me a unique position at the company. While being kept on retainer and providing piecemeal advice here and there, I had caught the attention of Mr. Guillot, who put me in charge of the security overhaul the company was undertaking in order to ensure all branches had uniform hiring checks and procedures.

Originally, Martin had been my boss, but once we became intimately involved, he relinquished security matters to his second-in-command. After agreeing to the meeting, I dragged myself out of bed, relieved the pertinent information was sent via e-mail. After showering and dressing, I flipped through the PDFs and PowerPoints, making notations as I went.

At one o'clock, I arrived at the MT building, greeted the security guard, and took the elevator to the top floor. My MT provided office was across the hall from Martin and down the hall from Guillot, so it made sense to stop there and drop off my things. As I turned on the coffeemaker, Martin strode past my open doorway. He stopped and checked his watch before coming inside and shutting the door behind him.

"Hey, gorgeous." He kissed me, which was completely inappropriate for work. "What's going on?"

"I have a meeting with Guillot and some security types on the upcoming project."

"Why can't you ever just be here to see me?"

"In case you don't remember, every time I've been here to see you, it's never been good." I took a seat at my desk, expecting him to go back to work at any moment. Instead, he sat on the small couch and patted the cushion next to him. "Seriously, you need to stop being ridiculous." I adamantly opposed public displays of affection, so he was doing this for his own twisted amusement. "Don't you have a company to run?"

"Actually, I'm going home for the day, but I might be persuaded to wait until you're finished. We're dealing with the Russians tomorrow morning, three a.m. to be exact. So since I'll be working all night, I get the afternoon off to rest and prepare. Want to rest with me?"

"There wouldn't be much resting involved," my eyes glinted evilly, "but unfortunately, I'm booked for the day. Meeting here, then a quick bite while I review my notes, and last stop – training."

"Training?"

"I'm waitressing now," I deadpanned.

"If money's tight, I can give you a loan."

"It's not that."

"Just promise before you start selling your body, you'll come to me first."

"Mr. Martin, I'd suggest you watch your tone, unless you want to deal with a sexual harassment lawsuit." We enjoyed our banter and verbal sparring too much sometimes.

He rolled his eyes and switched to something less playful. "What are we doing this weekend?"

"Shit. I'm working nights."

"As a waitress?" His face fell. "Then we're just going to have to work around our schedules." When did he become so compromising and insistent on seeing me? "After you're done here, we can get an early bird special somewhere, and I'll watch you read your notes or whatever. Then tomorrow morning after my teleconference, we'll—" His words were cut off by a knock at the door. He opened the door, smilingly warmly at Guillot. "Ms. Parker was just filling me in on the progress we're making on our security endeavor," Martin lied, hoping to keep our private relationship a secret. Guillot didn't seem suspicious, but I couldn't help wondering if he suspected there was something else going on.

"We're ready for you, Mademoiselle," Guillot intoned in his French accent. "James, feel free to join us."

"No, I have some paperwork to read and the Kiev files to take home. I'm leaving everything in your trusted hands." Martin walked out of the office, and I followed Guillot to a conference room down the hallway.

After two and a half hours of excruciatingly boring detail and hashing out the finer nuances in emergency security measures, Guillot thanked everyone for their time and scheduled a follow-up meeting in a month. At least I wouldn't be bored senseless for the next few weeks. I went back to my office and looked at my untouched coffeepot. Filling my travel mug with the brewed contents, I grabbed my purse and locked my door, only to turn around and find Martin waiting for the elevator.

"Ms. Parker," he grinned, "funny running into you again."

"It's almost as if it were fate. Or planned." I looked at him pointedly, and he smirked as we waited for the doors to open. We remained professional as we exited the building and went to the parking garage.

As I unlocked my car door, Martin leaned against my trunk. "I'm going home to change. Should I bring food over, or do you want to go out? You have homework, after all," he said. The best thing would be if he went home and left me alone, but it would take more effort to argue with him then it would just to give in.

"Pick up whatever you want. I have to stop by my office and grab some files, so I'll meet you at my place in an hour. I have to be at work by seven."

He glanced at his watch. "See, this works out great." His definition of great wasn't very accurate, but I ignored it as we parted ways.

*   *   *

Martin brought over Indian food, and after we finished eating, I reviewed the employee files. No one seemed criminal or suspicious. I was almost completely sure Infinity wouldn't be robbed Saturday night. As Nick and Mark had insisted, I wasn't responsible for figuring out what would be robbed, so the only thing left to do was determine the best place to stake out the club after close.

"Tomorrow morning, if all goes well, I should be done for the day by ten a.m. Want to get breakfast?" Martin asked, acting clingier than usual, and we had been doing so well lately with just seeing each other on the weekends or for the occasional weeknight dinner.

"At ten a.m., I will be asleep. Why the sudden need to spend every moment together?"

"Won't this weekend be two months?"

"Two months for what?"

"Since you agreed to this. To us."

Two months already. On the one hand, it felt more like a year since it was a closer estimate of how long we'd known one another, and on the other hand, two months normally felt more suffocating than this. My internal clock hadn't registered it'd been that long, maybe just a few weeks. But there was a strong possibility I was a commitment-phobe. Then again, Martin didn't have a great track record for long-term relationships either.

"Uh-huh. Right." I went back to reviewing Sam's personnel file. Still, nothing on any of the employees set my radar buzzing. The backroom financier drove me batty, but I didn't need to get involved with a crime family. I liked my kneecaps and my life, and neither needed to be jeopardized.

"Okay, so tomorrow, after my teleconference, I'll crash at your place until you have to get up for work. Deal?"

"Come on, it's just two freaking months. You can go back to your castle and get some actual sleep. Probably by Sunday, I'll be done with this job, and next weekend, we'll do whatever you like. I'll even spend the time at your place if you want."

"My castle," Martin snickered, "does that make me king?" I glared at him. "I didn't think so. Next weekend, I have a conference in Los Angeles. And who knows what you'll be doing by the following weekend. By then, you might be opening your own burger joint if this waitressing thing goes well."

Picking up a piece of scrap paper, I balled it up and threw it at him. "Fine. I'll give you tomorrow until I have to go to work at seven. But I swear to god, if you don't let me go back to sleep when you get here, I will hurt you."

He smiled happily, content in the belief he had won a great victory. I decided to let him believe it since he didn't need to know I wanted to spend time with him too. Emotional attachments were easily exploited weaknesses, but they were also important tethers to keep the world from turning into a completely merciless and disenchanted mess.

FIVE

My first night waitressing turned out better than I expected. Not only did I manage not to spill anyone's drink, but I also walked away with a couple hundred dollars in tips. Maybe I would deduct my earnings from Ernie's fee, but it would depend on how the next two days went. In between shouting orders to Sam and the two other bartenders, Barry and Brian, I noticed Mindy and Gretchen huddled in the corner, talking or taking breaks together. Unfortunately, I was never close enough to hear what they were saying.

My shift ended when the bar closed at four a.m. By five, we had cleaned the entire place and restocked all the glasses and bottles for tomorrow night. The three bartenders and four other waitresses decided we should celebrate a job well done by going out for breakfast.

Over eggs and waffles, I got to know everyone. Barry and Brian were brothers who had worked for Ernie for the last six months and loved bartending. They had moved from Miami, and their mother's brother-in-law was Ernie's uncle. Family connections were daunting enough, but it was just another example of who you know and not what you know.

The four waitresses were pleasant, but I found Tina and Mary easily relatable. They were women working odd jobs while supporting their families or going to school. Mary was writing her thesis on some type of applied physics theory, which was over my head, but her waitressing gig would pay the bills until she found a science job. Tina was married and had a business degree, but until she could find a more permanent position, the tips supported her and her husband. Gretchen was an immigrant from Germany, waitress by night and nanny by day. Mindy was the oblivious type, who had nothing in common with her co-workers. She was sweet, but she might have suffered a serious blow to the head during her formative years. The more time I spent with my co-workers, the more confident I became that Infinity was not going to get knocked over. None of them were evil criminal masterminds.

Bidding the group good night, I made it home a little before seven. I had only been asleep for two hours when constant knocking dragged me out of bed. It better be Martin because if it were a salesman or a religious zealot, a homicide would take place in the hallway.

"We made the Kiev deal," Martin said, pulling me close for a kiss. I stared at him, unimpressed with anything that wasn't a pillow, and locked the door behind him. "We should celebrate."

"Sleep first. Celebrate later." I went back to the bedroom, assuming he would follow whenever he was done prancing around. "If you shut up and go to sleep, I'll make it worth your while later on," I mumbled as I got into bed.

He joined me a few minutes later, having changed out of his suit.

*   *   *

Seated at my dining room table, I went through the Infinity employee manifest and recorded my notes in the margins. Martin emerged from my bathroom, freshly showered and dressed. He wrapped his arms around my shoulders and kissed my neck.

"That was a hell of a way to celebrate," he cooed. Blushing slightly, I giggled. "However, the paperwork needs to go." He took a seat beside me and attempted to read over my shoulder. I dropped my pen on the table and turned to face him, noting the clock on the wall. "What's the rest of your day look like, sweetheart?"

"Damn, it's already four. In three hours, I have to be at the club." I rubbed my eyes and tried to think. It was important to make sure any suspicions I had about the staff or bartenders were written down for later consideration since I was hard-pressed for time. Once again, no one seemed criminal or sinister, except for Ernie's liquor supplier and Mafioso ties. Neither of which I planned to investigate. Sighing, I noticed Martin assessing me appreciatively, which as usual was uncomfortable. "Stop that."

He smiled and looked at the table. "Let's get out of here and go somewhere nice for lunch, dinner, a senior citizen early bird special. Whatever." He looked up with his green eyes. "Do you mind driving? Marcal dropped me off."

An hour later, we were two of the only people sitting at Giovanni's. By six, the bar would fill up, and at seven, the tables nearby would be occupied. But right now, it was nice having some privacy. Finishing my chicken parmesan, I took a sip of iced tea before answering Martin's question about my current investigation.

"There isn't much to tell. Honestly, I'd say he's paranoid because nothing indicates his club is a target." I left out key details so Martin wouldn't know where I was working or who I was working for. "Comes Sunday morning, I'll be finished, one way or another." He chewed thoughtfully, but before he could respond, his phone rang. "Duty calls."

"Sorry," he apologized, wiping his mouth and answering. After a couple of moments, I knew it was work. I swirled the straw around my glass, waiting patiently. When he concluded the call, he put his phone away. "Since Kiev's been secured, I have paperwork and board meetings to contend with. The Board wants an update, and they want the merger documentation ready to go by Monday. Since you're working Saturday into Sunday, I might as well catch up on things and put in my eight to four workdays this weekend."

"Workaholic," I quipped.

"Et tu, Bruté?" He handed the waitress his credit card, and I thanked him for dinner. "So when are we doing this again?"

On the drive back to my place, we tried coming up with some mutual free time. The problem was I didn't know what was up with Mark and Nick or if I wanted to jump aboard on their joint venture. Martin was out of town next weekend, so we were playing it by ear. The one good thing was we were both okay putting work first. He got it, and so did I.

"You have everything, right?" I did a quick sweep of my bedroom and bathroom.

"It would be nice to have a drawer here. Or, I don't know, some counter space in the bathroom. Even just a toothbrush. You have a drawer at my place."

"When you go home, I want you to look in the drawer and see what's inside. Then we'll have this conversation again." It was true. He had given me a drawer at his place. Although, the drawer was more accurately the guest suite on the second floor since I had some issues when it came to certain levels of his compound, namely the top level which unfortunately was where his bedroom was situated. The symbolic drawer was in the dresser in the guestroom, and the only thing inside was one of his shirts which I had claimed as my own. Jones, his bodyguard whom I nicknamed Bruiser, knocked on my door, interrupting our argument. "I'll give you a call Sunday."

"Good, and we can discuss the drawer dilemma in more detail." He kissed me goodbye.

*   *   *

Friday night at Infinity was a veritable replay of Thursday. The crowds were larger, but the work was the same. Ernie schmoozed with some VIPs, but I didn't get a chance to talk to him. After the club closed for the night, I went home and got some sleep before Hoskins called.

"Are you still looking out for some paranoid club owner?" he asked as way of greeting.

"Uh-huh," I grunted, getting up and checking the time. It was a little after noon, and there was too much to do to go back to sleep. "Did you hear something?"

"No. Still digging into third party vendors, hoping to find a lead. What are you planning on doing?"

"Just keeping my eyes open for anyone suspicious. I plan to hang out at the club until close, wait around a bit, and call it a job well done. You got eyes on any particular locations tonight?"

"Hopefully, the fourth heist was the final heist. Whoever it is must realize how much greater the risk will be."

"Criminals aren't usually geniuses," I said before disconnecting. I was surprised Hoskins called, but maybe he just wanted to make sure I hadn't infiltrated the robbers. My reputation was stellar, but when a case went cold, even I couldn't heat it up.

Deciding some menial labor might help my brain recognize unseen factors, I did the laundry, changed the sheets and towels, and otherwise cleaned my entire apartment. When this failed to send me into a tailspin of theories and answers, I grabbed my uniform for Infinity and headed to my office. Once there, I re-familiarized myself with the blueprints of the club, the exits, entrances, surveillance equipment, and security measures. There wasn't much to do except wait.

I arrived early for my shift and found Ernie seated at the bar, going over expense reports while eating a churro. As soon as we were alone, I sat down next to him and reiterated a few helpful suggestions.

"You're emptying the safe tonight, right?" I asked.

"I guess. You did say it would be a good idea, right?" The way he questioned things made me wonder how he could be in charge of a place like this. Maybe his silent partners weren't so silent.

"Really, I don't think anything is going down tonight, but if you want to be on the safe side, it wouldn't hurt. You changed the combination and made sure all your security measures are up and running?"

He nodded emphatically. "What are you going to do?"

"Plant myself outside and run surveillance until

daybreak, unless you have a better idea." He shook his head. "If something happens, you do realize I will call the police."

"Yes, what else would you do?" Ernie was genuinely confused by my comment. At least he didn't expect me to personally apprehend the guilty parties or make them sleep with the fishes.

"Not a thing." Mary and Tina walked in, so I got off the barstool, thanked the boss for Monday off, and followed after the girls.

We were in the ladies' room, changing into our uniforms when Gretchen burst in, speaking vehemently on her cell phone in German. She was upset, and from my limited knowledge of the language, it sounded as though someone insisted she do as she was told. This piqued my interest, and exiting the stall, I stared at my reflection in the mirror, reapplying my makeup while watching her out of the corner of my eye. The only part of the conversation I understood was her repeatedly saying no and she couldn't do it.

With my luck, it was probably Gretchen's boyfriend who planned on robbing Infinity. Digging through my purse, I continued the ruse of looking for mascara while I tried to recall if she worked at any of the other clubs. Something was starting to feel off. Nanny by day, robber by night? And what was it she had been huddled in the corner talking to Mindy about? Could the airhead routine be an act?

Gretchen hung up and noticed me watching her.

"Sorry." I tried to look empathetic. "Is everything okay?"

"No. Stupid men and their stupid ideas," she huffed, and I reassessed my position on Ernie's paranoia.

SIX

Saturday night could only be properly described as a maelstrom. The bouncers and linemen were occupied with keeping a proper count of how many people entered and exited in order to ensure the fire codes weren't violated. Barry, Brian, and Sam served drinks so quickly I had no idea how they got any of the orders right, and the five of us waitressing should have been wearing tennis shoes, instead of stiletto heels, with all the running back and forth, not to mention catering to the VIPs upstairs in the lounge. Working undercover was designed to provide an opportunity to scope out anyone suspicious, but at this rate, I was lucky to remember which table got which tray of drinks.

"Oh my god," Mary panted as we practically collided at the bar, "this place has never been this busy. You'd think it was New Year's Eve with the crowd here tonight."

"At least the tips are nice," I said as Barry put the final drink on my tray, and I headed for the steps.

All the VIP areas were full, and I studied the group

situated closest to the office as I put the drinks on the table. This would be the perfect vantage point to enter the office and clean out the safe. Loading up my tray with empty glasses, I wondered if the burglaries could have happened during business hours but had remained undetected until the next day.

"Watch it," a tall, pudgy guy yelled as he ascended the steps.

"Sorry, sir." I continued downward, reminding myself to pay more attention. Spotting Mindy scribbling orders at a nearby couch, I came up beside her. "Do me a favor and cover my tables for a few minutes. I need a bathroom break." Not waiting for her protest, I dumped the tray on the bar and went toward the ladies' room to call Hoskins.

"You got something?" he asked.

I backed into the far corner of the club, hoping not to be overheard. "Probably not, but things are a little strange. Based on the four other incident reports, do you think it's possible the safes were emptied while the clubs were still in operation?"

Hoskins blew out an audible breath. "Stop grasping at straws. If you have something solid, let me know. Otherwise, stop playing detective." The phone slammed in my ear. For future reference, I would call his cell instead of his desk to avoid the dramatic hang-up.

Shutting my eyes, I took a breath and went back to slinging drinks until the crowd died down around two a.m. Everyone who remained had mellowed. Brian cleaned up the storeroom and reorganized the shelves while Sam and Barry continued to fill orders at a much more reasonable pace. Gretchen was sitting on a barstool, taking a break, when I returned with an empty tray and no requests for refills.

"Remind me never to work another Saturday

again." I smiled at Sam. He snickered and put a drink in front of a guy who was chatting up some woman. "Lucky," I turned to Gretchen, hoping to get a bit more out of her, "if I sat down, I'd never get back up."

"Ja, you'll get used to it. We all get used to it." It didn't seem like she was talking about work, but before I could ask anything else, Mindy appeared behind me.

"Alexis, those guys on the couch are looking for you." She jerked her chin at the back wall. "They probably need refills."

Sighing, I picked up my order pad and pen and headed across the room.

"Don't think you can cool your heels when you're dressed so smokin' hot," Det. Thompson mocked. From the snickers, it was obvious Thompson, Heathcliff, and O'Connell were enjoying themselves, and there was little I could do about it since I was technically undercover.

"Gentlemen, what can I get you?"

"A round of beers. Heathcliff's buying." O'Connell smiled evilly.

"Don't you think you might be more comfortable at the bar?"

"Nah, the couches are pretty nice," O'Connell replied.

Turning on my heel, I went to the bar and retrieved three long necks. As I placed the beers on the ottoman, I spoke to O'Connell and Heathcliff since Thompson's comment earned him a spot on my shit list. "The VIP table upstairs next to the manager's office got me thinking. Maybe the safes were emptied during business hours. I gave Hoskins a call, but the son of a bitch flew off the handle and hung up. Are you guys sticking around to keep an eye on things?"

"Do you think something's going down tonight?"

Heathcliff's hand automatically moved to his concealed weapon.

"I have no idea. I don't think so, but Gretchen," I jerked my head in her direction and saw Nick shift his gaze to the bar, "came in acting strange, but I'm probably just on edge."

"We might stick around and loiter for a while," Nick said. "Are you gonna comp us the beers?"

"On the house." I retreated to the bar.

Twenty minutes later, Ernie descended the staircase with his duffel bag and nodded to me on his way out of the club. I kept a watchful eye on everyone who left afterward, but no one tailed him. When the three detectives finished their beers and Thompson returned from snooping upstairs, they left the club, planning to remain close in case something happened. It was nice someone had my back, even if I was just a paranoid lunatic. It was more than what Det. Carl Hoskins was doing.

After the frenzied rush of last call, the club quieted as the music stopped. The remaining stragglers slowly trickled out. Once the bar was closed, I changed out of my waitress get-up and into my street clothes and sensible shoes. The cleanup didn't take nearly as long as I imagined, and by five, everyone had left except Sam. He was busy making sure all the bottles were properly organized and capped while I vacuumed and scrubbed the ottomans.

"Are you almost ready?" he called.

I had delayed leaving since I wasn't about to let any of Ernie's workers remain inside the club unattended. After all, any one of them could be a master safecracker. "Getting there. If you're ready to go, you don't have to wait for me."

"Not a problem. It's late. I thought I'd walk you to your car. In this neighborhood, you never know." Sam made surveillance an even greater challenge.

"That's sweet, but I can take care of myself."

He wouldn't take no for an answer, so I finished tidying up the barstools and went to grab my purse from the storeroom. I noticed I had a text message from an hour ago. My detective posse had been called away. Just as I realized I wouldn't need them tonight, the double doors clanged closed.

"Sam?" Maybe he was locking up. I put my jacket on and slipped my handgun into my pocket. "Sam?" I tried again. I heard two male voices, but they weren't loud enough to decipher. Then I heard one of the worst things imaginable.

"Police. On the ground, now."

I wondered what was going on. Was Sam in on the heist, and the police intervened in the nick of time? My first instinct was to surrender in order to avoid getting caught in a raid, but before I even cleared the bar, a single gunshot rang out. Automatically, I took cover against the doorjamb.

No other voices surfaced. There was no radio chatter, only the sound of heavy footsteps walking through the club. The mirror behind the bar provided an obscured view of a man with a badge circling around, the gun still in his hand. It wasn't an inside job.

I tried to study his reflection, but he moved out of range of the mirror. The reflection provided little help anyway since it only showed the assailant from the chest down. Slowly, I leaned around the doorjamb, checking to see where he went. The rules of the game had drastically changed.

I fumbled for my phone, placing the 911 call. Before the operator connected, the heavy footsteps came down the main staircase, and in my haste, I knocked over a vodka bottle that shattered on impact. Great.

Just fucking great.

"Police. Come out with your hands up," an intentionally unrecognizable voice bellowed.

The operator connected, and I gave her the address and reported a shooting still in progress. Come on, O'Connell, please don't be too far away. The storeroom had one advantage which was the second staircase leading up, but that would be my last resort. I needed to buy time until the actual cops arrived.

"Do you mind giving me your badge number, first?" I glanced around, assessing my options. There were liquor bottles galore but not much else. When no response came, I wondered if he was going to come around and surprise me using my intended escape route. Checking the clip in my gun, I risked a peek out of the storeroom, and he fired. The bullet ripped through the doorjamb, splintering the frame as wood shards and debris pummeled into my side and back. Ducking my head and turning my body away from the door, I reached around and fired blindly in his direction. "I'll take that as a yes."

Picking up a bottle from the stockroom, I threw it in his general direction and fired again. It was meant as a warning. "Do you want me to light this place up? Because I'm sure there's enough alcohol to make quite a boom. Then again, that might draw a little too much attention, don't you agree?" Sirens sounded in the distance, and I could make out hurried footsteps going toward the double doors. Now was my chance.

I ran up the steps, across the narrow second floor walkway, and down the central staircase to the back doors, hoping to surprise the bastard. Sam was on the ground, a bullet through the center of his back. Biting my lip, torn between checking on him and stopping the shooter, I continued pursuit to the doors when I heard the gathered police presence exchanging information.

I caught a glimpse of the back of the shooter, his clothing and jacket completely recognizable. He raised his arms as black and whites pulled in and officers leapt from their vehicles with guns drawn. "I was in the neighborhood." He held up his shield, and the officers lowered their weapons. Only then did it dawn on me that he wasn't a police impersonator; he was actually a dirty cop. "The suspect is female and armed. She attacked the bartender and is holding him hostage. I just heard shots fired. I was about to breach. We should consider her armed and dangerous. Take her down. Use extreme prejudice."

On instinct alone, I fled. Sprinting to the side door, I threw it open, expecting to find a tactical team, but no one covered the side. Zipping my jacket and shoving my gun inside my purse, I headed down the street. When I made it to the end of the block, I reverted to a full out run for the next half mile until the pain in my side forced me to slow down.

It was pouring rain and almost dawn. Remembering my phone, I pulled out the SIM card and battery and threw them in the nearest dumpster, knowing my 911 call would be easy to trace.

Finally, I found a cab and went home. After paying the man in cash with my tip money, I ran upstairs, keeping an eye on the time. Three detectives had seen me in the club, and none of Ernie's employees owed me any loyalty. It wouldn't take the police long to come looking for me. I unlocked my apartment and changed out of my wet clothes, noticing long pieces of splintered wood imbedded in my bleeding side, along with the bullet. There was no time to deal with this right now, so I poured some peroxide over the injury and wrapped gauze around my torso before throwing on a fitted tank top to hold everything in place.

The police were searching for Sam's killer. Hopefully, ballistics would prove I wasn't the shooter, but the realization that a cop could manipulate evidence to hide his involvement frightened me. I knew I had to run. What other choice did I have in a corrupt system where I'd either be framed for murder or killed while in custody? It was the only way I could prove my innocence.

Quickly, I went through my apartment, packing the bare essentials and leaving everything out in the open that the police would search my house for – my club clothing, gun, and evidence related to Infinity. I laid my nine millimeter on the kitchen table, unloaded, with the partially used clip sitting next to it. Unlocking my gun safe, I removed my secondary weapon and stowed it in the bag and left the safe open so the investigators wouldn't break the lock.

Picking up my home phone, I dialed Mark. When he answered, I rapidly filled the empty air space with as much pertinent information as I could muster. "Mark, it's a dirty cop. He was at Infinity. Get someone to check on Ernie Papadakis. He emptied the safe before leaving, but he can vouch for me, I hope. The bartender, Sam Harrigan, was inside the club when it all went down. He's probably dead. He took a bullet to the back, but I didn't get a chance to check his vitals."

"Alex, take a breath." He was probably tracing the call. Other agents were in the background, asking questions. "You need to come in."

"I don't know exactly what happened, but the cop shot Sam and then came gunning for me. When the police arrived, I ran. I didn't have a choice."

Remembering Martin had been in my apartment on Thursday, I wiped every flat surface and doorknob I could think of, hoping to prevent him from getting dragged into this. The police had no reason to dust my apartment for prints, but in case they were looking for leads on my whereabouts, I couldn't be too careful. Going to my desk, I pulled out the resignation letter I printed two months ago when we started dating and wrote last Thursday's date at the top and signed the bottom. Martin Technologies didn't need any more negative press than it already had in the last year, and the powers that be could insist I quit before going on a shooting rampage. I shoved the letter in my bag and emptied the drawer that housed my waitressing tips from the last few days. I had five hundred dollars in cash, but I needed more untraceable liquid resources.

"Parker, listen to me," Mark said, calm but forceful, "you need to turn yourself in. We will get this sorted out. Running is not the answer. How many times have you said the guilty always run?"

"If I turn myself in, the evidence could be influenced. He could bury me."

"I'll bring you in and keep you safe. What I'm seeing doesn't read well. This is all over the wire. There's a description of you, and from the preliminary radio chatter, you're the only person of interest."

"Since it's that bad, I'll have to figure something else out." I swallowed. "In case you're tracing this, I'll save you the trouble, I'm at home, but by the time you get here, I'll be long gone. Try not to trash my apartment too badly. I'll leave as much for you as I can, and I'll be in touch when I have more." The lump returned to my throat. "Mark, buy me some time." Pushing my fingertips against my side, I felt the painful protuberance. "I've got his bullet, and I will find a way to get it to you." Leaving my phone off the hook, I grabbed my brown leather jacket and a baseball cap and fled my apartment.

SEVEN

Parker, you need a strategy. The words rang through my brain as I got into a cab and headed as far from my apartment as the driver was willing to go. It was six a.m. on a Sunday morning. The city was still asleep.

Walking a few blocks, I found a twenty-four hour diner and went inside to get some coffee and sustenance. Staying in any one place for too long would be detrimental, so I needed to keep moving. I also needed cash, a few untraceable burner phones, and some solid leads. I ate quickly and left a decent tip, hoping not to be noticed.

It would have been nice to have my car, but the police could track my plates and pinpoint my location too easily. Moving east, I found a convenience store and purchased four disposable phones with cash. The numbers couldn't be tracked, and the phones themselves would remain anonymous. I'd have to use them sparingly because if I called Mark, he'd have the number, and I'd have to toss it. What was I doing?

The rain picked up again, and I sought shelter under the awning of a bus stop. I was running scared, and the constant fear and adrenaline made it difficult to think clearly. Who was the dirty cop? Detectives O'Connell, Heathcliff, and Thompson had been at Infinity, but it made me physically ill to think any of them could be dirty. Although, the only one I was certain of was Nick. We had a long history, and he had my back more times than I cared to admit. He wouldn't do this. At least there was one cop I trusted. The problem was he was still duty-bound.

My immediate goal was to get off the street and out of the rain. More importantly, I needed to cut the bullet out of my side and get it to Mark. My cash was dwindling after the cell phone purchases and cab rides. Where could I go for resources?

My mind went to the only feasible option. There had to be ways to mitigate his involvement. Fortuitously, I spotted a bike messenger service across the street, and I scurried over as soon as someone unlocked the door. Most services didn't run on weekends or this early in the morning, but maybe one thing would actually go right today.

"I need a package delivered." I picked up a blank manila envelope from the counter and pulled out one of the cell phones. Inputting the number into a different phone, I slid the phone inside the envelope and addressed it to James Martin, CEO.

"When do you want it delivered?" the guy asked, looking out into the storm.

How long would it take the police to properly identify me, search my apartment, and traipse down to the MT building? Although, for all intents and purposes, the MT building was shut down on Sundays. No one knew Martin would be working, so they wouldn't be monitoring building communications.

"At eleven. Can you guarantee it will get to the right person?" I had never used a messenger service before, but I couldn't afford to have my calls recorded or traced.

"Sure, you can require a signature." The guy handed me a clipboard to fill out with name and address, and I paid for the service and listed the sender as Lola Peters, my only undercover alias Martin would remember.

"Make sure it's there by eleven."

Leaving the bike messenger, I had four hours to get to Martin's compound. Taking a taxi directly there wouldn't be a good idea. This wasn't supposed to happen. I was not a criminal. I chased criminals. Sighing, I tried to get my bearings. Finding an open drug store, I stopped in to get out of the rain and scour the aisles for supplies. Unfortunately, they didn't sell anything surgical.

Entering the restroom, I flipped the lock and unbandaged my side to assess the splinters and obviously lodged bullet in the mirror. It wasn't at a good angle to remove it myself, especially since the bullet needed to stay as pristine as possible for a proper identification to be made. Goddammit, I slammed my palm on the sink, rewrapped the gauze, and pulled my soaking wet shirt down. When I emerged, a uniformed officer was standing at the register, chatting with the cashier. My heart pounded in my chest, and I ducked my head as I hurried past him. It took two blocks before I breathed a sigh of relief.

Being out in the open was asking to get caught or worse. Reading street names, I did some quick calculations and took out one of the phones. Although three of the four were the most basic model available, the fourth had a few nicer features, like internet capabilities. Bringing up a map, in another mile and a half, I'd be at a small secluded shopping center, and if I headed through the wooded area behind it, I should happen upon the back of Martin's compound in another two miles. There was a vague recollection careening through my mind of Bruiser mentioning he had used that method to arrive at Martin's when the media hounds had been circling the front. Too bad I didn't wear hiking boots.

*   *   *

Trudging through the woods between Martin's compound and the shopping mall, I had a renewed admiration for Bruiser. Soaking wet, I shivered uncontrollably as I searched for a clearing. Thank god. It was five after eleven, and it had taken hours to navigate the dense woods. I had gotten turned off course twice and had to retrace my steps. The outdoors weren't meant for me. Roughing it would be a cheap ass motel, not camping in the forest. I leaned against a tree. My gaze darted around the back of Martin's compound as I made sure there were no flashing lights or signs of activity.

Dialing the only saved number in the phone, I waited. With any luck, the messenger delivered the package promptly to Martin himself. After four rings, I was ready to give up when the ringing abruptly stopped. I held my breath and waited for a confused hello.

"Don't say my name. You know who this is, right?" My voice shook, and my teeth chattered.

"Are you okay? Why did–" Martin sounded anxious.

"Listen to me carefully. Are you alone?"

"Yes."

"Okay. Call the security office and say you have a teleconference and cannot be disturbed for the next few hours. Then," I ran through the advanced security system and cameras I had installed, "take the elevator down to the twelfth floor, get out, and go to your left. Get on the freight elevator, and when it opens, immediately go to your right and out the emergency exit. The alarm isn't rigged to sound. Walk two blocks, heading east on Forty-Ninth. Keep your head down, and once you get to Rolston, catch a cab and meet me at the castle. Use cash to pay the cabbie. Do you understand?"

"Not in the least," he replied. "Are you there now?"

"Don't let anyone know we spoke. Please hurry." I hung up before he could ask any more questions. Making him go to such extremes would hopefully thwart any eyes that might be on him, and if he was stopped, he couldn't provide any solid information to my whereabouts.

Pulling my jacket tighter around my body, I left the slight protection of the trees and walked briskly across his yard, past the pool, and up the steps to the back deck. His security camera caught me, and I reached into my bag and pulled out my gun in sight of the camera. Eventually, the cops would come here, so I had to make it look good.

*   *   *

Waiting in the alcove near the back door, I turned my collar up and pressed my body against the brick, trying to shield myself from the cold, stinging rain. Where was he? He should be home by now. Did he get caught or detained? I shouldn't even be here, but I had nowhere else to go. The security camera continued to monitor my presence on the back deck in the freezing rain. I held my jacket closed with only my left hand because my gun was in my right, down at my thigh.

What felt like hours later, the inside lights turned on, and footsteps sounded from inside the house. Using my gun hand, I rapped my knuckles against the door and waited for him to answer. My heart pounded loudly as he approached the door. The constant adrenaline rush wasn't helping matters. He pushed the curtains ever so slightly to the side, and as the lock slid out of place and the doorknob began to twist, I brought my gun up.

Martin opened the door to find my gun leveled at his chest. Stepping into the door so he couldn't shut out my intrusion, I tried to look as threatening as possible. His face reflected confusion, and he stepped back. "Alex, what are you doing?"

"Turn off your security system, now," I barked, looking up at the camera and knowing the damage was already done. He hesitated uncertainly. "Do it now, and make sure you shut off the cameras too. I know they're on a separate system." I jerked my gun toward the control panel on his wall. Since I had worked private security for him, it made everything that much easier, but Martin wasn't making a very good hostage as he slowly turned to the panel.

"Why are you doing this?" His tone held nothing but confusion. After he hit a few buttons and the green light flipped to red and then went blank, I shut the back door, went to the wet bar, dropping my gun on the countertop, and attempted to take a seat on the barstool. In my drenched state, my shoes lost traction, and I slid from the stool. He reached out and grabbed me before I landed on my ass. "You're ice cold and soaking wet." He pulled his hand away from my side to find his palm covered in crimson. "And you're bleeding."

"Unfortunate side effect of getting shot." I headed for the bathroom. "I don't have much time. You got any towels?"

"Alex," he was at my heels, and before I made it past the kitchen, he blocked my path, "come on, I'll take you to the emergency room."

"I'm fine. It's just a graze, sort of. I caught a ricochet, or I don't know." I pressed my lips together, knowing everything I said would either implicate him or be used against me. "I didn't want to drag you into this, but I didn't know where else to go. Mark, Nick, and everyone in law enforcement is gunning for me. I'm wanted for murder. The less you know, the better." Stepping past him, I continued to the bathroom. Once inside, I stripped off my jacket and tank top.

"You're drenched." He pulled towels from the cabinet. "You must be freezing. How long have you been out in the rain?"

"I don't know. Hours." Pulling the dripping, pinkish-red gauze away from my body, I twisted in front of the mirror to assess the damage. "Do you have tweezers and a paring knife?" He put his warm hands on my shoulders and spun me, so he could examine the extent of my injuries. Watching his reflection in the mirror, I saw his face grow ashen. "It's okay. I can do this myself. Oh, and a zippered sandwich bag would be good too. I didn't think to grab evidence bags on my way out. Shit, I have to find a way to get the bullet to Mark."

"You're not cutting into your own flesh. This is insane. How can you be so matter-of-fact about this?" He pulled supplies from the cabinet in the vanity. "A bullet and half a tree are projecting from your back.

You're ice cold and wanted for murder. And you're just going to stand here and ask for a damn sandwich bag?"

"It could be worse." Another shiver wracked my body, and he draped a towel around my shoulders.

"Go sit in the kitchen. I'll grab whatever you need, and we'll figure something out."

Unwilling to argue and unable to remove the evidence myself, I wasn't left with much of a choice. For the first time today, I did as I was told and flipped the chair around, leaning my chest against the backrest. Even my bra was saturated. He came into the kitchen with tweezers, first-aid supplies, and a book of matches. He sterilized the tweezers and began to remove the wood shards from my side.

"Fuck," I growled, digging my nails into the chair.

"You're bleeding," his voice was neutral, but he wasn't prepared to deal with any of this. "Are you sure I should pull them out. Wasn't there some kind of thing about if you are impaled, not to remove the object or you could bleed to death?" Clearly, his knowledge of field medicine came from watching too many doctor shows on television.

"I'm not impaled. They're just splinters." Looking down at the one he removed, I felt a little woozy. "You know what, they're not bothering me. I just need you to get the bullet out."

"How?"

Remembering the way it felt and looked in the mirror, I tried to describe the process. "Sterilize the paring knife and slice horizontally below where it's lodged, then you'll be able to dig it out."

"Hang on." He went to the basement door. Was he abandoning me? "Jones, I need your expertise."

"Bruiser's here?" I had no idea Martin's bodyguard was home, and I wasn't sure he wouldn't implicate me. "I can't involve anyone else in this."

"And I can't cut into my girlfriend with a goddamn paring knife." Martin locked eyes with me. "He was a Navy corpsman. He's bound to be better equipped to handle this than I am. And he'll keep his mouth shut. You trust him with my life, so you can trust him with yours."

"Mr. Martin?" Bruiser stood in the entryway to the kitchen, probably surprised to find me sitting backward in a chair in nothing but my jeans and a bra. "Ms. Parker?"

"Don't worry, it's not some weird fetish thing," Martin offered in an attempt at levity.

"We're in need of your medical expertise." I explained the current dilemma and my insistence on having the bullet removed intact.

"Get on the table." Bruiser unbuttoned the cuffs of his sleeves and rolled them up. "I'm going to need more rubbing alcohol. The injury itself isn't severe, but with the bullet still inside and all that damn wood, your biggest worry is infection. How long since it happened?"

"It was around five this morning," I said as Martin finished laying some clean towels on the table and went to find more antiseptic. "It's been a long day."

Bruiser let out a small chuckle as I lay flat against the towels, oddly relishing in getting to lie down somewhere warm, dry, and safe, even if I was about to be sliced open like a Christmas ham.

Bruiser washed his hands at the kitchen sink and poured copious amounts of rubbing alcohol over them. Martin stood around nervously, and I seriously considered taking a nap while I waited for things to get underway.

"Alex," Martin brushed my wet hair off my back and to the side, "we can still go to the emergency room."

"No. You know why I can't. If I do, I'll either be framed for murder or killed."

"Parker, this will sting, and then you're really not going to like what follows," Bruiser warned.

"Wait a minute," I remembered how important it was to maintain the veracity of the evidence, "Martin, take some photos. Just remember, I forced you to do it at gunpoint. In case Mark hits any snafus concerning where the bullet came from, he'll have photographic proof."

Martin picked up his phone and did as I asked. When he was done, I nodded to Bruiser and gripped the edge of the table, preparing for the pain to get worse.

EIGHT

My breath came in ragged gasps, and my side throbbed from where Bruiser had to dig around to locate and extract the bullet. At least it was over. As soon as I could get it to Mark, he would run it through ballistics. Hopefully, it would match the bullet used on Sam, and I would be cleared. Sam, I hadn't had time to think about him. Poor guy. He stuck around to walk me to my car, and this was the thanks he got.

"Alex," Martin traced small circles along my shoulder, "are you okay?"

"Yes." I tried to sit up, but I winced back against the table. "Help me up. I need to get out of here." Tilting my head, I saw him exchange a glance with Bruiser.

"Although amateur, you just had surgery with no anesthesia," Bruiser said. "It'd be best to hang around just to make sure you don't go into shock. I'm not a doctor."

"Nice disclaimer. What time is it?"

"It's two." Martin climbed off the table.

"I have to get out of here by four. Sooner would be safer, but with the way the investigation should be going, four is the absolute latest." I rolled onto my non-injured side, and before I could say another word, Martin lifted me into his arms and cradled me against his chest. He was warm. I missed feeling warm. He carried me to the couch and was about to put me down when I insisted my blood on his sofa wouldn't sell the story of being taken hostage. Bruiser covered the cushions with some extra towels, and Martin laid me on top of them. "Thanks, Jones."

"Anytime." He disappeared into the kitchen to clean off the table.

Martin retrieved a blanket, and once I was covered, I shimmied out of my damp jeans and asked if he could rinse my shirt and pants and throw them in the dryer. With my limited resources, staying wet all day wouldn't help matters. His expression was grim, but he did as I asked and returned with the dress shirt I had stuffed in my bequeathed drawer. At least I had something to wear in the interim.

"Try to get some rest. You look beat." He rubbed his thumb across my cheek, and I shut my eyes, knowing I had to sleep whenever I could. There was no way to predict how long I would be out in the cold, but until I was cleared, I couldn't turn myself in. As I started to drift off, I heard Martin and Bruiser exchange mumbled words.

"It's not a question of if it'll get infected. It's a question of when."

"Only she understands what's going on. I won't tell her what to do," Martin said. "It's her call."

"She's tired, hurt, and scared." Jones sighed. "It's a deadly combination."

*   *   *

Martin softly stroked the lock of hair framing my face,

and my eyes fluttered open. His forehead creased, and his jaw clenched. Sadness clouded his eyes, and every argument I had ever made for the reasons we shouldn't be together played through my head.

"It's 3:30." He sat on the edge of the couch, next to my hips. "I'll do whatever you want. I have resources. A private jet. We can be wheels up in an hour. Or we can get in the car and drive until we run out of gas. Please let me help you."

"You've already helped. I might be on the run, but I'm not running away. If I leave now, I can never come back. I trust Mark. Nick, too. They'll find a way. Once I know it's going to be okay, I'll turn myself in." Sitting up, I noticed my side felt better, and so did I. "But if you're offering resources..."

"Anything."

"Can you lend me some cash? I can't use my credit cards or anything they can trace. And can I raid your bathroom for first-aid supplies?"

He offered a bittersweet smile and got off the couch to get some money. My messenger bag remained on the bathroom floor where I dropped it. Opening it, I pulled out the resignation letter. Then I took the bottles of ibuprofen and acetaminophen from the cabinet, a container of peroxide, and all the medical tape and gauze I could find and stowed them inside.

Martin brought my clothes into the bathroom, along with a thousand dollars. He watched as I dressed, and then he went back upstairs to get a sweatshirt and umbrella. "You don't have to leave. Maybe they won't make the connection."

"You're already too involved. You don't have to do anything else." He knew I had another request, and he wouldn't deny it. "But I need an hour's head start before you call Mark and report the assault. Tell him I burst in here with a gun and forced you to remove the bullet. Make sure he gets the photos for evidence. And remember, you did this against your free will. My dramatic entrance will help sell it when they review your security footage." I picked up the resignation letter and handed it to him.

"You quit?" He attempted to tease, but there was no mirth behind his joke.

"MT has enough problems without dealing with blowback. If I quit before any of this happened, it should insulate your company. Maybe you should call your legal team and be prepared to threaten lawsuits if necessary."

"Alex," he tried to interrupt.

"I never wanted to hurt you. I'm so sorry. I'm trying to mitigate it as much as possible, but if they turn up the heat, I'm leaving you the cell phone. You're the only one who has my contact number. If things go south, call. I will surrender and take all the blame and culpability."

He put his thumb and forefinger on my chin, and we shared a long, passionate kiss. "Stay safe."

"One more thing. Do you mind if I borrow a car? I'll ditch it at the first parking garage I find, and—"

"Take it. Just remember, Jones is concerned about infection. Avoid the bad guys and the germs."

"Sure."

*   *   *

Driving around would lead to capture. Time was not on my side in any regard. If no one was investigating my connection to Martin, I would have an hour until Mark was notified, and soon after, they would track Martin's missing vehicle.

Finding a parking garage less than five miles from his house, I parked on the third story and locked the doors. As I walked down the steps, I slipped the car keys into my bag. Once outside, I opened the umbrella and continued walking.

Going back to my apartment would be asking for trouble. Checking into the precinct would be a surefire way to get arrested or caught, and stopping by my office was just as dumb of an idea. How was I going to pinpoint the crooked cop when all avenues were barred? Ernie. Maybe if I could find Ernie, he could shed some light on what happened this morning and what the police were doing.

Out of options, I headed for the public library. Accessing a computer terminal, I ran a white pages search for Ernie Papadakis, which led to half a dozen entries. Switching tactics, I ran a more thorough people search, located the proper Ernie Papadakis, and cross-referenced it with the addresses. I scribbled down my destination and left the library.

I hailed a taxi to Ernie's apartment building. He lived in an affluent building, complete with doorman and high-powered security cameras. Smiling at the doorman, I insisted on seeing Mr. Papadakis and provided my first name. The doorman called up to Ernie's apartment, but there was no answer. My blood ran cold, but I tried to convince myself Ernie was probably out. His club had been robbed, and his bartender shot. Obviously, there was no reason to think he would be home. The doorman eyed me suspiciously as I walked away. I glanced back at him, finding he had picked up the phone and was speaking animatedly to someone.

Five blocks away, I heard the cacophony of sirens. An ambulance and two police cars darted past, en route to Ernie's building. Great. Was I about to be blamed for another crime? Even though I needed to keep moving, I found myself reversing direction and sprinting down the street after the cars. A couple blocks later, I slowed my gait and ducked into a café. The police lights reflected off the wet pavement, and a gurney rushed out the front door, carrying Ernie with an oxygen mask over his face. From this distance, I couldn't determine the extent of his injuries or what happened, but he was still breathing.

A few nosy onlookers stood in the street, watching the ambulance race away as police officers questioned the doorman. "Anyone know what happened?" I asked from behind the group. They shrugged and disbanded at the sound of my intrusion. How come they never did that when I had a badge and gun?

Things were rapidly going downhill for me. To be fair, things weren't going so well for Ernie either. I thought briefly about his silent partner, but I insisted on not knowing the man's identity. And even now, I still wasn't comfortable getting in bed with organized crime.

The rain picked up, and I shivered. My focus should be on finding shelter. It was getting dark, and I had no plan of attack. Muddling through the city, I found a chain motel with exterior doors. The sign out front said they were still open, despite their ongoing renovations. Since there weren't many cars in the parking lot, I thought I'd give it a try. Spotting the maid's entrance, I pulled the baseball cap lower and removed my lock picks.

In two minutes, the lock popped. Finding a master keycard hanging from a peg, I palmed it and put the snap-closure grey smock on over my clothes and took off the cap. Picking up a stack of folded towels, I exited the room and pulled the door shut behind me. My messenger bag would probably be a dead giveaway I wasn't a maid, so I obscured it from view with the towels as I headed up four flights of stairs.

Motels tended to fill the bottom floors first so cleaning and services could be provided more easily. The fifteen cars in the parking lot were likely half employees and half guests. By my estimation, the fourth floor should be vacant, especially since most of it was roped off for renovation. I walked to the far end and knocked on the door.

"Maid service," I hollered. There was no response. "Sir, I have your towels." I glanced around; no one opened a door or shouted a response. All the drapes were drawn on the other rooms. There was a distinct possibility no one was even occupying this level. Carefully, I slipped the keycard into the lock and opened the door. "Sir? Ma'am?" The place held nothing except motel-provided amenities. Noting the light layer of dust on the surfaces, I knew business hadn't been booming for a few weeks.

Immediately, I went to the wall unit and cranked up the heat. Then I went back to the door, slid the security bar into place, and shoved the standing wardrobe in front of it. If someone wanted to get inside, I wouldn't make it easy for them. Taking a deep breath, I hoped this would be a safe place to stay the night. Discarding the maid's uniform, I took off my jacket and wet clothes and hung them in the wardrobe in front of the door. No reason it couldn't serve multiple functions. Then I dumped out the contents of my bag and assessed what was left. All I had were two unused burner phones, the one for contact with Martin, roughly a thousand dollars, car keys, lock picks, peroxide, some pain relievers, gauze, a change of clothes, some extra underwear, an umbrella, and my gun and bullets.

Shivering, I stripped out of my underwear, removed my bandage, and took my gun into the bathroom. Stepping into the shower, I turned the water on as hot as I could stand and tried to force the chill from my bones. My side was sore and bleeding. The hot water made it worse, but like Bruiser said, it needed to be kept clean so it wouldn't get infected. Being out in the rain all day didn't help, and I prayed my temporary shelter would remain secure. When I was finally warm, I got out of the shower, dried off, poured copious amounts of peroxide over the wound, and redressed it. Luckily, there was a motel-provided hairdryer.

When I emerged from the bathroom, I was clean, warm, and exhausted. I took my wet clothes from the wardrobe and hung them over the heating unit so they would dry faster. Then I pulled down the covers in one of the two full-size beds and shut the light.

I awoke a little after four a.m. to the sound of voices on a lower level. Quickly, I got up and traded the motel towel for my now dry clothing. Throwing everything back inside my bag, I put it on the floor, reached for my gun, and listened through the darkness. The voices quieted, and I didn't hear any other sounds. My eyes closed, but I forced myself to stay awake for another twenty minutes until I was sure it was safe. Then I buried myself under the covers and slept until eight.

The sun filtered in from the window, and I squinted against it. At least it wasn't raining. Risking a quick look outside, I didn't see any movement on my level or any police cruisers in the parking lot. My safe haven remained secure. In the bathroom, I found soap, lotion, shampoo, a toothbrush, toothpaste, razor, hairdryer, and coffeemaker, all courtesy of this fine motel chain. Brushing my teeth, I turned on the coffeemaker and listened to it whistle and sputter as the coffee brewed. Parker, you need a plan.

Taking my full mug into the main room, I got back

into bed, wincing as I propped myself against a few pillows and put pressure against my injured side and back. Locating the remote, I turned the television to the local news. There was no coverage on the club shooting. Uncertain of everything, I picked up the burner and called Martin's disposable phone.

"Are you okay?" The sound of his voice broke my heart.

"Yes. Are you alone?"

"Yeah, I'm in my office."

"Did you get everything to Mark? Have they been following you? They're not filing charges against you, are they?" A million questions bubbled to the surface.

"Mark's on it. He said they'd put a rush on ballistics, so hopefully, they'll hear something today or tomorrow. There's a lovely group of federal agents parked outside my place and another set who followed me to work. No one's asked any questions except Mark, and," Martin lowered his voice, and the sink in his office washroom turned on, "he has a message for you."

"I'm listening."

"He and O'Connell are looking into allegations of police corruption. The cop who shot you is probably the same guy they're after."

"Holy shit."

"He thought you'd want to know, so he asked that I pass it along, figuring you might contact me."

"You're not a go-between. It's too dangerous. I just wanted to make sure you were okay and tell you where to pick up your car." I gave him the address. "Call if there's an emergency. In the meantime, I have to find a way to talk to someone in charge."

NINE

Hoping the motel wouldn't rent or renovate my occupied room while I was gone, I left the nonessentials inside the wardrobe, shoved everything else into my purse, grabbed the master room key, made sure the coast was clear, and stealthily exited the motel room. Martin said ballistics might get a match later today, so I needed to figure out a way to set up a meeting with Nick or Mark.

I caught a cab to the precinct, hoping no one would recognize me. Walking into the lion's den was ludicrous, but leaving a note on O'Connell's car might work out okay. Entering the back lot, I spotted the beat-up sedan in its usual space. During my taxi ride, I scribbled a location and time to meet and addressed it to my favorite detective. Nick would know who left it. I just wasn't sure if he would show up alone or if he would invite a tactical team to join us. Sidling up to the car, I expertly maneuvered the plain white paper, having cut off the motel name from the top, into the doorjamb.

Mission accomplished. I returned to the main thoroughfare to find another cab. As I passed, a few fresh-faced uniforms exited the precinct. Two of them chatted happily, paying me no heed. Incompetence and obliviousness were my allies at the moment.

Rounding the corner, I practically collided with a beat cop returning from his tour. He initially smiled, and I swore for not ducking my head a millisecond sooner. I took three steps past him before he called out, "Excuse me."

Parker, keep walking. My pace remained unchanged, but he called out again, approaching quickly. I could either run or see what he wanted.

"Yes?" I played dumb, focusing on the ground and refusing to fully turn around.

"Hold on a second." His voice sounded uncertain, and I knew I had been made. "Turn around slowly and take your hands out of your pockets."

"Really, I don't have time for this." I continued to walk away, and he put his hand on my shoulder to halt my procession. I spun around and delivered an elbow to his jaw with a crack. He dropped to a knee in surprise and pain, and I slid over the hood of a parked car and darted across the street.

Genius, my sarcastic internal voice mocked as I ran down an alleyway. In the distance, the sounds of radio chatter polluted the air as the cop called for backup. All of this over a damn meeting with O'Connell. What the fuck was I thinking? A swarm of officers would be on me in a matter of minutes. I needed to get off the street, which meant there was only one way to go. Up.

As my rubber soles screeched to a stop next to a fire escape, I didn't have time to process the rationale as I jumped up and tugged the ladder down. I climbed flight after flight, all the way to the roof. The original beat cop was two levels below and gaining quickly.

Despite my fear of heights, I did the only thing I could think to do. I ran full speed off the roof and jumped to the next rooftop, landing hard and rolling. Movies always made this seem exciting, but in real life, it was a miracle I didn't turn kamikaze or break my ankle.

Thankfully, the door leading to the inside was unlocked, and I shut it before the cop emerged onto the roof of the first building. The building I entered appeared to be an insurance firm, and I received many awkward looks as I made my way down the stairs. Running down flight after flight, I couldn't help but think the elevator might have been a better idea. Finally, I made it to the ground floor and slowly opened the door to the lobby. The police hadn't penetrated the building yet, so there was a chance I could still slip by.

Taking off my jacket, I twisted my hair tightly and secured it in place with a pen from a nearby desk. Finding a pair of sunglasses on another desk, I slid them on before heading out the door. My disguise wasn't much, but it might be enough to throw off some confused rookies. I strutted down the street as a dozen police officers surrounded the building I ascended. A block away, I got into another cab and gave the driver Mark's home address.

As we pulled into Mark's neighborhood, I scanned the area for surveillance vans. Nothing looked suspicious or particularly nondescript. I had no reason to think the authorities would consider me a threat to Mark or dumb enough to go to his house, so this was already a better plan than leaving a note for O'Connell.

Getting out, I paid the driver and walked around to the fence at the end of the row of townhouses. Unlatching the gate, I went behind the connected buildings and counted four across before stopping at

Mark's back door.

Even though he was a federal agent and knew crime intimately, he still kept a spare key underneath the ugly frog statue in his backyard. I picked up the key and opened the door. Mark's car wasn't parked out front, and I didn't believe he was home. However, it was better to be safe than sorry, so I announced my presence as I entered. After getting no response or hearing any other sounds, I opened the fridge and made myself a sandwich.

I was famished, and I didn't know where or when my next meal would be. As I chowed down on some turkey and a glass of orange juice, I grabbed a sheet of paper and outlined everything I knew. There wasn't much. Everything relating to Infinity was in my office. The LEOs must have cleared it out by now. Would the dirty cop use whatever was in my office to bury me?

Internal affairs and the FBI investigated police corruption. Since Mark was an OIO agent, Director Kendall probably kicked him over to the Bureau to help investigate. His long history with O'Connell's superior, Lt. Moretti, and the brief cooperative ventures they had in the past made Jablonsky and O'Connell the perfect pair and would explain why they both approached me about assisting them on another case.

Making another sandwich, I tried to pinpoint who in the police force might have an axe to grind. But the crooked cop could be anyone. The way he acted made it seem like he didn't know anyone else was in the club besides Sam. Then again, EMTs rushed Ernie out of his apartment. Did a cop come for Ernie too? Or did his mafia partners get pissed because he brought the fuzz into their establishment and emptied out the safe the night before? Did Ernie deposit the money like I told him? I had too many questions and not enough answers. I sat back in the chair, instantly regretting it.

Checking the time, I went to the bathroom to see how well I was healing. All the physical exertion wouldn't let the wound close. It was red, tender, and warm to the touch. So much for avoiding infection. I found some rubbing alcohol and cleaned and redressed my injury. Mark's hospitality would not go by unnoticed. Whenever this was over, I'd send him a nice fruit basket to express my gratitude.

Back in the kitchen, I left a few notes on Ernie – the emptied safe, some shady silent partners, his speculation on the new staff. Then I wrote everything I knew about the shooter. My description only described him from the chest down, and I wished I had gotten a better look at his badge. Closing my eyes, I tried to sketch what I had seen. When I opened my eyes, it was a detective's shield. At least that would narrow it down.

He wore a pale grey t-shirt underneath a blue windbreaker with the shield hanging from a chain around his neck. He fired one shot into Sam Harrigan and another into me. The son of a bitch was two for two. I fired twice, missing both times. After finishing my brief incident report, I scribbled a quick thank you for the sandwiches and headed to the door.

Just as I was exiting out the back, Mark came in the front with his weapon poised. I ran for cover, cowering behind the picnic tables and ancient playground equipment the neighborhood provided. As soon as Mark realized it was me, he holstered his gun, and we watched each other uneasily. I took a seat at the table, far enough away to outrun him if he wanted to pursue but close enough so we could see one another. Reaching into my pocket, I pulled out one of the two unused burner phones and dialed Mark's home number.

"Making yourself comfortable?" he asked.

"Thanks for the sandwiches. I wanted to make sure you had some more information. Did you get anything back on the ballistics yet?"

"Mi casa es su casa." He picked up the notepad and skimmed the pages. "The bullet you delivered didn't match your gun. It's from a Glock, probably police issued. But right now, we have nothing to compare it to. Our team pulled two slugs out of the wall. The striations match your nine millimeter. Didn't I train you to be a better shot?"

"What about the one that went into Harrigan?"

"Do you want to come in?" Mark asked. I wasn't sure if the invitation was to his house or to turn myself in, so I shook my head. "The son of a bitch removed his bullet from the vic."

"What about the autopsy? Maybe they can take a mold or something."

"Alex, Harrigan's not dead. He's in critical condition and under protection by the U.S. Marshal Service." I pressed my lips together and said a silent prayer of thanks to any deity who might be listening. "The problem is proving you didn't shoot him."

"I didn't shoot him."

"I know. Evidence doesn't say you did. It just says you fired a few wild shots into the wall. If Harrigan wakes up, maybe he can tell us who did this. In the meantime, Papadakis was found this afternoon bludgeoned in his own bed. Apparently, a woman was snooping around, and it set off some red flags, causing the doorman to call up to his apartment. The management heard Papadakis crying for help and phoned an ambulance."

"Any leads? Or do you want to pin this on me too?"

"It's being investigated." He slumped further in the chair as we stared at each other through the screen door. "Parker, none of this looks good. Your office was full of information on the best way to conduct the heist. Infinity's safe was empty when we got there, and the bartender was shot. You were the only other civilian at the scene, at least according to the responding officers. We won't be able to substantiate any of your claims until we track down this fucking dirtbag. Right now, the arrows all point to you."

"Once again, this is exactly why I can't turn myself in."

"With any luck, Papadakis will be able to shed some light on the matter once he's out of intensive care, and when Harrigan wakes up, we'll see if he can't clear you completely. In the meantime, stay away from the precinct unless you have a death wish."

"Don't worry. I'm staying away from everyone if you catch my drift." I was talking about Martin. "Mark, you once asked me to protect him because you couldn't. Now I'm asking you to protect him because I can't. He doesn't need to get caught up in this. Our communication has been severed. He's not a go-between."

He nodded in understanding. "Are you okay? You were shot for god's sake."

"I'll be better once I can stop running. Here's my phone. You'll want to call this in and run a trace, so I'll just leave you the damn thing." Placing the phone on the table, I walked away.

*   *   *

Everything in my unpaid motel room remained undisturbed. Eventually, I would have to escape my safe haven because staying in one place too long would lead to capture. If Nick got my message, we would meet in the morning to exchange information.

There was a good chance he would bring me in, but I had to risk it. My discussion with Mark had left some important questions, and since O'Connell was a cop, he'd have a better idea of who was dirty. His commentary on having no friends in burglary replayed through my mind, and I wondered if Hoskins might have some idea who on his team might be crooked.

My head pounded, and I tried desperately to stay warm as I burrowed under the blankets. Maybe some sleep would help matters. Waiting was the only thing I could do without having any real leads or means of investigating. An hour later, I pulled the blankets tightly around me before getting up to search for the acetaminophen. Popping two, I fell into an uneasy sleep as dreams of being arrested and murdered in a prison cell played through my unconscious mind.

When I awoke, I felt slightly better. I prepared for my meet with O'Connell as I watched the morning news for any stories on Papadakis, the shooting, or me. Still, nothing was mentioned. Dressing in layers, I put Martin's sweatshirt on over my tank top and button-up blouse. I was freezing and suspected I might be feverish. Maybe it was from spending the day out in the rain and not from some infection that would turn gangrenous and eventually kill me. It brightened my day to think O'Connell could arrest me or sell me out, and at least then I would die from a crooked cop's bullet, instead of necrotic flesh.

I arrived at the diner and took a seat in the back corner next to the emergency exit. I wasn't above running out the door. Ten minutes later, O'Connell showed up alone in civilian dress and sunglasses.

He scanned the room and removed his aviators. "Are you trying to get me fired?"

"If it'll make you feel any better, you can consider

me your CI."

"Dammit, Parker, I should arrest you right here," he hissed. "The radio calls yesterday at the station were ridiculous. Have you lost your fucking mind? You could have gotten killed."

"Ah, Nick, you're worth it."

"Cut the crap. I can't be seen with you. So what the hell is going on?"

"Everyone who can vouch for why I was at the club is getting attacked. I gave all my information and the dirtbag's bullet to Mark, but I'm not coming in from the cold until I know I'm not getting pinched for this." The waitress approached the table and refilled my mug with hot water and handed me another tea bag. "Do you think it might be someone in burglary? I'm guessing the same guy who hit the four clubs was one of burglary's guys, and that's why it looked like an inside job each time."

"You're quick." His eyes continued to sweep the room. "We've narrowed it down to a particular division, but we don't have enough to get a search warrant. It's too circumstantial right now. Are you sure you don't remember anything else about the shooter?"

"I only saw him from the chest down." I lifted my mug and held it close, hoping to absorb the heat from the ceramic. "Any word on Ernie Papadakis or Sam Harrigan?"

"Last I heard, Papadakis left before the shooting, but he said he hired you to protect the place. It adds corroboration to your story."

"What else am I going to have to do to clear my name?"

"You need to surrender and tell your side of things. It might be enough to get a warrant."

"When Harrigan wakes up and points the finger at

the crooked cop, I'll see you at the precinct with a set of matching bracelets. Until then, I can't risk evidence being fabricated or lost in the shuffle. I trust you and the guys in major crimes, but I need assurances." Dropping a ten on the table, I went out the emergency exit and through the alleyway before I came out on the other side and caught another cab.

TEN

The rest of the morning and afternoon I spent talking to Infinity's staff. Sneaking in and out of buildings was rapidly becoming my new hobby. After exchanging a few words with Mary, Brian, and Tina, I started to question my own recollection of Saturday night. Things had been busy, but no one had noticed anything out of the ordinary. It was just another insane shift.

Deciding to give it one more shot, I traced Gretchen's whereabouts to the park where she was pushing her charge on the swings. Approaching her slowly, I sat down on a nearby bench and surveyed the area. A few mothers chased their toddlers. A sole father rocked a stroller back and forth while yelling at his son to put something down. Thank goodness I wasn't the maternal type, or this could be my future, assuming I had a future.

Gretchen left the child on the swing and turned to find me sitting on the bench. She looked shocked, and I suspected she would call the police. Those were the instructions everyone had been given in case they encountered me, but I doubted anyone else wanted to get involved. Common sense dictated the best approach was to do nothing and hope the problem went away. No one wanted to get dragged into drama that wasn't their own.

"You got a minute?" I asked.

"I shouldn't be talking to you. You shot Sam."

"I didn't shoot Sam, but I'm trying to find out who did. What happened Saturday night? Did you see or hear anything suspicious? Do you remember any cops loitering around? Maybe someone was outside when you and the rest of the gang left for the night?"

She looked thoughtful. "Ja, there was a police car on the corner. You must be one crazy bitch to shoot someone with a policeman right there." If she honestly believed I was a crazy bitch, she shouldn't call me out on it, or I might have to shoot her too. "I have to leave. Don't follow me, or I will call the police."

"Gretchen," I called as she grabbed the child's arm and dragged him down the slide, "did you notice the number on the car?"

She didn't answer. Instead, she took out her phone as she fled the scene. That was my cue to scram.

Walking out the park's western exit, I was considering going back into hiding and hoping something would surface when a limousine pulled up to the curb. The window rolled down a few inches, and a man looked out. Something about the car and his appearance didn't bode well.

"Ms. Parker, do you need a ride?"

I ignored him and continued walking. This guy knew who I was, and that couldn't be good. The limo continued to roll along beside me.

"Did it sound like a question? Let me rephrase. You need a ride. Carmine, assist her in getting in the car."

Before I could react, the front passenger's side door opened, and a man in an expensive suit with a very large gun exited the vehicle and stood with his hands folded in front of him.

"I guess I could use a ride after all." There was no way out of this.

The large man opened the rear door and waited for me to get inside. Sizing him up, I ran through some possible strategies and decided to get in the limo. Once I was seated, the door closed, and I was face to face with one of the city's infamous organized crime bosses.

"Welcome." He gave me a joyless smile. "Do you know who I am?"

"Let's pretend I don't."

"Excellent." The corners of his eyes crinkled slightly. "You can call me Vito. Care for a drink?" The limo had a well-stocked fridge in the back, but I wasn't taking anything from a gangster.

"No thanks, Vito."

He shrugged and leaned back in the seat. "Looks like you were helping out a mutual acquaintance of ours, Ernesto Papadakis. We appreciate the care you took to ensure the safety of our," he paused and scratched his chin, "business capital."

"I'm glad someone appreciates me."

"I'm aware of the current predicament plaguing our fine police force, particularly the nearest precinct. The gentlemen who are supposed to be protecting this city might just be doing it the most harm." His accent was classic mafia don, and I wondered if he watched the *Godfather* to get the gestures correct. "Needless to say, I feel there is a debt owed to you. I am prepared to take care of your current problem."

"Sorry, but I think working within the system is better than superseding it."

"You handle things your way, Ms. Parker, and we handle them ours. Most of the time, our way is faster."

"Doesn't make it better."

"Not much goes on in this city without word getting back to me. To express my gratitude, a surveillance tape is being delivered to Detective O'Connell as we speak. The footage is from a hidden camera used to ensure Mr. Papadakis wasn't skimming off the top. Although your crooked cop," his eyes lit up a little, "can't be recognized, a man can be seen shooting the bartender. This should clear your name and get you back on the job."

"Why are you helping me?"

"I make good on my debts. After this, we will be even, and our business will be concluded. Shall we cross paths again in the future, I hope you will remember this kindness I have extended to you." The car slowed to a stop.

"Thanks, but I can't make any promises."

Carmine opened the rear door. Our meeting was over. He bowed his head slightly, and I stepped out of the car. Carmine shut the door, got back in front, and the limo drove away. Turning around, I was only a few blocks from my motel. Could it be a coincidence? Maybe Vito wasn't kidding when he said he was aware of everything going on in this city. A shiver traveled down my spine, and I wasn't sure if it was from my constant paranoia or if the fever returned.

*   *   *

After the IT department analyzed the footage to ensure its legitimacy, I should be cleared of any involvement in the near-fatal shooting of Sam Harrigan. In the morning, I would call Mark and ask for verification before surrendering to the boys in major crimes. Only one more night as a fugitive and then maybe I would be free to return to the world of the not guilty.

On my way up to my room, I stopped at the vending machines and bought a few things to eat. It was slim pickings between chocolate candy bars or salty snacks, so I settled for both. If Vito had offered a hot meal, I might have agreed to more than just letting his involvement at Infinity go unnoticed.

My room remained a safe haven, and the paranoid parts of my brain wondered if that had anything to do with Vito's influence. Stop it, Parker. After my dinner of chips, cheese puffs, and some chocolate peanut butter thing, I made a pot of decaf coffee and drank it as I wrapped the blankets tightly around my body. It was barely six p.m., and I was exhausted.

Dragging myself to the bathroom, I cleaned the incision and punctures in my side and back, but the area was inflamed. The flesh was red, puffy, and painful. After doing all I could, I returned to the main room and pulled the blankets off the second bed and got underneath the double layer of covers.

Waking in the middle of the night, I was dizzy and parched. I surfaced from under the covers, the air frigid against my skin. It felt like I was walking across Antarctica in a bikini. I got a glass of water from the bathroom sink and squinted against the harsh, blinding lights. Going back into the main room, I took a few ibuprofens since I finished the acetaminophen the day before and pulled myself into the fetal position to conserve warmth. Slipping in and out of consciousness until daybreak, I welcomed the prospect of turning myself in.

I gathered everything inside my messenger bag and dialed Mark on the last remaining unused burner phone. White-knuckling the banister, I made my way slowly down the stairs. My head pounded. The world was hazy, and my body ached from being wracked by uncontrollable shivers all night.

"Jablonsky," he answered.

"Don't bother tracing this. I'm on my way to the precinct to surrender. Can you verify new surveillance footage has surfaced, making my involvement in Sam's shooting less likely?"

"Parker, I'll send agents to meet you there. You no longer look good for this, but until it's sorted, we can't recall the warrant for your arrest. Other charges are still pending."

"It'll be nice to get out of the cold." Discarding the battery, I tossed the phone into a dumpster and hailed a cab.

*   *   *

The precinct was abuzz with crimes, cases, and newly discovered evidence. As I entered, I expected to be tackled to the ground or held at gunpoint. Instead, not a single person paid any attention as I took the stairwell up to the major crimes division. Exiting the double doors into the bullpen, I watched a few officers and detectives rush around, but still, no one tried to stop me. Had I known this, I would have gone upstairs, talked to Nick, and left without having to body-check a car to get away from an overzealous beat cop.

Wincing, I went to O'Connell's desk and sat down. I could wait for someone to return before begging to be arrested. It's not like I had anywhere else to be. Maybe while I waited, Mark and some federal agents would show up and take credit for collaring a notorious criminal genius.

"Parker?" Heathcliff sighed audibly. "Are you

armed?"

"Right jacket pocket." I placed my purse and bag on top of the desk, but I couldn't be bothered to reach into my pocket because that would have involved unwrapping my arms from around my body, and right now, they were the only things holding in the warmth. Heathcliff reached into my pocket and removed my handgun and started Mirandizing me. "Yeah, I know. Silent, counsel, uh-huh. Can we skip all that and just say I surrender?"

O'Connell, Thompson, and Moretti came down the hallway, and O'Connell and I locked eyes. He had missed the perfect opportunity to throw me in the slammer. Heathcliff was confused by my appearance, but he was a cop first. By walking in off the street and surrendering, I had thrown him off his game. He held out his handcuffs, waiting for me to unfold my arms in order to be cuffed, but I wasn't cooperating. In the meantime, Thompson rummaged through my bags, and Moretti went to make a call.

"You look like shit," O'Connell offered.

My teeth chattered, and Heathcliff touched my cheek with the back of his hand. "You're burning up. What's going on?"

"Bullet hole in my side seems to be infected. You don't happen to have a blanket by chance, do you?" The hazy harshness of the lights pulsed with the pounding in my head.

"Should I call for a bus?" Thompson asked. I was no longer part of the conversation; instead, I was relegated to the position of silent observer.

O'Connell took his jacket off and wrapped it around me. "We're not waiting. She's one of us. Let's get her in the car. I'll drive convoy, and we'll figure out how to process and report this after the fact."

Heathcliff lifted me out of the chair, and he and

O'Connell headed down the steps and out of the precinct. After strapping me in the passenger's seat, Heathcliff turned on the siren and flew through red lights. O'Connell drove his cruiser at our flank.

"It's nice getting celebrity treatment," I murmured.

In the emergency room, my police escort got me bumped to the top of the waiting list, and the nurse took my temperature which was dangerously high at nearly a hundred and five. Typically, I liked being considered an overachiever but not in this instance. So many things and people shuffled around that I lost track of it all after the IV was painfully inserted in the back of my hand. A few minutes later, the lights dimmed, and everything faded to black.

ELEVEN

Time lost all meaning in my drug-induced fog. One minute, people were around, and the next, I was alone in a room with my wrist cuffed to the bedrail. My heart raced, and my chest felt tight and heavy. I coughed but couldn't catch my breath. Someone in a white lab coat entered the room and disconnected the tubing from the back of my hand and injected something into my arm as I struggled against my bindings. Then my airways opened, the pressure eased, and the world went dark.

When consciousness returned, the shackle was gone, but it felt like I swallowed sand. Everything was numb, and I wasn't sure I could feel my face. O'Connell sat in a chair, filling out paperwork.

"Nick," I croaked.

He glanced up from the file folder in his lap and smiled before focusing his gaze behind me. I tried to shift off of my right side in order to turn around, but something blocked my movement.

"I'll find a doctor." He left the room.

"Alex?" Martin was still out of visual range, but that changed as he knelt next to the bed. "Hey, beautiful."

"You look like hell."

He was unshaven with dark circles under his eyes. "I'm too kind to say the same to you," he quipped.

"What?" To say I was confused would be an understatement. I looked at the tubes taped to the back of my hand and tried unsuccessfully to shift onto my back as Martin stroked my hair. "What's going on?"

"Easy, you're not supposed to lie on your back. But it looks like I'm your emergency contact." He grinned.

"No. Well, yeah." My brain was foggy.

"From what I've been told, you checked in with a serious infection. They gave you some intravenous antibiotics which triggered a pretty bad reaction." He got off the floor and sat on the edge of the bed. "You've been out for a few days, but you're fine."

"Days?" Oh god, how much time had I lost. Did they identify the crooked cop? Was I still under arrest, or were they waiting to make sure I didn't drop dead to save on the paperwork?

"It's Saturday," he supplied. My gaze followed the intravenous line to the two hanging bags, and he glanced up to see what had caught my attention. "Some pain meds, fluids, and a final round of antibiotics."

"Good, then I won't be needing this much longer." Before I could unhook myself, a doctor entered the room.

"Ms. Parker, glad to see you're finally awake." He checked my chart.

After I insisted on having everything nonessential removed and getting a general update on my condition, a nurse came in to implement my requests. With the exception of completing the antibiotics, medically speaking, I was almost free to go. The doctors had inserted a drain in my side to remove the excess fluid that had built up, but it had been removed yesterday. At least I had an explanation for why I was lying on my right side with a pillow keeping me propped uncomfortably in place.

I had the dire need to move around after being prone for days. Getting up on a numb leg and hobbling on unused muscles to the bathroom was an ordeal in itself. By the time I returned to my hospital bed, Nick and Martin had come back from their brief exile in the hallway. Nick gave the nurse a quick peck as she left.

"That's Jen," Martin informed me, "Nick's wife." He fell silent as I tried to untangle myself from the IV tube before lying flat on my back, most certainly against medical advice.

"Don't worry. You're no longer under arrest. Harrigan regained consciousness and corroborated the security cam footage that was delivered." O'Connell approached the bed and gave my hand a squeeze. "I'll wait in the hallway for Jablonsky to relieve me. You gave us quite a scare. I'm glad you're okay, Parker."

"Me, too. Tell Heathcliff thanks."

"You can tell him yourself when he fills in. Until further notice, you're in protective custody." O'Connell didn't wait for my questions or protest before he disappeared out the door.

"Do you want to get some rest?" Martin asked, returning to his spot on the bed.

"According to you, I've been resting for three fucking days. Please tell me what's going on. I turned myself in Wednesday, and now it's Saturday. How long have you been here?"

"The hospital called Thursday night." His features

darkened. "You were cleared of the murder charge, and since the members of your protection detail were more than willing to vouch for me, I came to keep you company. You had a negative reaction to the first set of antibiotics, and whatever they administered to counteract it knocked you for a loop. Some emergency contact I am. When I arrived, they asked what medications you were allergic to, and I had no idea what to tell them."

"Sorry, I should have given you the heads up. It just made sense since we've been together for a while. Although, I never expected I'd need an emergency contact. Mark was always my emergency contact." I tried to get comfortable, shifting onto my stomach, but this made conversation difficult.

He sensed my discomfort and repositioned himself, so I could lean against his shoulder. "O'Connell, Heathcliff, and Mark have been taking turns keeping an eye on you. Bruiser's outside, just in case they need assistance."

"Why?"

"No one's been apprehended yet. There's still a cop gunning for you."

All the other questions I had were about the investigation and what happened to my apartment and office. I would wait to ask Mark about this, instead of Martin. Shutting my eyes, I knew I wouldn't be much use until the remaining drugs worked their way out of my system. Being a lightweight when it came to medication had its downfall.

"You've been here since Thursday?"

"Thursday night. It provided the perfect opportunity to get to know your cop buddies and meet Jen." Martin always put a positive spin on things.

"What about work?"

"Work can wait." Even in my impaired state, I

picked up on the hesitation of his next question. "Alex, we don't talk about our pasts too often, but why am I the only one here worried about you?"

"Someone has to do it, but if you don't want to, Mark can." I found resting my eyes made it easier to focus on the conversation.

"No, I meant family."

"I don't have any."

He stopped speaking and traced random patterns on my upper back as I drifted off to sleep.

* * *

When I came to, the lights were off, and Martin was asleep beside me. Falling asleep on his shoulder didn't leave him any other option but to stay. I shifted off my hip, which now ached, and squinted at the clock. It was almost five a.m. My brain felt clear. The IV had been removed. With any luck, I'd be discharged in a few hours.

I did my best to remain still, trying to let Martin sleep. Running through our previous conversation, I suspected he hadn't left my side since Thursday night. He failed to hold up his end of our agreement to put work first. I would have to remember to ask about the Los Angeles conference, which he must be missing.

When my new position proved to be even less comfortable than my last, I leaned back, and Martin's hand, which rested on my hipbone, tightened to keep me from rolling onto my back. His constant concern, even when he was unconscious, could be irritating. Reaching down, I eased his hand off of my hip and lay flat against the mattress. Anything was better than staying on my numb, uninjured side for another second.

"Are you okay?" he asked.

"Go back to sleep." I stared at the ceiling, replaying everything I remembered and had been told about the past week.

"You're still awake."

"All I've been doing is sleeping. It's physically impossible to sleep any longer," I said. He carefully snuggled against me but didn't go back to sleep either. "What happened with your conference?"

"I sent Luc. There will be other conferences."

"You didn't need to stay here. I have friends with guns to keep me company."

"It's about time I get to do more than practice my surgical skills on you. Surprisingly, it's kind of nice to be included in your life and hang out with your friends. Nick's not so bad. I might have misjudged him. But Heathcliff's a bit stiff, not much for small talk. Oh, and I told Mark we're dating."

"Lovely." My old friend, sarcasm, was back.

We were silent for a time until another stray thought entered his mind. "Maybe I'm prying," he apparently decided in my current state I would be more forthcoming about who I was and where I came from, "but why are you so opposed to medications and doctors?"

Sighing audibly, I turned to face him. "When I was fourteen, I found out I was adopted. For all I know, my birth mother may be a drug addict. There is only so much nature versus nurture to consider once you start running the statistics, and I've always been afraid I'm genetically predisposed to turn into a substance abuser." Even though this was how I felt, the words sounded silly coming out of my mouth.

Smiling sadly, he rubbed his thumb across my cheek. "You won't. It's not in you. You're too much of a control freak." I laughed at the absurdity of our early morning conversation. Something about hospitals and near-death experiences always turned me into a talker. "Is that why you said you didn't have any family?"

"The people who claimed to be my family lied my entire life, and once I turned eighteen, we parted ways. It was a mutual thing. They paid my tuition, but all other communication ceased. They still have bragging rights for taking in a charity case and making a difference, but they made it perfectly clear their job was done. And so was I."

It wasn't a topic I ever talked about and the first he had heard of it. Unsure of what to say, he enveloped me in his arms, and we remained silent until daybreak when the medical professionals examined my back and brought my discharge papers.

*   *   *

Leaving the hospital seemed to be an even more daunting challenge than my arrival. Mark sent an agent to my apartment to retrieve a change of clothes, and once I was dressed and ready to leave, we had to deal with the travel arrangements. The exchanged glances between Mark and O'Connell tipped me off to some type of plan being in play, but no one gave me any details. Mark drove me in his car, and Nick followed us. Martin went home alone, but his driver, Marcal, was instructed to take circuitous routes and watch for tails and police vehicles.

We went straight to the OIO building which housed offices for the FBI and OIO. Even though I was given a clean bill of health, I wasn't quite ready to go back to work yet. Director Kendall was waiting for us, and once Nick emerged from the elevator, the three of us were ushered into his office.

"Parker," Kendall spoke, "you've stepped in it

again, haven't you?"

"Sir, this time, I think it stepped on me."

"Either way. Although there is no longer a pending murder charge, you did resist arrest, assault a police officer, trespass, break into an agent's domicile," he glanced up from reading the list of offenses, "should I continue?"

"No need. I'm pretty clear on how that half of the week went."

"Police corruption claims are always investigated by the Bureau. The police department has its own IA investigation going, and we've been exchanging information. The slug you provided should be a conclusive match to the guilty party. However, all other evidence has been slim. Our only witnesses are being protected by the Marshal Service, but Mr. Harrigan has yet to provide a usable sketch of his attacker."

"From what you've told us," Mark said, "your own certainty over identifying the scumbag isn't substantial either."

"I didn't see him. Not enough of him, anyway." My jaw set as I considered if Vito might have more information. He did know a lot about what was going on in the city, but his way of getting results wasn't legal.

"I'm prepared to offer you a one-time only deal," Kendall continued. "We'll deputize you. Your badge and gun will be returned, and you will resume your position at the OIO for the duration of the police corruption case. You will be assigned to the joint task force the FBI and PD are running, and all charges against you will be forgiven under the guise of necessary in the line of duty." Kendall knew I was leery of coming back on a permanent basis or anything resembling a permanent basis, but it was a good deal.

"Why?" There was always a catch.

"Right now, you're not up to the physical reqs. So we want to stick a decoy at your apartment until you are. It will give you a chance to catch up and provide us the perfect opportunity to disseminate some misinformation concerning your ability to positively identify the corrupt son of a bitch."

Now things were falling into place. I was bait.

"Where do I sign?" Bait or not, some asshole shot me, framed me for murder, and nearly killed a damn good bartender. The gloves were coming off.

After I was formally deputized and my two handguns were returned to my custody, I would be escorted to my apartment where I could pack a bag and leave. I would meet with an agent of a similar build and coloring who would impersonate me and return to my apartment until I was deemed fit for duty. Having a stranger live at my place wasn't a comforting thought, but knowing a dozen agents and police officers had already ransacked my home made the thought of one more person invading my personal space seem less intrusive.

"Welcome back, Agent Parker," Kendall said.

TWELVE

Being homeless was turning into a way of life. Mark drove to my place and waited in my living room while I shuffled through the mess, grabbed everything I imagined I would need, and threw it all into a very large duffel bag. If someone were watching, he'd probably think I was disposing of a dead body.

We left my apartment in separate vehicles and returned to the OIO offices. A female agent, who I didn't think looked anything like me, met us in the garage where I gave her my jacket and keys to my car and apartment. She left without a word. Alex Parker's body double was going home for the rest of the evening.

"O'Connell grabbed the pertinent files. He's setting everything up for you at Marty's," Mark said. Just what I wanted, to drag Martin even deeper into my occupational hazards.

"Can't I sleep on your couch instead?"

"No," but he regretted his tone and added, "federal agents will be outside at all times. You'll have your own protection detail, and Martin has Bruiser working nonstop. It'll be fine. Once you're fully recovered, you can go home."

"Great."

"So the two of you finally hooked up?" He kept his eyes on the road, but his tone hinted at smug amusement. "Took you long enough."

"Watch it, Jablonsky, I just beat one murder rap. I can probably overcome another one."

* * *

Arriving at Martin's compound, Mark nodded to the agents sitting outside who radioed ahead. The garage door opened, and he pulled inside. O'Connell stood at the top of the stairs, waiting impatiently for us to join him. Mark carried my bag, which was the least he could do, and I instructed him to put it in the guestroom as I performed a quick visual sweep for Martin. I hated intruding on him when the two of us hadn't discussed this.

"Where's Martin?" I asked O'Connell.

"Upstairs. He said we could have the office down here and the run of the living room."

"Did the two of you have fun planning this?" I despised being uninformed and out of the loop. Letting other people make decisions was asking for trouble.

"Yep, and next time, we're going to braid each other's hair."

When Mark returned, we got down to business. An hour into the briefing or debriefing, at this point I couldn't tell the difference, Martin came down the stairs, annoyed with whoever he was speaking to on the phone, and went into his downstairs office to collect a fax. He smiled at me as he disappeared back up the steps. The distraction did not go unnoticed by my male counterparts.

"Alexis," Mark said my name, and I turned to him, "are you listening?"

"Can we take a break?" It was mid-afternoon, and I was tired and hungry. "In case you forgot, six hours ago, I was stuck in a hospital bed. I thought you guys planned to ease me into this."

"We'll stop for today. You can read the rest of the files when you get the chance. I'll be back tomorrow after work, and the three of us can go over this again. Maybe by then you'll be more apt to pay attention," Mark said.

After he left, I turned to O'Connell who appeared intrigued by something in the folder he was holding. "Are you sticking around?" I asked, going into the kitchen.

"Well, I was invited for dinner," Nick said. "So eat something light. You don't want to spoil your appetite. I've been promised a feast." It sounded as though Martin and Nick had become best friends or lovers. Either way, I was frightened. Settling on an apple, I returned to the living room confused and perplexed by the strange turn of events. "You don't look so good."

"Thanks." I bit into the fruit and shuffled through the stack of files. "Paperwork is exhausting."

"Right. It has nothing to do with everything you went through over the past week. Where did you even stay when you were on the run?"

Before I could answer, Martin descended the stairs and joined us. O'Connell made himself scarce, claiming to need to use the restroom, and Martin sat down next to me.

"I'm sorry. I didn't plan on staying here or taking over your office and living room."

"It's okay. I insisted, and you heard the docs. You

need to take it easy for the next few days. At least if you're here, I can keep an eye on you. The way I figure it, this way, you'll be less likely to hold me at gunpoint again and demand I cut a bullet out of your side."

"Point taken."

"Plus, I offered Nick a nice meal after everything he's done."

"So the two of you are pals?"

He nodded thoughtfully and grinned. "That's what happens when you spend several hours together in a very drab hospital room. They couldn't even splurge on cable."

"If you're trying to make me feel guilty, it's working."

He kissed my forehead and went into the kitchen. I picked up another folder from the pile to read, but I was useless. The print blended together in an inky haze. By the time I set the folder down, O'Connell had returned.

"Does Jablonsky really believe you'll get through all of this by tomorrow afternoon? I've only skimmed half of this shit, and I wrote most of it."

"Give me a breakdown." Leaning back against the couch cushion, I unclipped my newly acquired badge and put it on the table next to my firearms.

"We've narrowed it down to four potentials, but we're having issues running alibis and conducting searches. The union rep has been all over IA's ass. Normally, I'd side with the union and tell IAD to go fuck themselves, but corrupt cops give us all a bad name."

"Everyone in major crimes is clear, I assume."

"Yeah, that's why we're pulling double duty, assisting the FBI. Well, me, the LT, Heathcliff, and Thompson. Everyone else is still working cases. It's not like crime stops when the cops are fighting amongst themselves."

"The focus is on the guys in burglary, right?"

"See, you did read and retain something."

"Actually, I'm just a kick ass investigator. It says so on my business card."

Before our conversation could return to serious, Martin asked about salad preferences and pasta choices. Food was food, but Nick offered to help. I remained on the couch, staring into nothingness as I pieced together everything I knew about the robberies and what was in the reports. If someone in burglary was behind this, each heist would need to be re-examined. The facts were probably inaccurate or downright fictitious. Too bad I couldn't hide in my unpaid motel room until the investigation concluded.

After we finished eating, O'Connell helped organize the piles based on suspects, police reports, internal reports, and other miscellaneous information. Martin thanked him again for taking care of me, which I found aggravating since I was in the room and not deaf. And before he left, Nick promised to drop by around noon tomorrow to run through everything again before Mark joined us.

Once Martin and I were alone, I announced my desire to take a shower and change. He covered my wound with plastic and tape. I didn't deal well with being taken care of, and more importantly, I didn't handle being controlled by everything around me. Tonight, I would play nice, but if things didn't change, heads would roll. When I finished showering, Martin untaped the plastic and re-bandaged my side.

"Why am I here? Did anyone even ask before turning your house into headquarters for this investigation?"

"I already told you I offered. As far as I can tell, you don't have anywhere else to go. This is your home too."

"Actually, my home has an agent pretending to be me, probably sleeping in my bed and raiding my fridge."

"Alex," he tried to be patient, "a home is a safe place with people who care about you."

"Aww, you care." My sarcasm was flippant, as usual. "I'm sorry. You've gone out of your way. It's just–"

"Like I said, you're a control freak. No one bothered to ask. Not even me."

"Winner, winner, chicken dinner." I graced him with a genuine smile.

"I'll make a note for the future," he teased.

I spent the next few hours perusing one of the stacks of folders while he argued with Luc over a business plan concerning information obtained at the conference. When my head started to droop, I shut the folder and placed it in the proper pile. That was enough for today. Waking up at five a.m. had an adverse effect on my ability to remain functional and lively. Glancing up, I noticed Martin studying my badge.

"Is this the same one you had while on the job?"

"Yes. Kendall must have kept it for a rainy day."

"Maybe you should consider going back permanently." This seemed particularly odd since during our one and only short-lived breakup I told him I needed time to choose between him and the job. Maybe I had chosen wrong. "At least you'd have friends with guns watching your back. There would be no solo work. You couldn't be framed for murder."

"This was just a one-time fluke." Getting off the couch, I glanced toward the guestroom. "I'm going to get some sleep. Don't feel obligated to join me since I'm sure I've kept you awake the last few nights and not in the good way, but you can if you want."

"Well, after that kind of invitation, how can I possibly resist?" He disappeared up the steps to change before meeting me in the guestroom.

The doctors said to take it easy, and my only desire was not to wake before the sun came up

*   *   *

The next morning, I jumped at the sound of Martin's alarm clock. He reached over and blindly hit snooze. Once he got up, my day would start. Fifteen minutes later, he disappeared from the room, and I carefully stretched, making sure not to pull my healing side. Thirty minutes later, I gave up trying to use Martin's new, expensive coffeemaker. The struggle of woman versus machine wasn't worth it, and I went into the living room and dove into the second stack of files, coffee-free.

After Martin's early morning workout routine, he went upstairs to shower and dress. In his zombified state, he didn't notice me. Maybe I finally broke him of his annoying morning person habits. Unfortunately, my victory wasn't as gratifying as I hoped. Before he left for the office, he provided a brief tutorial in brewing fancy individual cups of coffee. At least I could say I achieved something today.

I spent the rest of the morning reading reports. The information swirled together, and no set of facts called attention to themselves. Either I was off my game, or there weren't any solid leads. Shuffling back through the paperwork, I pulled out the dossiers on the four potential suspects. On a sheet of paper, I listed the commonalities: detective, assigned burglary division, involved in working the club heist cases, male. Not much more to go on.

Maybe height could be determined based on the reflection. A field trip to Infinity might be helpful. Also, Ernie could be of some use. If we let him look through a six-pack, he could point out anyone familiar from the photos. Vito was the only possible problem with going near Ernie. I didn't know who attacked Ernie. It could have been the dirty cop or one of Vito's people. There was no way to know for certain, and I didn't want anyone to know of my brief connection with organized crime if it could be avoided.

The door opened, and I grabbed my nine millimeter and pointed it at the intruder.

O'Connell held up his hands and shook a brown paper bag. "I brought lunch, don't shoot."

Lowering my gun, I got up from amidst the files to grab a few bottles of water.

"Making any progress?" O'Connell asked.

"Do you think it's possible to knock down a brick wall by slamming my head into it repeatedly?"

"From your metaphor, shall I assume that means something's gotta give?" He scooted the paperwork off the coffee table, placing the food in front of him.

I handed him a bottle and sat down. "Let me tell you what I've determined, and you can add your wise, detectively insight to it." He unwrapped a burger while I ran through the commonalities among our suspects. "Is anyone in burglary free of suspicion?"

"Schwartz and Andrews. They're women. You said a man shot you, and Harrigan's shooter was obviously male. Although, how we've come to the conclusion it's a single party acting alone makes zero sense. General cop code, you watch your partner's ass. Nine times out of ten, if your partner's dirty, you know."

"I only spotted one shooter inside Infinity, but who's to say he didn't have help on the outside. Do we know who declared it was a single dirty cop acting alone?"

"It came from above my pay grade. Might have even come from your side, Agent Parker." Nick enjoyed putting the screws to me on my reinstatement.

"Do you think the proclamation is for PR purposes or because it's a rogue cop?"

Nick shrugged.

"Out of the four potentials, are any of them partnered together? Where did they even come from?"

"It's burglary division. They all work together, just like us major crime guys. The video footage you miraculously had delivered gave the IT geeks a basis for height, weight, and hair color. These four are the closest matches."

"Hoskins, Packard, Metz, and Fisher," I read the names out loud. I encountered Hoskins but not the others. My brief communication with him wasn't enough to base anything on. "What do you know about them?" O'Connell reached for the employee files, but I stopped his hand. "Do you know any of them personally?"

"We've never worked together. There's never been a reason for our paths to cross. Heathcliff worked with Fisher on a jewelry thing a couple of years back, but he hasn't said yea or nay about the guy."

"Sounds like Heathcliff." I picked up the stack of reports on the four burglaries and checked to see who the responding officer and detective in charge was. "Hoskins is primary on two. Metz and Fisher are primary on one each, and Packard is included because..." My voice trailed off as I stared at an evidence photo from the second heist.

"He assisted on all of them."

I skimmed the other three files; all the clubs had a VIP lounge near the office. This reminded me of working Saturday night at Infinity and pondering if the safes were emptied out before the club closed for the night. "Do you have surveillance footage from all four clubs?"

"Yes, it's at the precinct. The Bureau has a copy, but nothing's caught on tape. Remember, the footage was wiped. After hours, the clubs were empty, and the footage just blanks out to static."

"What if the heists were orchestrated during business hours and then made to look like they happened later?"

"You need to go back to sleep because you're dreaming up some pretty crazy things." He threw out his empty lunch wrappers. "I have to get back to work. Jablonsky, Heathcliff, and I will be here after five to make sure you're caught up and to work out a better game plan. In the meantime," he pulled a radio out of his jacket pocket, "you might want to stay in communication with the agents out front. They'll let you know when you have friendlies entering so you don't accidentally shoot someone."

"When have I ever accidentally shot anyone?"

"There's a first time for everything," he replied, leaving me to ponder the intricacies of the robberies and the influence a dirty cop could have on the investigations. This gave the conspiracy theories I normally locked away plenty of time to run rampant through my subconscious mind.

After I finished picking at my lunch, I settled on the couch with a notepad and started over on my own list of leads. Everyone working at Infinity should be interviewed again. Gretchen said a police cruiser was outside. This could be something worth checking out. Maybe starting at Infinity and working backward would lead to an unforeseen discovery. Could our dirty cop have forgotten to recover the stray shell casings or left a footprint behind?

I was scribbling notes furiously on the paper when the radio chirped. Martin and his driver were approaching the house. It was a little after two; something was up. A few minutes later, the door opened, and Martin stepped into the living room. Marcal and Bruiser remained downstairs.

"You're home early." I continued working on my list.

"Alex," he distractedly greeted before heading up the steps and mumbling about incompetent idiots. Twenty minutes later, he was back, speaking into his phone to make sure his itinerary had arrived and someone double-checked the flight plan. When he concluded the call, he studied me. "How are you feeling? Are you okay?"

I gave him a suspicious look. "Are you planning on smuggling me out of the country to harvest my organs? Because I'm feeling absolutely horrible, and my kidneys aren't viable."

He snorted, amused. "The conference has been extended, and my presence is requested. I'm flying out in a couple of hours."

"Have a safe trip." I went back to reading my notes.

"Are you sure you're okay by yourself? I can stay if..."

I cut him off midsentence. "Go. I am fine. Work first, remember? You should have left Friday like you were supposed to. I'll figure out how to use the coffeemaker, and there are armed guards out front. What more does a girl need?" Not to mention, I'd feel better knowing he was thousands of miles away from this.

"I'm not sure when I'll be back, but I'll call and let you know. Try not to get shot while I'm gone."

"Try to stay out of trouble while you're gone."

Neither of us had a very good track record. "Make sure Bruiser goes with you everywhere. I have too much to handle as it is."

He smirked and went upstairs to finish packing. When he returned, he had a garment bag and a rolling suitcase. "Before I forget, you might want this back." He handed me the resignation letter I shoved at him last week. Across the page, he had written in bright red letters *Denied.* "You can't quit your only stable job, particularly now that you don't have your waitressing income to fall back on."

"In that case, make sure you call before you return. I'll need the warning in order to finish stealing all your fine art and priceless possessions." I hesitated. "Are you sure it's okay I'm staying here?"

"Of course." He rubbed his thumb across my cheek and leaned in for a kiss. "Plus, now you have the perfect opportunity to rob me blind. It's okay. My homeowner's insurance will cover it."

"My god, you might just be a genius." I kissed him excitedly and hurried back to my file folders. "Oh, and have a safe flight."

THIRTEEN

Martin had uttered a few magical words, sending me spiraling back on track. Insurance – what types of protection would the clubs have established as reimbursement for theft and damages? There were a lot of avenues to consider, but insurance companies needed official reports. If a cop was on the take, the reports could be fabricated, the investigations could be completely bogus, and everyone could be walking away with thousands without any real robbery ever having been committed.

The large, glaringly obvious hole in my theory was noted in my aching side. Some things were a pain in the ass; this was a pain in the side. Our unknown subject had gone to Infinity and attempted to silence everyone inside. There would be no reason to do this unless an actual physical robbery was taking place.

"Dammit." I threw my notepad across the living room. Focus on the facts, Parker. No supposition or testimony by anyone, including Ernie Papadakis, counted as fact. I needed to come up with the truth on my own. The only certainty was our unsub had attempted to kill Harrigan and frame me. He had entered through the double doors in the back where deliveries occurred, and when he claimed to be responding to a call, he had left through the same set of doors. The police vehicles were out back, waiting for him.

Why would the police be out back? When I made the 911 call, I gave the operator the address but little else. Sure, surrounding all exits was sound practice, but to have even more black and whites stationed out back than in the front made no sense. The son of a bitch must have been in a police cruiser and already parked out back. When the rest of the cavalry rode in to save the day, they followed his lead.

"Do we have surveillance footage from outside the club?" I asked as soon as Mark answered the phone.

"Cameras were disconnected. No footage. What are you thinking?" he asked, so I filled him in on my current theory. "He must have been planning it for a few days. The last time the cameras held any data was the Thursday before."

Thursday had also been my first day working at the club. The uneasy feeling returned to the pit of my stomach. Were my conspiracy theories running away with me, or did one of the boys in burglary, who knew the details of my work with Ernie, devise a plan to set me up to take the fall?

My memory was a total blur. After spending the past week on the run and drugged to the point of unconsciousness, my recollection of the previous week was somewhat shoddy. The only detective I had been in contact with was Hoskins, but this didn't mean he hadn't shared the information with someone else in his department. No matter what angle I explored, it always led back to a giant question mark. Anyone could be involved. With any luck, we'd make some progress tonight, and by tomorrow, I would be pounding the pavement, looking for answers.

Like clockwork, by a quarter to six, the guys were assembled around the table with a six-pack and a few pizzas between us. The files and casework left too many holes to be helpful. Mark gave another briefing over the FBI's assumptions and leads, and Heathcliff updated me on the IAD investigation. The only conclusion both teams had drawn was our unsub was a burglary detective.

"Hoskins?" I asked the room. Heathcliff and O'Connell exchanged a brief glance before shrugging their shoulders in unison. At least they had their *Patty Duke* routine down. "Okay, Patty and Kathy, is anyone more obvious than Hoskins?"

"Like I told you this afternoon, it could be anyone. Or any combination," O'Connell said.

"We'd love to bring the entire department in for questioning," Mark added. "Will your union reps let it happen?"

"Dragging the names of good men through the mud won't help anything." Heathcliff was a cop, and sometimes, I wondered if he was capable of being anything else. Then again, he had kicked protocol to the curb when it came to driving me to the hospital.

Mark was getting impatient, and before it turned into us versus them, I intervened. "I agree. The look of impropriety is almost as bad as a conviction. We don't want to risk slandering the wrong person, especially when it's a fellow crime fighter." I added the last part for Mark's benefit, and he sunk back in his chair. Even though we were equally matched, federal agent to police detective, my allegiances were fickle, and I was stuck acting as the go-between. "Can Moretti do anything behind closed doors?"

"He's trying, but no one wants to say anything," O'Connell said. Mark muttered something under his breath about the whole lot being dirty. "Like I was telling Alex, I don't know how we came to the conclusion it's just one bad apple acting alone."

No one offered an explanation. Before long, our investigation would turn into a witch hunt. I got up to clear the table, and Heathcliff offered to help while Mark and O'Connell continued to throw friendly jabs over the other's incompetence.

"You doing okay?" Heathcliff asked quietly. We stood near the sink, avoiding the crossfire.

"Yes. Thank you for not slapping on the cuffs and tossing me into holding."

"I can't make any guarantees for next time, but I'm glad you're feeling better. Where's James?"

"Out of town at a conference." Narrowing my eyes, I was curious to see where this conversation was going.

He nodded thoughtfully and put down the dish towel. "He's a good guy." Apparently, Martin had made quite the impression. Without another word, Heathcliff went back to the table and commandeered the attention of our two co-workers. "There's at least one dirty cop, maybe more. Are you two planning on throwing insults all night, or shall we figure out a better way to handle this situation?"

The four of us worked until the early a.m. hours. Beginning with the shootout at Infinity, we narrowed down potential suspects. As soon as Heathcliff and O'Connell reported in at the precinct, they'd run records of everyone in burglary to see who could be accounted for. It was a time-consuming task, but it would yield the best results possible. From there, our police counterparts would work backward through the other heists until a reasonable suspect list was compiled.

Jablonsky and I would report to the FBI offices. I was getting introduced to our federal agent leadership. The Bureau was busy sifting through phone records, radio calls, and surveillance footage in order to identify anyone suspicious at the time of the heists. The Feds were also re-examining the evidence and crime scenes to ensure everything matched up, and there were no obvious signs of tampering. Neither side had a particularly glamorous job.

Until we had a list of possible leads, my job was to keep a low profile and stay out of the limelight. It had already been decided, once again without my consent, the misinformation circulating around my involvement in this case was that I was currently a cooperating witness in the identification of our shooter. This didn't seem reasonable since I didn't believe our perp had gotten a clear view of me either, but it might be enough to scare him off. It was still a widely held belief that Harrigan was unresponsive and not assisting in a more usable sketch of his assailant.

"Can you get me cleared to talk to him?" I asked Mark after O'Connell and Heathcliff left for the night.

"Send your request through Kendall. It'll be your best bet. Although, I doubt the marshals will risk their star witness when we still don't know who we're protecting him from."

True. We'd need more concrete evidence in the meantime. "How am I supposed to visit the scenes or talk to anyone from Infinity if I'm assumed to be a witness?"

"Parker, we'll figure this out tomorrow when you run your cockamamie ideas by the FBI agents in charge. In the meantime, do you care if I crash here? It's almost three a.m., and we're supposed to be at work by eight."

"Take the couch. I'll be down the hall if you need anything."

Calling it a night, I went to the guestroom, ignoring the confused look on Mark's face. He didn't understand why I wasn't sleeping upstairs in Martin's room, but after surviving a firefight on the fourth floor almost a year ago, it shouldn't be that hard to put two and two together. It was something else I needed to work on. I had gotten over the uneasiness of being in Martin's house. Maybe one day I would conquer my anxiety over the indelible images of him being shot in his fourth story office.

Morning came all too soon, and I fought bitterly with the coffeemaker from hell. What was the point of brewing a single cup at a time? Obviously, the inventor didn't understand the need for a constant supply of caffeine.

"Are you sure you're doing that right?" Mark asked, coming into the kitchen. The creases across his dress shirt made it obvious he slept in his clothes, but then again, he always looked like he slept in his clothes.

"No, it's a torture device meant to be the bane of my existence. On the way back, we're stopping at the store to buy an actual coffeepot, unless I'm allowed to go home."

Mornings typically annoyed me, and going back to work in an official capacity made me even bitchier. He kept his mouth shut, and after more cursing and my obvious defeat, he produced two cups of coffee from the infernal machine. Searching the cabinets, I found a few to-go cups, and we went on our way.

FOURTEEN

"Agent Parker," Special Agent in Charge Steve Cooper extended his hand, "it's a pleasure. I've heard excellent things about your work." Cooper was head of the joint task force and looked like a cross between a varsity jock and an accountant. His boyish features lacked the liveliness or vivacity of someone in their mid-thirties. Dull would accurately describe his monotone expressions and voice.

"Don't believe everything you hear."

"Back to business then." Cooper gestured to a seat at the conference table. By the time I sat down, he had turned on the Smartboard and flipped to the crime scene photos. "You've already been briefed on our current findings, but I thought emphasizing some of the more obvious facts would be helpful." Glancing at Mark, I stifled a yawn, and he shot a warning look my way. "Each location relied on digital surveillance, but the hard drives were wiped. Our forensic IT team is working on it, but it doesn't look promising. Moving on," Cooper flipped to some different photos, "we didn't find tool marks or other signs of tampering at any of the clubs." Next slide. "With the exception of Infinity, there was no apparent property damage, no gunshots, and no vandalism aside from the actual thievery."

The monotony continued as I contemplated the benefits of a ten cup coffeemaker compared to a four cup. The prices weren't too dissimilar, so there was no reason not to indulge in the ten cup. Martin's kitchen had plenty of room. Plus, if I had to work with SAC Comatose, I'd need the extra six cups.

"Do you want to add anything I might have missed?" Cooper asked.

Dammit, I always zoned out at the wrong times. Assessing the photo array, I tried to wing it. "The slugs you pulled out of the back wall are mine. The casings on the floor behind the bar, also mine. When I pursued the shooter to the back door, he didn't have time to stop and pick up his spent casings. Then again, when I was forced to flee in order to evade capture, I don't recall seeing anyone digging through Mr. Harrigan to retrieve bullet fragments either."

"Any idea how long the unsub was alone in the club before reinforcements arrived?"

"He wasn't. When I fled the scene, our shooter was outside, speaking with the responding officers. Any evidence tampering occurred after uniforms were on-site," I clarified as Mark leaned back in his chair and bit absently at a hangnail. From past experience, this meant he had a thought.

"Bring in the rest of our crack team of investigators," Mark told Cooper, "and we'll start breaking things down." Cooper wasn't used to being told what to do, but Mark had seniority, even if it wasn't in this office. "Parker, you saw the guy's reflection, and you saw him speaking to the officers outside. Why can't you identify him?"

"You all look the same from the chest down and from the back," I replied, annoyed.

Mark snickered, enjoying riling my feathers. "The bastard must have sent the reinforcements away while he retrieved the damning evidence, or someone's working with him."

"Agent Parker," Cooper returned with three other agents, "meet Sullivan, Webster, and Darli."

Corinne Sullivan had auburn hair and a freckled face. She had worked bank robberies in the past and been made the poster girl for a recruitment campaign a couple of years ago, but Nate Webster and Andrew Darli were a mystery. The three of them looked uneasy, and I wondered if it had anything to do with my questionable status or how often I had been shot or otherwise injured in the past year.

"Don't worry, I don't think being accused of attempted murder is contagious," I said in lieu of a greeting. My witty banter was lost on the group who grew even warier.

Our crack team of investigators got back to business, thanks to the cajoling of our fearless, monotone leader. Every single incident report was rechecked, and the crime scene photos were re-examined in connection with the reports. Any recorded fact had to be verified by two sources before we were willing to accept it as true. The day proceeded at a painfully tedious pace as we slowly recompiled the reports for the first two heists.

"Let's break for dinner, and then we'll continue with the next two heists," Cooper announced. Leaning back in the chair, I stared at the mess of paperwork and splayed photos. My eyes were dry and tired, and I wondered when I last blinked. "Let's finish up the original reports today, and tomorrow, we will have fresh eyes to examine Agent Parker's shooting." The way he said it made it sound like I was running around with a gun, just for the hell of it.

Mark and I ordered delivery and worked through dinner. At the OIO, we were used to long hours, and breaking for dinner just meant that much more sleep we'd miss. Together, we closed the file on the third club robbery and were working through the details of the fourth when our FBI associates returned.

"Webster," Mark said, "read our compilations and look for any similarities in the first three heists. Darli, take everything down to the lab and have them go over the forensic conclusions and lab results the police department developed."

The two agents did as they were instructed, and Cooper began working on the fourth heist.

"Jablonsky, did you notice this?" He held up a photo of the cash register. Mark squinted, and Cooper slid it over, along with a magnifying glass. "Do you think it was there before the robbery?"

"Only one way to know for sure." Mark passed the photo to me, pointing to scuff marks on the drawer. Maybe the perpetrator couldn't get it open as easily as we were led to believe. "Want to send a team to find out?"

Cooper grinned. "Are you volunteering?"

If it wouldn't have seemed completely infantile, I would have grabbed Mark's arm and jumped up and down while begging to go.

"Sure. Parker and I will be back in the morning. Is that okay, sir?" Mark might have realized he overstepped his boundaries, or he wanted to get the hell out of the conference room as much as I did.

"Good night, agents."

*   *   *

"I could kiss you right now," I murmured as we got into Mark's car. "One more minute of the monotony and I might have jabbed my own eyes out."

"Please don't. Are you talking about Cooper or the paperwork?"

"What's the difference?"

He chuckled, turning right and heading for the main strip that housed all the clubs.

For a Tuesday night, the place was as crowded as could be expected. There was no line to get in, and the bouncers seemed too bored to pay any attention to us as we entered. Wearing the classic black dress pants, button-up shirts, and black blazers, we were either die-hard fans of the *Blues Brothers* or federal agents. Mark went in search of the owner while I attempted to work my womanly wiles on the bartender.

"What can I get you?" he asked.

"Is that a new cash register?" I jerked my head at the ancient contraption, and he turned and followed my gaze.

"What do you think?" His response was sarcastic and abrasive. Maybe he could be my new best friend.

"I'm guessing it was here when the robbery occurred."

He narrowed his eyes, realizing he was slow on the uptake. "Your guys already questioned me. They dusted the thing for prints or whatever, and it came out clean."

I pulled out my newly acquired badge and showed it to him. "Federal agent," I smiled sweetly, "mind if I check the scratches on the front?" He audibly exhaled and waited for me to come around the bar. "Do you remember seeing these before the place was cleaned out?"

"Look, lady," he wasn't the patient type either; we

must be soul mates, "I told the cops I didn't remember those before. They ran some tests or whatever it is you guys do with tape and shit, and when the bar was allowed to open again, the cash register was still here."

"Sir, did you assist the robber in opening the cash drawer?" It was fun to make people sweat. Sometimes, valuable information would surface.

"Are you fucking with me? You're fucking with me, right? I wasn't even working Saturday night. I don't work Saturdays."

"Have you ever jimmied open the register? It's old. Might get stuck every once in a while."

"Yeah, maybe once or twice, but I didn't rob this place."

"Show me how you get the register to open."

He twisted a key, and the drawer popped open. He looked to me for approval or verification. Instead, I slammed the drawer shut and took the key from the corner.

"Now show me how you get the drawer open."

He shot a disgusted look my way and reached into one of the alcoves under the bar and pulled out a crowbar. After some prying, the drawer popped open. "Happy?"

"Thank you for your cooperation, sir." I handed him the key and met Mark on the other side of the bar. "Get anything from the owner?"

"He stuck with the same story we read in the reports. He doesn't know anything about the scratches on the drawer."

"The bartender keeps a crowbar handy to pry the register open when it gets pissy. Anyone could have used it to open the drawer, so we're back at square one."

On the way home, Mark stopped at a twenty-four

hour discount store where I purchased a stainless steel ten cup coffeemaker which matched the other appliances in Martin's kitchen. At least tomorrow morning would begin on a brighter note. When we arrived at Martin's, Mark held up his badge to the agents stationed outside, and we were allowed to enter the house.

"If the scratches were already on the drawer, why didn't the police record the discrepancy in the report?" he asked.

"My guess is our suspect jimmied the drawer open, and when he prepared the report, he left the scratch detail out because he didn't want to make this scene stand out compared to the others." Grasping at straws was always my way of handling supposition.

"That or he was afraid the scratches would lead back to him."

"How?"

"I don't know, but you aren't the only one who can throw around insane theories. Shall I update Cooper?"

"Please." I got out of the car and grabbed my coffeemaker from the back seat. "Are you staying tonight? Because I promise I am perfectly capable of taking care of myself."

"Was I that obvious?"

"The only thing more obvious is the nagging feeling Martin put you up to it." I gave him a pointed look, knowing he'd cave if I pushed.

"He called and asked if I could check in on you. He worries."

"You know it's ridiculous."

"Yes, and I also know, regardless of what the surveillance tape would have me believe, you came to him wounded and asked for his help. Newsflash, Alexis, Marty isn't the kind of guy who walks away from a crisis."

"The crisis is over. It was over the moment I surrendered to Heathcliff."

He looked skeptical. "Fine. The agents are outside, and you have a radio upstairs in order to remain in contact. I will be back in the morning to pick you up. Try to figure out how to make coffee between now and then."

FIFTEEN

The four FBI agents stared at me as I concluded the briefing on the Infinity heist and subsequent shooting. I didn't enjoy being the center of attention, and with no one saying a word, I wondered if I left something out.

Finally, Webster asked the only reasonable question. "If you didn't know about the corruption case, why didn't you go outside and clear matters up immediately?" He had a point.

"Obviously, it's because I was sent here to infiltrate your operation and discover how much you know about the crooked cop in order to report back. The bullet in my side and my stint in the hospital just make my story more believable."

Darli reached toward his belt, and Mark intervened. "Parker, cut the crap. The gentlemen and lady would like an answer. We'd all like an answer."

"When an ally, someone with a badge, gun, and authority, tells a group of six other officers you just shot someone and should be considered dangerous,

I'd like to see how you react to the situation. Keep in mind, until three days ago, I was a civilian. What choice did I have?"

"Where'd you go afterward?" Darli asked.

"Home. I'm sure you've seen my place. I packed what I could carry, called it in, and took off."

"You should have followed procedure and turned yourself in," he berated. "We'd have this SOB if you had followed orders."

"Or your office would have been forced to turn me over to the police and I could have been killed in custody. We can ponder a dozen what ifs, but it won't change what happened. I reacted based on the circumstances and knowledge I possessed at the time." I took a breath. "What about the incident reports filed that night. Why can't we identify the shooter that way?"

"Only the six officers responding to the 911 call wrote reports. We asked them to identify the detective at the scene, but no one recognized him. He didn't provide his name, and the dashcams didn't get a clear view of him. It's a dead end," Webster said.

"Dammit."

"While you were on the run, did you collect any hard evidence?" Cooper asked.

"No, sir. The bullet was all I had. I spoke briefly with the staff from Infinity. Gretchen admitted to seeing a police cruiser outside. You should bring her in for questioning. Also, when I sought out Mr. Papadakis, I was made aware of his condition. Do you have any leads on who attacked him?"

"Papadakis isn't talking." Sullivan glanced at her notes. "He's at his apartment with a protection detail on him."

"I can take a crack at him." Maybe Ernie would open up to me.

Cooper nodded. "Get to it, Parker. Sullivan, go with her."

Tossing a brief glance at Mark, I got up from the table and headed for the exit with Sullivan at my heels.

*   *   *

"Agents Sullivan and Parker to see Mr. Papadakis," Sullivan said to the men stationed outside the door. We pulled our credentials, and they examined them closely before allowing us inside Ernie's apartment.

"Ernie," I called, "it's Alexis."

He emerged, wearing a silk robe. His face was badly bruised, and he was limping. The way he held his side indicated a few broken ribs to top it off.

"Nice to see you again. Please make yourselves at home."

I introduced Agent Sullivan, who pretended to find something in the kitchen of particular interest. "What happened?" I asked as I sat across from him in the living room. "Who did this to you?"

He waved his hand in the air and smiled warmly with his disfigured face. "I'm fine. Can't keep a good man down, right?"

"Mr. Papadakis, please," I lowered my voice and checked to see what Sullivan was doing. She was out of earshot, contemplating the view from the kitchen window. "After I was shot, I came to see you. I spooked the doorman. When he called up to your place, he heard your cries for help and sent for an ambulance. You deposited the money like I told you, right?"

"Yes, of course." He looked serious. "Alexis, my financiers didn't do this. I was visited in the hospital by the person you said not to name, and he said a dirty cop was responsible and not to speak to the police, especially about his involvement."

"Did you see who did this? When did it happen?" Ernie's willingness to listen to Vito exasperated me. Then again, I wasn't sure acting against Vito's wishes was sound advice either.

"I'm not sure. I was asleep. The sun wasn't up yet because my room was still pitch black." He paled and swallowed. Reaching for his hand, I tried to comfort him, hoping it would encourage him to continue. "It all happened so fast. I didn't know why they were there, but it was a warning to remain uninvolved."

"They? Uninvolved? How would you be involved?" I shook my head, trying to make sense of the details.

"There were at least two of them. I heard talking when they left, but I didn't see anything. The one in charge said not to admit to knowing you or hiring you. My involvement with you was what I was supposed to keep quiet."

"Did you?"

"Not really. When I was in the hospital, some federal agents asked if I knew your whereabouts, but I said no. I told them I just hired you a few days earlier for security, but I didn't think you would shoot Sam. However, I told *him* what happened," Ernie said, referencing Vito again. "He said no one else could ensure my protection, and since he has eyes and ears around this city, he'd make sure it was fixed."

"But you had to keep your mouth shut."

He nodded uncomfortably. Sullivan had grown bored in the kitchen and came back into the living room. She looked to see if our meeting was over.

"Take care of yourself, Mr. Papadakis," I said.

We were almost to the door when Ernie called, "Alexis, I'm sorry for the trouble."

"It's just part of the job."

After we left the building, I filled in Sullivan on Ernie's assailants, but I left out the part about Vito. I would have to mull over this tidbit before deciding if it should be divulged to the FBI and what the consequences might be for Ernie and me. Sullivan was content to believe he was simply frightened his attackers would be back if he didn't follow their instructions, and that's why he hadn't spoken up sooner.

At least my conversation with Ernie disproved the theory of a sole unsub working alone. One other person was involved, maybe more. We were almost back to the office when Sullivan's phone rang, and after answering, she handed it to me.

"Parker," Heathcliff sounded more business-like than usual, "an attempt was made on the agent posing as you at your apartment. O'Connell is on his way to investigate. Everyone's okay, but Jablonsky decided it'd be best to turn it over to 911 dispatch and hope the guilty party might surface in response to the call. If you can get here, it'll appear we were questioning you about the incident and not blow your decoy's cover."

"On my way."

Sullivan u-turned, and we headed for my apartment building. It was never a dull moment.

Pulling up in front of my building, Heathcliff met us in the lobby and escorted me up the steps. Sullivan continued on her way to the actual debrief with my clone and the federal protection detail. Heathcliff remained silent until we were inside my apartment.

"The detail in the lobby caught sight of a suspicious looking man and radioed ahead. The agents on the sixth floor stopped him, and he disappeared down the stairs. Dark jacket, bandana obscuring his face, and a cap, so needless to say, no positive ID can be made."

"Maybe Bandana wasn't here for me."

"Right, and you believe in the Easter Bunny too."

Shrugging, I did a sweep of my apartment. Dishes were in the sink, and a blanket was balled up on my sofa. "Now what? I wait around and see who else shows up?"

"Not much else for you to do." Heathcliff took a seat at my dining room table, and I joined him. "At least you're home."

Ten minutes later, O'Connell knocked on the door. The call had gone out over the wire, and he attempted to react normally. From past experience, when calls went out concerning me, he'd show up. The three of us sat at the table. When I couldn't take the silence any longer, I washed the dishes, folded the blanket, and did my best to resist the urge to go into my room to see what had or hadn't been touched. Giving in, I entered my bedroom and found my bed made and everything else as I had left it. At least the fake me was sleeping on my couch and not being overly intrusive.

When a knock sounded at the door, O'Connell answered it. Heathcliff put his hand on the butt of his gun, and he signaled for me to remain out of sight. Detective Hoskins stood on my doorstep, wearing a dark jacket and looking confused.

"Guess I'm a little late to the party," he said casually.

"Hoskins?" I asked. Was he the dirty cop? His jacket fit, and he walked right into our trap.

"Parker, I'm glad you're doing better. We never got a chance to discuss the Infinity shooting. I was just on my way to meet a CI when the call came over the radio. I wanted to make sure the bastard didn't come back."

Heathcliff and O'Connell did a decent job appearing nonchalant. There was no need to tip Hoskins off this was meant to be a sting, and I took a breath and reminded myself of the details only the shooter would know so as not to divulge anything relevant. We needed proof he was the shooter before we could arrest him.

"You didn't have to come here. The guys outside just overreacted. No big deal." Turning my back to Hoskins was the last thing I wanted to do, but I had two armed detectives for support. "Obviously, you all had the same idea. Coffee anyone?" Everyone declined, so I decided it best to get this over with.

Hoskins sat at my table. "I should have responded more appropriately to the call you made two Saturdays ago. I apologize." Cocking an eyebrow up, I waited for him to continue. The overwhelming urge to confront him as the son of a bitch who shot me and nearly killed Harrigan needed to be quelled. "Any idea who the shooter is?"

"We're working on it," O'Connell said. "It's need to know, and you don't."

"Last time I checked, we're on the same team," Hoskins said, but O'Connell fixed him with a hard stare. "Are you guys done asking about the intruder today? Because I'd like a chance to discuss the heists and Infinity."

Heathcliff and O'Connell exchanged a look. "We can finish up afterward," Heathcliff offered. They needed an excuse to stay in my apartment.

"I'm supposed to discuss my investigation in front of you, but you can't talk in front of me?" Every time Hoskins opened his mouth, he painted himself a deeper shade of guilty.

"Gentlemen, oddly enough, there's plenty to go around." The whorish reference was not lost on me, and I feared Martin's adolescent sense of humor was catching. "Like you said, you are on the same team. Carl, we'll get the burglary stuff out of the way first because I'm sure I'll be looking through mug shots all night." Carefully choosing my words and limiting the details, I gave Hoskins a basic recollection of my first and only Saturday at Infinity. "The thing is, as far as I know, the place wasn't robbed, so why do you care what happened?"

"If you weren't there to stop it, it would have been. This bastard strikes once every two weeks, and we're almost out of time. Another place might get hit this weekend. So I need clues. Weren't the two of you at the club earlier that evening?" Hoskins scrutinized Heathcliff and O'Connell.

"Where'd you hear that?" Heathcliff asked.

"Scuttlebutt around the precinct. One of my guys said he heard some of the detectives in major crimes talking about backing Parker up. You did a real fine job."

O'Connell was getting pissed, but Heathcliff remained his usual stoic self. "Well, when she called burglary, no one gave a shit. Unfortunately, the man pushed in front of the train required our attention instead, so we weren't around when she needed us," Heathcliff said.

"Shame really," O'Connell continued where Heathcliff left off, "I would have loved to get my hands on the burglar turned shooter."

"Me too." Hoskins got up from the table. "Glad you're still breathing, Parker. Try to keep it that way. If you come up with any theories concerning his next potential target, let me know. The clock's ticking."

SIXTEEN

Given Ernie's insistence that more than one merciless bastard attacked him, the FBI decided to reassess their position. Like O'Connell said, cops knew if their partners were dirty. Based on the evidence, we assumed a burglary detective was our shooter, and his partner helped conceal the crime. We just didn't know which burglary detective was responsible. But when Det. Carl Hoskins showed up at my place in response to the call, all eyes focused on him.

"He had opportunity and motive." SAC Cooper blew out a breath. "Too bad we don't have any hard evidence."

"What about the bullet fragment?" Mark asked.

"Tough sell without proof, but we might have enough to get a warrant for Hoskins' service piece."

"And if he's not the guy, we're tipping off the entire department that we're on to them," I muttered.

"Let's see what Moretti's sent us and if the detectives from major crimes have anything to add before we show our hand," Cooper declared.

When the FBI trio returned from analyzing the records Lt. Moretti sent over, Mark and I waited patiently for their assessment. Detective Packard was the only one of the four original suspects cleared from our pool of corrupt candidates since he had been teaching a class on nighttime weapons and tactics at the academy during one of the Saturday heists. Additionally, he had been alibied out for the night of the shooting by a few members of vice who needed additional UCs to impersonate gigolos. One down, three to go.

I was getting a cup of coffee when Thompson emerged from the elevator, carrying a copy paper box full of files. He spotted me and smiled.

"Those for us?" I asked.

"Yup, where am I going with these?" he asked. Leading the way, I opened the door to the conference room, so he could enter and set the box down. "Mail's here." Pulling four stacks from the box, he placed them on the table. "IAD files on Packard, Hoskins, Metz, and Fisher. Every complaint, every report, everything."

"Put Packard back in the box. We cleared him five minutes ago." Mark scooped up the Fisher files.

Everyone divvied up the work, and I was left standing near the doorway unsure of my role. Thompson raised a questioning eyebrow as if to say *now what.*

"I'll get everyone some coffee." Turning, I left the room, Thompson right behind me. Once the door shut, I faced him. "Did Heathcliff and O'Connell fill you in?"

"Yes. O'Connell's on his way. He got held up by a personal call. Moretti's talking to IAD, and they're keeping a tail on Hoskins. It's all hush-hush, but we want surveillance on him just in case."

"Better safe than sorry."

Countless hours later, our suspect pool remained at three. Hoskins looked guilty as sin for showing up at my apartment before the unsub had been identified as positively leaving my building. The forensics team was going over every inch of surveillance cam footage to see if the subject could be seen leaving the building, but so far, nothing turned up. My apartment building had shoddy equipment, and only the lobby and my floor had working cameras. He easily could have disappeared, changed, and walked out without a hitch.

O'Connell and Thompson provided their rendition of the facts, the situation, and their leads. The FBI agents hid their scoffs masterfully, and the potential pissing contest was avoided for today. By the time we decided when to reconvene, there was an obvious feel of progress in the air. One, two, or all three remaining suspects could be involved in the heists and the attempted frame-up job. We were monitoring Hoskins, but unless we had solid evidence pointing to either of the other two, we didn't have enough for a warrant. Honestly, I doubted we had enough to convince a judge to let us test the ballistics from Hoskins' gun, but the others seemed so hopeful, I didn't want to rain on their parade.

O'Connell offered a lift back to Martin's, and the two of us discussed things more fully in the privacy afforded by the plastic and steel box with wheels. Unfortunately, even though we were trained investigators, we didn't have much insight on the matter.

"How long has the corruption case been going on?"

"Two months." O'Connell's eyes constantly moved as he watched for tails and other traffic.

"It started before the first burglary?"

"A week before, two anonymous calls came in. The first was to internal affairs and the second to the Bureau. Whoever it was wanted to make sure we took notice."

My suspicion rested on Vito being the tipster. More than likely, Stoltz Bros. was a front company for his illegal enterprises. Vito might have heard rumors about a renegade cop and wanted to put a stop to things before they got blown out of proportion and interfered with his business.

"How was the investigation going before I got roped into it?"

"It could have been better. Almost everything we had pointed to corruption in burglary, but we had no hard evidence. Just like now. You pointed out the detective shield, and at least we have a bullet fragment whenever we get enough to run comparisons." Nick sighed deeply. He didn't have to say it. I already knew; he didn't like investigating others in the brotherhood.

"You think it's Hoskins."

"Don't you? There is something wrong with him. He reeks of it. And why show up now? You've allegedly been home for the last four days. If he was so concerned about your well-being or tracking potential leads, he should have banged on your door three days ago. He never showed up at the hospital either. Nothing." Nick was angrier than I realized.

"Is something wrong?" Thompson mentioned O'Connell being held up by a personal call.

"It's late, and I'm sick of this shit." He pulled up to Martin's and flashed his badge at the surveillance van. They ran through the checklist of approved police personnel and let him proceed.

"Is Jen working late? I can offer you dinner or coffee or something," I said. He shook his head and stared out the windshield, waiting for me to exit. "See you soon. Get some sleep." Entering the security code, I walked through Martin's front door and re-engaged the security system. There was so much to think about. Why did everything have to happen at once?

*   *   *

The ringing phone startled me awake, and I jumped up from the couch, scattering papers everywhere. My narcoleptic habits and unnatural attachment to Martin's sofa had resurfaced after being forced to spend my nights at his place while dealing with a particularly daunting case. Old habits die hard, I suppose. Getting up, I grabbed the handset from the wall and held it against my ear.

"Martin's residence." I stifled a yawn.

"Did I wake you?" Martin asked, amusement in his voice. "It's three hours earlier here, so I didn't realize this would be an issue, especially on a Thursday. Did you invite a dozen of your girlfriends over for a slumber party and lingerie pillow fight last night? I hope it was in front of the security cameras, so I can watch when I get home."

Squinting, I noted the microwave's illuminated nine a.m. I should have been at the office an hour ago. Shit. "Damn couch."

I heard a distinct chuckle before he returned to the matter at hand. "Can you do me a favor?"

"Yeah, of course."

"Upstairs," he began, and I swallowed. The shootout on the fourth floor occurred almost a year ago, but I hadn't set foot up there since. My heart raced at the nightmarish thought, but I pushed it away. I had to get out of my own head sometimes. "You'll find a USB drive on my dresser. If you can e-mail me the contents, I'd appreciate it. In all the rushing around, I must have forgotten it."

"No problem. I'll send the information to your corporate account. If you don't get the files within the next ten minutes, call back. Then I have to get to work." Why didn't anyone pick me up this morning or at least bother to call? Something was up.

"Alex," he stopped mid-hang up, "I miss you." It was our pathetic attempt at an inside joke. Honestly, it made little sense, but most things which amused him made little sense.

"Jerk," I teased, rallying my nerves for the walk upstairs.

It was anticlimactic. After the initial adrenaline rush hit on the third floor landing, the next flight made little impact. The hallway was carpeted now instead of hardwood, but the bedroom remained the same. The office down the hall, where Martin had lain bleeding, had been walled up and a new room created. Not having time to take a full tour, I ducked into his bedroom and located the USB drive on the dresser next to a set of car keys. At least this trip upstairs remedied my lack of ride. Two birds, one stone. Maybe things were looking up.

Back down the stairs, I turned on the computer and e-mailed the files. Then I got ready and drove to the federal building.

When I walked into the conference room, Mark and Cooper looked confused. They were listening to Agent Sullivan recap the information Agent Maureen Navate, my clone, had provided.

"Glad you didn't start without me," I said pointedly, taking a seat. Luckily, neither Mark nor Cooper wanted to make a scene, and they both turned their attention back to Sullivan.

Agent Navate didn't see or hear anything. Frankly, she was bored and wanted to go home. So did I. The suspicious man hadn't made it to my apartment or resurfaced since yesterday. Apparently, we were debating if keeping an agent staked out in my apartment was a waste of resources. I thought so.

"Why don't you let me play the part of Agent Parker?" I whined. "I've been told I'm a dead ringer for her. Same height, weight, hair. Need I continue?"

"Same smartass attitude too," Mark muttered. "Are you even cleared for field work yet?"

"I haven't checked, but I'm pretty much healed. Want to make sure? I'll take my shirt off, if you want."

"Parker," Cooper interjected sharply. Being unfamiliar with my quirkier personality traits, he had yet to figure out when I was serious and when I was using exaggeration as a technique to reinforce my point. "Regardless of your field readiness, Director Kendall doesn't want a temporarily deputized agent placed in a position to take lead on an arrest. Therefore," he turned back to Sullivan, "Agent Navate will remain in Parker's apartment until further notice. However, please inform her we'll find a relief agent so she won't be expected to live there."

"Aye, sir."

After Sullivan left, I did my best to deflect the accusatory and semi-angry stares I received from Cooper and Mark. "Why didn't I get picked up this morning?" Shifting my gaze from one to the other, I watched a dark cloud settle over them. "What happened?"

SEVENTEEN

"But she's okay?" I asked for the third time, and Mark nodded.

O'Connell's wife, Jen, was accosted in the hospital parking lot by uniformed officers the night before. They suggested she ought to be more careful, and her husband needed to mind his own business and watch out for his family instead of spying on his brothers in blue. The threat was obvious, but thankfully, it was all bark and no bite.

"Were they the bastards from burglary?" I couldn't get my mind to wrap around the details.

"From what O'Connell said, they were just some rookie uniforms who were told by their TOs that screwing with your own kind is sacrilege. They wanted to send a message and make a point." Mark looked pensive. "The scandal is in the open now, and the cops know who's looking into departmental corruption."

"Always have your partner's back." I sighed. It was the code law enforcement lived by. If you couldn't trust the person next to you, you didn't have anything.

The only problem with this ethical code was how to deal with a scumbag who got confused which side of the line he was on.

"O'Connell's not backing down," Cooper said. In his monotone voice, it sounded like he was reading the stock market report. I understood Nick's aversion to rolling over, but some things weren't worth it. Although, I would dig my heels in too. "But Moretti's sending him to work the ongoing subway homicide case instead."

"Let's get back to business." Mark produced a notepad with the day's itinerary.

With the long hours and my current physical condition, my days blended together. A part of me feared it wasn't just days, but weeks, months, or even years, that were turning into an unending blur, broken only by monotone dialogue and changing images on the screens. If there had ever been any doubt in my mind why I hadn't returned to the job I walked away from a year and a half ago, I now had my answer. Being human, I bumbled around, got into trouble, and typically pissed off anyone who happened to be in the vicinity, but things were ultimately figured out without sitting in a windowless conference room, staring at the same reports.

"Agent Jablonsky," I could be formal when necessary, "I'm not coming in tomorrow. In fact, I might not be back the rest of the week."

"That's not the deal you made with Kendall."

Resisting the urge to say Kendall could shove it up his ass, I chose to be diplomatic. "I'm no good here. Pushing papers isn't solving the problem. Give me some time to let the facts ruminate. If something pops, I'll let you know."

"Everything from your office is in evidence storage. Don't go back there. And stay away from your apartment too. Other than that, if you have the overwhelming need to chat with someone, particularly a witness or suspect, take an agent as backup. Understand?"

"Aye, sir."

By the time I pulled out of the garage, it was dark outside. The stars were hidden by a thick blanket of foreboding clouds, indicative of the impending downpour. April showers brought May flowers, but it was early March. Damn global warming. While driving, I paid attention to police vehicles in the area, traffic cams, and other motorists. The old adage, *you break it, you buy it*, worried me because I couldn't afford to replace Martin's car or even pay the insurance deductible. Luckily, I arrived at his compound unimpeded and without incident.

"Aren't you guys bored?" I asked the federal agents acting as guards.

"It'd be worse if we weren't." Truer words had never been said.

Flashing my credentials, I figured they were tired of me by now, but I didn't have the authority to send them away. And the people who could wouldn't consider it.

Once inside with the security system reactivated, I opened a can of soup and left it on the stove to simmer while I transformed the second floor into a usable workspace. By the time I finished, my soup resembled gravy.

A large whiteboard stood in the center of the living room with copies of the files splayed in workable order on the coffee table and a desktop computer and desk occupying the space where the couch had been. I wouldn't win any awards for home decorating, but at least everything was together in one room.

The only way I knew how to work an investigation

was to gather information. And since we couldn't pinpoint the perpetrator, analyzing the locations of the crimes was the next best thing. As I dug deeper, it became apparent many aspects of the club heists linked to Vito, from the liquor supplier to Ernie's silent partners.

As I ate my dinner, I performed a search on Antonio 'Vito' Vincenzo. The last thing I wanted was to tango with one of the strongest crime families in the city, but Vito knew a lot more than he should. He knew of my involvement, and after his visit with Ernie, he located me at the park. A shiver ran down my spine as my paranoia pondered if he knew where I was now. *Vito's not your enemy*, I reminded myself. *The corrupt cops are.*

Following the information where it led, I moved on to the liquor supplier. Stoltz Bros. Liquor Emporium was originally founded by the Stoltz brothers in 1948. The name became synonymous with restaurateurs and bar owners for quality and low-cost. Even when the company switched hands in the sixties, again in the eighties, and finally in the early twenty-first century, business remained booming. The company was in the black. The most recent owner was one of Vito's lieutenants. Although, from the tax records and public documentation, no obvious crime connection could be made.

"Strike one," I said to the screen. Next, I checked financial records and ownership documentation of the four burglarized clubs to see what other ties to Vito might exist. Each club, including Infinity, had some connection to Vito. It seemed financially unsound to have one enterprise provide a product or service to another, particularly when it appeared not all of the clubs were pulling their financial weight, but I was no corporate genius. My assumption was Vito used the clubs to clean dirty money. With the number of cash-only patrons and cover charges, it'd be easy for the dirty money to filter in, get laundered, and be paid back out through purchases made to Stoltz. What did I get myself into this time?

Unfortunately, it was completely out of the question to go to the gangs unit at the precinct or the organized crime unit at the Bureau with any of this. Vito made it clear I owed him. But I felt certain I just stumbled upon the motive for the heists. A police detective could theoretically find justification for committing crimes if the victim was a criminal. Maybe he rationalized stealing the money as helping get drugs, guns, or prostitutes off the streets. Stop the funding, and the crime would stop. However, things were never this cut and dry.

What to do? I paced the room. Eventually, I stopped in front of the whiteboard and diagrammed the connections, making Vito the sun in this particular solar system. He was a mob boss, so dozens of police personnel had an axe to grind with him. But who would be insane and corrupt enough to try to take down a kingpin, especially by staging robberies at a few clubs that barely traced back to him? Knowing I couldn't stop now, I performed background checks on all the employees from each of the clubs and their known associates. Before I finished reviewing the personnel files for the second club, dawn had broken.

Brewing a strong pot of coffee, I continued running down names. Every club had at least two employees who worked for Vito or were suspected of having connections to someone who worked for him. Having two inside men made it easy to keep an eye on things and make sure no one got greedy and skimmed off the top. Did they even know about one another? I stared at my theory board, but the notes and lines ran together. I needed sleep.

Shutting down the computer and taking the radio and my nine millimeter with me, I settled into the guestroom. After sleeping for a few hours, my nightmares returned. The trip upstairs had brought back bad memories, along with demons from my past. Thankfully, despite the rain, it was still daylight, and I was relieved not to be alone in the dark. I drank the remainder of the now cold coffee while reassessing my work with fresh eyes.

Everything was sound. Vito was at the center of this. He used his liquor company to provide goods to the clubs, where someone from his organization held a position as primary investor. To ensure everything ran smoothly, he had eyes inside. Holy shit, if he had a security cam in Infinity, he might have others in the four other clubs. He might possess the evidence needed to stop this. *Wait*, my thought process came to a crashing halt. If he did, he would have taken care of the problem already.

The footage may still exist, but there might not be anything useful on it. Tabling this thought for later consideration, I rummaged around for Infinity's personnel information. After hours of searching, I realized Gretchen and Mary were working for Vito.

Picking up the phone, I was halfway through dialing Mark's number when I noticed the time. It was after one a.m. And I thought staying in the conference room was a time suck. At least I made clear connections in a little over twenty-four hours. Putting the phone down, I headed to bed, but ghosts from my past haunted me.

Getting up, I took the radio and my handgun and methodically searched the house. Darkness was my enemy, and to kill the spirits lurking in the shadows, I flipped on light after light as I went from floor to floor.

On the third level, the radio chirped, and the doorway to the laundry room almost took a bullet. Luckily, I restrained myself as I answered the call. All the activity and lights had thrown up warning bells for the protection detail outside.

"Sorry, I was just looking for something," I radioed back. They asked for the all clear verification phrase, and once I gave it to them, they resumed radio silence. Finishing my check of the third floor, I went up another flight and looked warily down the hallway. This was a dumb idea. Chasing ghosts to the place where I had slain a mercenary was not the way to free my mind from past demons.

Somehow, my search concluded in Martin's bedroom. Nights like this I wished he was here. Actually, I wished I wasn't. Snorting at the absurdity, I stared out the French doors and watched the rain cascade in sheets onto the stucco balcony. Time stood still as the raindrops fell. Eventually, I found some much needed solace, and instead of going down two flights of stairs, I crawled into Martin's bed. His scent, a mixture of cologne, shampoo, and his natural musk, lingered on the pillow, and I let oblivion replace the hours of work and worry.

Static interrupted my nonsensical dream. Opening my eyes, I forgot where I was until the radio chirped again. After listening to the message, I picked it up, replied with a clipped "copy", and hurried down the steps.

Mark was on his way inside, and I didn't need him examining the only lead I wasn't sure I wanted to divulge. In my converted office space which used to be the living room, I flipped the whiteboard over and shoved it against the wall just as he opened the door, and I detoured to the kitchen.

"What the hell?" He looked around the room with a

healthy level of concern mixed with amazement. "Marty needs to hire a better decorator."

"Coffee?" I turned on the machine, wanting nothing more than to take a shower and change my clothes. I'd been working for hours, and my break to sleep didn't involve bothering to get undressed.

"Sounds good." He examined my face. "I thought you wanted a break from the incessant work."

"I wanted a break from the monotonous work. This," I gestured to the living room, "not so monotonous." Casting a winning smile his way, I asked, "How about you make breakfast while I get cleaned up?"

He rolled his eyes and went to the fridge as I scurried down the hallway to take the world's shortest shower and dress faster than Clark Kent in a phone booth.

Ten minutes later, Mark sipped his coffee while trying to flip some eggs in the pan. Giving up, he stirred the mostly cooked eggs with the spatula. "It's not pretty, but it works."

"I'm sure you say that to all the ladies."

He looked annoyed, but he dismissed my jibe without comment. As we sat across from one another, he kept glancing at my workspace. "Theories? Guesses? Suspects?" He expected a call yesterday, and when he didn't hear anything, he had grown impatient.

"You mean those ace investigators haven't figured it out yet?"

"Parker, do you have anything?"

"I need to talk to Gretchen and Mary again. Also," I hedged, "I'm working on something, but right now, you don't need to know."

"Let me be the judge of that. You've gotten yourself into enough of a mess."

"I know." Remaining silent, I finished eating and poured us each another cup of coffee. "I'm just trying to avoid getting into another predicament. Do you trust me?"

"Dammit, Alex. I'm giving you some slack here. Don't hang yourself with it."

EIGHTEEN

Mark accompanied me to Mary Johannson's house. Mary had been waitressing at Infinity for the past four months while working on her thesis in applied physics. From what I gathered, she was the niece of Vito's right-hand man, but when her mother got divorced, she and Mary changed their names. It explained how I missed the obvious crime family connection. Perhaps Uncle Carmine had gotten her the job to help pay off her six-figure student loans.

"Mary," I knocked, "it's Alexis." No answer. "Mary," I tried again. Dropping the friendly tone and pretense, I rapped loudly against the door. "Federal agents, open up."

Mark tossed a furtive glance my way. "Admit it, you've missed saying those four words."

"Shut the fuck up. You mean those four words?"

Mary wasn't home, so we'd have to come back later. Mark chuckled, and after giving the door the quick once-over for signs of foul play, we headed to Gretchen's workplace.

Since it was early on a Saturday, she'd be fulfilling her child-rearing role as the Nunzios' nanny. Constantine Nunzio worked in an official capacity as Vito's personal assistant, but realistically, Nunzio made problems go away.

When I told Mark about Gretchen's connection to Constantine Nunzio, he looked apprehensive. He didn't have to ask; I already knew what he was thinking. It was the same question I asked myself since the shootout at the club – what did I get myself into?

Predictably, Gretchen had taken the littlest Nunzio to the park. When she saw me approach, she reached for her phone to dial either the police or her boss. Mark hung back to keep an eye on things, probably hoping to avoid a reenactment of *Goodfellas*.

I unclipped my badge and held it up. "Gretchen, I'm a federal agent. The man sitting on the bench is my partner." She looked at Mark, who displayed his credentials as well. "We need to talk."

"Ja? Here?"

"Here works." Lowering my voice, I continued, "I know who you work for. Why do you waitress at Infinity? Did Mr. Nunzio put you up to it? What can you tell me about the night of the shooting? You said you saw a police cruiser outside the club."

"Mr. Nunzio asked if I wanted to make extra cash and help his boss. All I had to do was make sure no one skimmed profits. In Germany, I went to university to be an accountant, but once I arrived in this country, there were no jobs. So every week, I sneak into the office and check the books." Her German accent sounded like something from a Mel Brooks movie since she pronounced the w's as strong v's.

"Did the accounts change? Did anything change?"

"The money remained, but you showed up. Mr.

Nunzio's boss wasn't happy Mr. Papadakis hired a new girl, and he encouraged Mr. Papadakis to fire you."

"But I'm so lovable," I protested. She looked confused, so I got back to the topic at hand. "What did you see Saturday night when you left the club?"

"A police car parked near the back. The lights were off. It looked abandoned."

"Did you get a number? Or a license plate? Anything that would make it identifiable?"

"There was a dent on the passenger's door, but I didn't see any numbers." She paused, recollecting. "Nein, that's not true. I saw black numbers written on the side and back. Nine-one-one."

My jaw dropped in awe at her idiocy. Every time I felt certain the rock bottom of stupidity had been reached, the floor fell through to another subbasement. Was it possible she was making a joke? I waited a few beats, but she didn't crack a smile or hint she was teasing. If I stayed near her any longer, my brain cells would die out of sympathy.

"Thank you for your time. I'll be in touch." Striding back to Mark, I made sure the coast was clear before exiting the park.

"Anything?" he asked.

"Dent on the passenger's side of the cruiser."

"We can run work orders and check the cars. Maybe we'll see who signed it out that night. Did she see the number?"

"Nine-one-one."

"You're kidding, right?"

"God, I hope so."

*   *   *

Dropping by the Bureau offices, Mark sent in his

request on the service records for all police cruisers. While we waited for the records department to get back to us, I went upstairs to the OIO to see if Director Kendall might be putting in some overtime weekend hours. He was gone for the day, probably fishing or relaxing, but his assistant was catching up on paperwork. When I asked if my request to see Sam Harrigan had been approved, she shuffled through some papers, said the U.S. Marshal Service was still considering it, and Kendall would notify me when he heard something. Before returning downstairs, I dialed O'Connell's cell phone from Mark's office.

"O'Connell," he answered on the second ring.

"I heard about what happened. How's Jen? Is everything okay?"

"It's fine. But I need you to pull some of that crazy theorizing out of your ass and have this thing end sooner rather than later."

"I'll do my best."

"Be careful. I work with some insane motherfuckers. You already got shot once. Let's not have a replay."

His admonition put me on edge. The hairs on the back of my neck stood up, and I forced the apprehension away as I went to consult with Mark. The dented cruiser hadn't been registered to anyone the night of the shooting. The precinct assigned cars randomly every tour, so there was no point in sending an FBI forensics team to look at it. Everyone's prints and DNA would be inside. We had hit another dead end.

"Calling it a day?" Mark asked as I sat on top of the conference table, kicking my heel into the table leg.

"Where is everyone?"

"Running leads. They didn't want me to play since my vest has different letters written across the front."

"Interagency cooperation at its finest." I hopped off the table. "When can I move back into my apartment or at least get some of my belongings out of evidence?"

"Try back Monday," he said in an automated consumer hotline voice. "In the meantime, shall I drop you at Marty's?"

"Guess so."

Our ride back to Martin's compound was brief and silent. I was mulling over my theories and considering paying Vito a visit. Based on my research, I knew he owned a small tavern. If I showed up at his secret hangout, I would find him or he'd find me. But the prospect made my feet drag. I didn't want to go down a road when I didn't know where it would lead.

"You're home," Mark announced, parking in front of the garage, but in my thought-induced comatose state, I wasn't sure how we got here. "Maybe you should take a nap or something. You look tired. How's the side?"

"Still attached." I shrugged. "A little sore but healing. I'm just really starting to hate this case. Correction, I've hated this case for the last couple of weeks, before I even knew what was going on. What are Cooper and his team doing?"

Mark gave his patented 'you're not going to like it' look. "He sent Sullivan and Darli to talk to the marshals guarding Harrigan. He and Webster are conducting another interview with Papadakis, and then they're going to the precinct to work some things out with Moretti."

"So why do they need us?"

"We add class to the operation," Mark said. Leaning back in the seat, I shut my eyes and decided he ought to know about the organized crime connection, but before I could say a word, he filled the silence. "Alex, I've been meaning to ask, when you were resisting arrest, where'd you go?"

I laughed. "You really want to know?"

"Maybe it'll provide some insight into fugitive recovery," he deadpanned.

"I snuck into a motel room at night. During the day, I ran errands. I might have gone to see O'Connell, stopped by to see you, threatened to shoot Martin, quit my job at Martin Technologies, took a lot of cab rides, and talked to some witnesses. Y'know, the usual."

"It must be nice to have luck and resources."

I needed to pay Martin back as soon as my credit cards and bank accounts were no longer frozen. "It would be nice to have some things again, a place all my own, an office, and money."

"It'll be cleared up soon enough. Until then, you have everything you could possibly need."

"Except my own space." I got out of the car. "My own bed. My own car. Hell, even my own phone." I bid him farewell and entered the security code to get inside the house. The federal agents keeping watch from their van were probably bored. At least they had their own van to sit in and homes to return to when second shift came to relieve them.

Spending the rest of the day working on theories, I practically jumped out of my skin when the radio chirped again. Pondering the activity of known mob bosses put me on edge, as did being in Martin's home. The nerve-wracking radio call announced Heathcliff and Thompson were stopping by for a visit. Maybe a plan had been devised with SAC Cooper.

"Pizza delivery," Thompson bellowed. "Heathcliff sprung for the beers tonight. The last time you comped us, things didn't turn out so well, and we didn't want to risk it a second time."

"Sorry for the intrusion," Heathcliff said. "O'Connell went home after shift, and I figured you might want to hear what went on today."

"Do tell." I got some plates, a few glasses filled with ice, and napkins. The detectives sat down in the converted living room, staring at the stacks of pages laying around. Once again, I was glad the whiteboard faced the wall.

"Nice job redecorating. If my girlfriend trashed my place like this, we'd so be over," Thompson commented.

"Good thing you don't have a girlfriend then," snarky was my devoted friend, "especially one who is armed and was accused of murder within the last few weeks." I gave Thompson my death glare, and he shut up and poured his beer into the glass.

"Seems you've been working harder than we have," Heathcliff said. "Today, Special Agent in Charge Cooper came to see us. He and Moretti have made arrangements to pair an agent with a cop and stakeout the clubs on the strip tonight."

"Saturday night, time to rock and roll," I said.

"Exactly. But if none of the clubs are knocked over, we won't know if it's because the corrupt cops are sitting next to federal agents."

"At least it'll be one less heist in the crime spree to process."

"Less evidence and fewer leads, but no one will get shot," Heathcliff said.

"So I take it the burglary boys have been partnered with FBI agents," I said.

"I don't know. We didn't get the details. Thompson and I were each assigned members of the dream team." Heathcliff was referencing the group of federal agents Mark and I were working with. "O'Connell's off this. He's at home tonight and not going anywhere."

The detective sighed. "We shouldn't be turning on one another."

"No, you shouldn't," I agreed, and we exchanged a meaningful glance. "I'm guessing I'm benched for this play."

"Yep," Thompson abandoned the silent act, "they want to double up on your protection detail in case the pissed off party makes a move on you. Although, we're hoping if that happens, they'll go to your apartment and not here."

"Tactical support is set up across the street from your building," Heathcliff chimed in. "Agent Navate's inside, and undercover agents are positioned throughout the building."

"Why me?" It was Saturday night, and while I could be a lot of fun, I wasn't a happening nightclub with thousands of dollars free for the taking.

"After Hoskins showed up at your place, asking for leads and details, we figured he might be upset you ruined his last big score. If he thinks you're standing in his way, he might want to exact revenge," Heathcliff stated matter-of-factly.

"Did you ever figure out why those particular clubs were targeted?" I wondered if the PD made the Vito connection like I did.

"Still working on it. Do you have anything?" Thompson glanced at the papers on the desk.

"They use the same liquor supplier." It never hurt to point the good guys in the right direction. It was information they would uncover eventually, and in the meantime, I could still tell Vito I didn't say a word about him.

"We'd better head out." Heathcliff was all business. "Planning an op takes time, but if anything goes down tonight, Parker, give me a call."

"Thanks, Derek." I glanced at the five remaining

beers in the six-pack. It was stupid they picked up beer when they were working, but maybe it was their way of contributing.

After they left, I straightened up the kitchen and made sure all the doors and windows were locked and the security system was functioning. The looming threat startled me, and once again, I found myself in Martin's bedroom, staring at the backyard and wondering when the culprit or culprits would be caught.

NINETEEN

My dream that night sent me back inside Infinity's storeroom. I was pinned down as gunfire ripped through the doorjamb. The gold detective's shield glowed in the mirror's reflection. *Two, nine, four,* I stared harder at the reflection, trying to read the reversed, backward numbers in the glass. The sound of a door being thrown open caught my attention, and scurrying up the secondary staircase and down again, I found myself at the double doors, staring out as he announced he was responding to the 911 call. His deep and slightly raspy voice probably came from years of smoking. He had short dark hair peeking out over the top of his upturned collar. Suddenly, I heard heavy footsteps and another door slamming shut.

"Parker, copy?" The staticky radio sputtered to life, rousing me from sleep. "Please respond."

Fumbling with the buttons as I clung to the last remnants of my dream, uncertain if they were memories or imagination, I replied, "Say again."

"Friendlies entering the house now." Who the hell

was showing up at four a.m.?

I headed for the stairs, spotting Martin giving Bruiser last minute instructions to stay on the second floor and not to disturb me.

"Too late." I smiled at him from the floor above.

"Jones, ignore that and make yourself comfortable," Martin called before turning to me. "I never expected to find you up there," he teased, but his voice didn't convey the sentiment. "My god, you're a sight for sore eyes." He closed the distance between us in the blink of an eye and grabbed me in a tight embrace. His shirt was damp, as was his hair. It must still be raining.

My brain was foggy from sleep, but something felt wrong. "You didn't say when you were coming back. Why'd you fly home in the middle of the night?"

He had yet to let go as he continued to crush me against him. His kiss tasted of stale alcohol, and I wondered if he was hungover. "It's late. Can we talk in the morning?" Releasing me, he entered the bedroom. I followed and watched him peel off his dress shirt and tie. "I'm glad you made yourself at home." He tossed a slight smile in my direction. "If I had known this was the trick to getting you into my bed, I'd have left a long time ago." Classic Martin.

For someone who wanted to talk in the morning, he had yet to shut up. His posture was unnaturally rigid as he climbed into his unmade bed, still wearing his suit pants. I retrieved a towel from the bathroom and found him sitting up in bed, having shifted my gun and handheld radio to the nightstand farthest from the bedroom door.

I quickly scribbled a note about the pertinent facts of my dream on a nearby sheet of paper for reconsideration in the morning and got into bed next to him. I ran the towel through his hair, but he tossed it aside and enveloped me in his arms. His eyes closed, but his jaw clenched. Tension radiated from him.

"Martin," I pushed against his chest, "a little space and the ability to breathe would be nice."

He barely loosened his vise-like grip. "Shit." His green eyes flashed in concern. "How's your back? Are you okay?"

"I'm fine as long as you don't suffocate me. What's wrong?" I ran my fingers along the stubble on his jaw. He was never this clingy. Something was off, and I hated not knowing what it was.

He went prone with both of his arms still around my waist, leaving me no choice but to lie down next to him. "Tomorrow." He shut his eyes and kissed my forehead. "Night, Alex."

Lying in the semi-darkness of his bedroom, thanks to the bathroom light being left on, I was certain he was still awake. His posture was tense and rigid, and his breathing wasn't slow and steady. The way he positioned himself and kept his arms wrapped around my body, I couldn't help but feel he was acting like a human shield, my protector from some unforeseen danger. With the exception of arguments, he wasn't one to put off conversation. That made his lack of discussion an unsettling harbinger. Letting out a sigh, I tried to relax, but the stress and intensity emanating from him put me further on edge.

Around dawn, I unhooked his fingers from the small of my back and managed to doze. My dreams were brief and horrific with mercenaries, blood, death, and torture haunting every image. I'd jerk awake each time, grateful not to be so sound asleep to wake myself screaming. Martin clutched me close to him with a single arm around my torso but didn't acknowledge my panicked breathing or jolting sleep patterns. Maybe he conked out, or he wanted to avoid conversation. The uneasiness grew as I waited impatiently for whatever was to come.

Sometime mid-morning Sunday, I opened my eyes to find him brushing a strand of hair from my face. He hadn't slept; his eyes were dark and rimmed with red. He looked forlorn, and I returned his gaze with a questioning look.

"I called Mark last night after it happened. He didn't think there was any reason you needed to know right away. You were supposed to have gotten at least one more night to sleep, but from all the jerking around you did," there was no mirth; with him, there was always mirth at juvenile jokes, "that plan failed royally."

"What are you talking about?" Being behind was one of my least favorite things.

"Alexis, please don't have a knee-jerk reaction."

What possibly could have happened? The anticipatory build-up was probably worse than whatever it was. Before I could respond, his phone buzzed, and he spun around to answer it. He got out of bed and headed for the bathroom, talking animatedly. Once the water turned on, I left the room. He deserved some peace, and I needed time to think about the shooter.

Downstairs in the guestroom, I showered and dressed, replaying the entire event multiple times. Maybe my imagination and reality had merged together, or maybe I remembered a partial badge number and slightly better description of the gunman. It was something else we could consider in the course of investigating.

When I emerged, I spotted Bruiser sitting at the kitchen table in the midst of a conversation with Martin. The unease returned when they both stopped speaking as soon as I entered the room. Bruiser excused himself, and Martin wished me a good morning.

"Spill," I shot out.

"Looks like you've been busy." He indicated the living room. "Make any progress?"

"I'm working on it. Why are you back?"

"I live here." His serious tone from the bedroom had abated. "The conference ended. Work resumes Monday. But it doesn't look like you got the chance to clean me out. Should I leave and come back?"

"Sure, but I'll need the code to your safe first. That's why I was in your room, trying to perfect my safecracking skills."

"Funny, I don't have a safe in my room." He was infuriating and avoiding the question at all costs.

"Damn, that must be where I went wrong." Narrowing my eyes, I waited for an explanation for his uncharacteristic behavior last night and again this morning.

"Alexis." His tone shifted to serious, and he opened his mouth to speak but shut it again. He turned away and rummaged through the fridge for a time before turning back. Despite my impatience, I had conducted a few interrogations in my day. I could wait him out if I needed to. "Once you know," he swallowed, "I honestly have no idea how you'll react."

"Try me." Things were going from bad to worse.

"Just promise you won't rush out of here half-cocked." He winked in a failed attempt at levity, and I leaned against the wall and waited. "God, you're really good at that." Still, I waited silently. "We, being myself, my driver, and bodyguard, were stopped last night on our way home from the airport. Everything's fine. Like I said, I already called Mark. Bruiser's cool with hanging around here, and there are nondescript vans parked outside."

"Who was it? What did they want?" I pressed my lips into a hard line. My heart pounded in my chest, but my breathing remained slow and my speech resigned. It was the calm before the storm.

"Alex."

"Who?" The intensity of my tone grew exponentially.

"Two police cars. One uniformed officer and one plainclothes. Plain-clothed? A detective, maybe. They weren't willing to divulge names or badge numbers. Not much happened really."

"Define not much." *Martin is not your enemy*, I reminded myself as I tried to rein in the hatred so it wouldn't splatter onto him.

"They were just screwing around, wanting to search my car, reminding me assisting a fugitive and providing refuge to a criminal was a felony. They had some positively lovely things to say about federal agents and private investigators," his tone seethed with bitterness. "But I was pleasant and told them they could search whatever they wanted if they had a warrant. And until then, they could speak to my lawyer. They suggested I be careful because, with the wet roads, it'd be a shame if I had an accident."

My stomach twisted in knots, and I forced a long exhale. I balled my hands into fists to stop the obvious shaking. The message was clear; you fuck with us, and we'll fuck with you and yours.

"I have calls to make." My insistence to move back into my apartment just went from a deep-seated desire to a dire need. Maybe distancing myself would keep the bull's eye off Martin's back. "Are you sure there are no other business trips you need to take. Maybe leave now and stay away until..." My voice dropped as his face fell. We were back to our constant dilemma.

"Are you walking away again?"

"Right now, I don't even know which way is up."

"If things ever calm down, I'd be more than happy to show you." His face brightened at the adolescent humor. "You just have to stick around until then."

Picking up the kitchen extension, I dialed Mark's number. Last night, another robbery might have occurred, and if not, then maybe my newly remembered facts would help. "Do you think you can identify the cops from last night if you saw them again?" I asked as I waited for Mark to answer.

"Pretty sure. Jones got a good look at them too."

Two eyewitnesses. I should be downright giddy, instead of homicidal.

"Parker, hang on a minute," Mark answered and immediately put me on hold.

"Why couldn't you have just slept with a flight attendant instead of this? You're supposed to be a womanizing millionaire, not some schmuck who has cops harassing him."

"My girlfriend has a gun. Do you think I have a death wish?"

"I'd only graze you. You'd live."

This time his embrace was gentle and sensitive. "Who's to say I didn't bang half of Los Angeles?"

"Did you?"

"No." He let go and started making brunch. "How many of your friends are joining us today?"

"A few."

Mark came back on the line and caught the tail end of the conversation. "Is Marty offering to make us brunch?" he asked. "If he is, the five of us will be over in thirty."

"You know what happened?" I asked Mark.

"Got the call in the middle of the night. O'Connell's

on his way to the OIO now, and Heathcliff, Thompson, and Cooper have been going over debriefs since six a.m."

"See you soon."

Before I could hang up, Mark offered his patented, unsolicited advice, "Parker, don't do anything rash. You and split second decisions rarely work out in the long run."

Rolling my eyes, I disconnected the call. "Maybe you should make the rest of those eggs," I suggested, and Martin nodded but didn't turn around as he continued to cook. I pulled out the coffee filters and coffee, brewing a pot. "Luckily for you, I invested in an actual coffeemaker and not a ridiculous mechanical paperweight."

"And here I thought I kept you around for your looks and wildcat bedroom antics."

"Not because I carry a nine millimeter and have precision aim?"

"Since you're no longer my bodyguard, my preference for your particular skill set has shifted." He turned with a questioning look. Would I stay or would I go? Things were quickly devolving into a Clash song.

"I'm still homeless, and with my bank account frozen, I remain indebted to you. Do you think you can put up with me for a little while longer?"

"If you really twist my arm, I suppose I can manage." His relief was evident, but he was never one to leave well enough alone. "But if you want to tip the scales more greatly in your favor, it might depend on your willingness to put out. In the name of full disclosure, there's currently a cocktail waitress and flight attendant vying for your spot. They were both more than willing to throw themselves at me twelve hours ago."

I slapped his arm for the poor attempt at a joke and

went into the living room to move my incriminating whiteboard away from prying eyes. I needed to make certain no signs of mob connections remained in sight of the impending troop of law enforcement officers. Now wasn't the time to have that discussion. Frankly, there might never be a time to have that particular discussion. Thankfully, we were investigating crooked cops who were knocking over nightclubs, not establishments used for money laundering. As I began scooting the desk back to the office, Martin came into the hallway.

"Are you trying to hurt yourself?" He shoved the desk back where it belonged. "Do you mind?" He reached for the hem of my shirt and waited for permission before lifting it to examine my scarred side. "Wow, I leave for a week and come back to find you in one piece. It's amazing."

"Time heals all wounds, right?" Something intense and poignant sizzled between us, but it dissipated when the front door opened, and Mark announced himself.

TWENTY

Martin provided sustenance to the troops and gave a full statement to everyone at the table. Thompson fought with the computer to display a photo array of police officers for Martin and Bruiser to identify. While they were occupied, I was brought up to speed on last night's surveillance.

The surveillance teams didn't run across anything suspicious. No one knocked over any of the clubs. More than likely, the guilty party or parties had been paired with federal agents and didn't have a chance to conduct a heist. But someone in the police department discovered Martin's arrival time and followed him from the airport to deliver a threatening message.

"Things at the precinct aren't good," O'Connell said. "Lines are being drawn. I wouldn't be surprised if by the end of the week we haven't turned on one another like rabid dogs."

"Where are you with this?" I asked Cooper.

"Surveillance teams have eyes on Hoskins, Fisher,

and Metz, but no one's stepped out of line or done anything suspicious."

"They don't have to. There are enough sympathetic old school brass and stupid newbie officers turning against us without anyone saying a word," Heathcliff said. "I'd bet my badge the guys who spoke to Jen and the chuckleheads from last night think they're helping out a wrongly accused brother-in-arms. As far as they're concerned, we're the enemy."

"We need to change their minds," I said.

We spent the rest of the afternoon devising an attack strategy. Defense wasn't cutting it, and heads would roll. While Cooper couldn't officially enact anything at the moment, he agreed to make sure I passed the physical requirements for a field agent. I needed to get off the sidelines and do something to set the crooked bastards off kilter. Before things concluded, Martin, Jones, and Thompson came out of the office.

"Nailed them," Thompson said. "We have two names, Officer Perkins and Detective Spinelli. Both have ties to Hoskins. Hoskins was Officer Perkins TO, and Detective Spinelli listed him as a recommendation for his promotion."

O'Connell and I exchanged a charged look. We wanted blood. "I'll run their mugs past Jen and see if she recognizes them." O'Connell pushed away from the table. "Are we ready to go?"

Cooper and Mark were coordinating something, so Mark waved them off. Thompson and Heathcliff followed O'Connell. Even when it came to riding together, it was still an us versus them situation.

I followed the cops to the door. "Nick, wait a minute." I wanted to talk to him without being overheard. Heathcliff offered a reassuring smile, and Thompson bumped against my arm as they walked out the door. Making sure the coast was clear, I pulled O'Connell aside on the front step. "The bastards came for him last night. I didn't even know he was flying in, and they stopped him. Who the hell are these people?"

"They're cops, Parker."

"If Hoskins wants to come at me, he better bring it." I thought briefly about Vito. An alternative solution might be a viable option, after all.

"Are you positive it's Hoskins?"

"No. Do me a favor, check these numbers as part of a detective's shield." I rattled off what I remembered from my dream. "See if the number correlates to a detective with a medium build and dark hair, who's probably a smoker. Someone with a deep, raspy voice."

"You just described half the precinct, but it's worth a shot."

*   *   *

After everyone left, I sat alone in the second floor office, burying my face in my hands as I tried to compartmentalize the rage. Mark was right; split second decisions tended to work out negatively for me. For someone with usually good instincts, my ability to rationalize was obviously impaired. I flipped the whiteboard around and stared at Vito's name written in the center.

O'Connell said lines were being drawn. How many of those lines was I willing to cross? The only hard evidence in this case was my statement, the bullet, and whatever Ernie and Sam provided. Martin and Bruiser identified a couple of policemen who theoretically could argue they made a routine stop last night. If Jen identified the same men, and that was a big if, then maybe they could be questioned. Of course, they'd get a union rep, and the whole thing would turn into a pile of paperwork with no real answers. Unions were great ninety-five percent of the time.

"Alex?" Martin asked from the doorway. "Can I come in?"

"It's your house, isn't it?"

"You do realize it's not my fault, right? I just wanted to surprise you. Getting home last night wasn't supposed to turn into this steaming pile of shit."

"No, it's my fault." Spinning around in the chair, I stared at him. "They're after me, and you're caught in the middle."

"Again, we're going to have this argument?" He pulled up a chair. "Let me get this out of the way for you. You're going to say something like 'run away and don't look back', and I'll respond with 'you can't control everything. I know what I'm getting myself into', and you'll disagree. We'll go back and forth for a while until one of us storms off."

"See, you don't need me around. You're perfectly capable of arguing with yourself. I'm sure you can do other things with yourself too."

"Hey, you were the one in my bed last night. Were you fantasizing about me? Because I'd like to remind you, I have some tricks up my sleeve you haven't even seen yet." He raised a challenging eyebrow and smirked. "I don't need you to protect me."

"So you say." Originally, I was hired to do just that, so it was difficult to shake that ingrained thought process after watching him nearly die before my eyes. "You know why it's easier said than done."

"Alex." He knelt on the floor and took my hand.

"If you're proposing, I will shoot you."

"God, no." He snickered. "It's been two months. I'm

not fucking psychotic." I laughed in relief, and he continued. "These last two weeks have been hell. Maybe you weren't bleeding to death, but you were shot. You showed up at my house and demanded I cut a bullet out of you. The hospital called to say you were admitted and no longer under arrest, but they almost killed you with whatever medication they administered."

"Dysfunctional much?"

"That's us."

"You've been through too much to walk away, I take it."

"We've been through too much to let some idiot with a badge think pulling over my car in the middle of the night will have any real effect on the way things work."

"Can't let the bad guys win, right?" Martin once said that, and it seemed applicable to repeat it now.

"Right." He stood up, pulling me with him. "Now let's go upstairs and make sure the springs in my mattress are decent."

*   *   *

The next morning, Martin left for the office with Bruiser and a federal protection detail in tow. Mark pulled some strings to make it happen, and I thanked him as soon as I stepped foot in FBI HQ. My next stop was Director Kendall's office. After signing off on a few legal notices and waivers, I was granted field agent status and permitted access to my bank accounts and credit cards. I was no longer persona non grata.

Taking a seat in Mark's office while he read the morning reports and checked office memos, I broached the topic of moving back into my apartment.

Initially, I wanted to distance myself from Martin, but after much consideration, one fact remained true. I was the last line of defense. How could I be sure the van out front with a few bored agents would save the day?

Mark considered the conundrum and suggested I stay at Martin's for the duration. Moving back into my apartment was more hassle than it was worth. As it was, I was supposed to be living in my apartment anyway, so it was unlikely the dirty cops would locate and attack Martin.

After reviewing a few of the finer details with Cooper and the other FBI agents, I borrowed a car from the motor pool and drove to the precinct. In hindsight, it would have been advisable to give someone a heads up, but I would have been deterred from enacting phase one of my plan. Stopping by the major crimes division, I knocked on Moretti's door.

He discussed the internal investigation and elaborated on just how divided the precinct was. Two schools of thought existed among the police department. One was to always have the back of your fellow officer no matter what. The other was to serve and protect while upholding the law. This led to fights in the locker rooms, requests for new partners and new TOs, and quite a few outside incidents. The whole place was going up in flames over the investigation. So much for keeping it an IAD matter.

"I want this resolved as quickly as possible. When we can't keep our house clean, how can we be expected to protect the neighborhood?" Moretti posed a good question. "The commissioner is busting balls. It's going straight down the line. Police corruption will not be tolerated by any stretch of the imagination. The whole thing is getting blown way out of proportion."

"In the event I throw more fuel on the fire,

remember, Lieutenant, it's because I only have the best intentions."

Moretti glowered but resigned himself to whatever I was about to do.

Exiting his office, I took my jacket off and hung it from the empty chair across from Heathcliff's desk. Perhaps it was posturing, but I wanted my gun and badge visible for what was to come. No one was in the bullpen, and I didn't need an audience in case things went horribly awry.

Sauntering up to burglary division, I found Hoskins sitting behind his desk. A quick sweep of the room supported O'Connell's claim that the description I provided matched half of the detectives in the department.

"How'd last night go?" I asked, sitting across from him.

"Nothing happened. I'm overjoyed. Did you remember anything you wanted to add about Infinity? The other day at your place, you were less than helpful with those clods from MC hanging around."

"You can't blame me. I don't know who I can trust in burglary."

"Follow me." Hoskins got up, and I assessed him. Medium build, dark, close-cropped hair, and a badge hanging around his neck. Was he the shooter? He led us to the space between the double doors, near the stairwell. "Well? Talk to me."

"The cop who attempted to knock over the club had a medium build with short, dark hair and wore his shield around his neck." I looked pointedly at his badge, spotting a two and a nine.

"Are you accusing me of something?" He stepped forward and forced my back against the wall. "Is this because I didn't come when you called? I'm not your pet."

"I don't know. Maybe it's because you showed up at my place at a particularly inopportune time. You fit the shooter's description, and you have the know-how. With years on the job, you damn well ought to know how to knock over a place."

"Bitch," he slammed his fist into the wall, inches from my face, "throwing around accusations right now isn't wise. In case you haven't noticed, we're all on edge."

"Why? Are you planning to send another couple of guys to deliver a second threat? Let me make something very clear." I leaned forward and got in his face. "Don't fuck with me. You should know by now I'm not so easy to kill." He slammed his palm against the wall, and his face turned red. "Furthermore, it's Agent Bitch to you. And assaulting a federal agent is a felony. Now back the fuck up."

He seethed, taking half a step back and allowing me to pass with no choice but to turn my back to him. "You should realize you have the wrong guy."

"We'll see." Storming down the stairs and back to major crimes, I brushed past Heathcliff as I grabbed my jacket.

He gave me a curious look, but I continued out of the precinct. This was hostile territory.

TWENTY-ONE

Taking a deep breath, I entered the dive bar. "I'm here to see Vito."

The hefty bartender ran a rag across the counter's gleaming surface. "There's no Vito here, especially not for a federal agent like you." He continued wiping the countertop, never looking up. How he even noticed my badge was astounding.

"Tell him Alex Parker would like to pay her respects." I unclipped my badge and laid it face-up on the counter. "And right now, try not to think of me as an agent."

The bartender barely shrugged, but it set something in motion behind the scenes. One of Vito's other lackeys went into the back room. After staring down Mr. Personality for another three minutes and regretting stepping inside the bar in the first place, I was surprised when Vito emerged.

"Ms. Parker, please." Vito gestured to a booth in the corner. One of his enforcers blocked my path and wouldn't move until I surrendered my handgun.

Removing the clip, I gave him my unloaded weapon but insisted on keeping the bullets handy. He didn't seem pleased by my insolence. "Tony, let her through."

"I just want to make sure you don't accidentally shoot yourself with my gun, Tony," I whispered haughtily.

Vito sat with his back to the wall, making it painfully obvious if anyone was about to get shot in the back it'd be me. "After our ride, I thought I made it abundantly clear our business concluded." Despite his words, my presence intrigued Vito.

"Mr. Vincenzo, I was hoping you might be amenable to providing further assistance."

His face betrayed a look of smug satisfaction. "You guys hear this? A federal agent is asking for my assistance. You believe that? We should go to church because the world must be ending."

Coming here was a mistake. He was posturing in front of his lackeys and hired help and at my expense. Too late now, Parker. I sat gracefully through the remarks and jokes, waiting for him to pay attention.

"Let's consider this a quid pro quo. The other burglarized establishments belonged to you. The liquor supplier is in your back pocket. It won't take competent detectives very long to make those connections."

"You came here to threaten me?" He didn't sound angry, just mildly interested.

"No. As far as I'm concerned, knowing people with entrepreneurial interests isn't a crime. What goes on beyond the black and white on paper, I don't need to know. Although, if you want to avoid the hassle from those with a less live and let live attitude, you might want to provide hard evidence as to the identities of the thieves."

He drummed his fingers on the tabletop to a rhythm only he heard while he considered my proposal. "I didn't realize Quantico taught a class in blackmail."

"It's not blackmail. It's mutually beneficial. You protect your interests, and I remove the dirty cops. Based on what you said earlier, you don't want them hanging around either."

"Who says I got anything to give you?"

"Maybe you don't, but since you're a businessman, I thought you might have protections in place in case someone develops sticky fingers. Maybe a hidden camera or two?"

"I'm not saying I have anything, but if security cam footage were to show up, you'd owe me."

Shutting my eyes, I swallowed. "Fine."

"Don't look so glum, bella. I'm not asking you to pop a guy, but don't confuse me for an altruist either. A favor's a favor, and I will collect."

"If something usable turns up, you have a deal, Mr. Vincenzo." Maybe I should slit my wrist in order to sign the contract in blood. Wasn't that the practicality of dealing with the devil?

"Funny how quickly you dropped the pretext of not knowing who I am. The goons with badges must have scared the shit out of you Saturday night for you to be here today. Are you sure you want this problem taken care of the legal way?"

How did he know everything about everyone? I suppressed the shiver traveling down my spine. He knew of my involvement with Martin and what happened Saturday. Was nothing sacred? He probably knew what color underwear I was wearing too, but if I asked and he did, I'd never sleep again.

"Remember, you are speaking to a federal agent. Any discussion related to the commission of a crime is considered conspiracy."

Vito nodded to Tony, who laid my gun on the table in front of us, signifying the meeting was over. "I'll be in touch."

Vito's words chilled me as I walked out of the bar, leaving the last remnant of my sanity inside. Things would get dark before the light triumphed.

*   *   *

What have I done? The words reverberated through my skull as the queasy feeling found a permanent spot in the pit of my stomach. Staring across the conference table at SAC Cooper, I tried to force myself to concentrate, but my mind wouldn't cooperate.

Pardoning myself, I left the conference room, but I couldn't escape the invisible shackles. Somehow, I ended up near my old desk. Meandering back toward Mark's empty office, I watched my replacement shuffle files around and retrieve a folder from the drawer. In another place and time, that would have been me.

"Taking a break?" Director Kendall asked from outside Mark's door.

"Sir," I immediately stood up straight, "I'm just…I don't even know."

"You're cleared for field work, and your bank account and credit cards should be working by now. The Marshal Service approved a meeting between you and Harrigan, if you still want it."

"Yes. Thank you, Director."

"I'll call you with the details. Maybe you ought to invest in a new phone since you're no longer on our most wanted list."

"I'll get right on it."

Sitting down in Mark's chair, I couldn't bring

myself to go back to work. Finally, when I couldn't come up with any other excuse to stay away, I returned to the conference room and picked up the briefing notes and made copies to take home.

"Are you feeling okay?" Mark asked as I gathered everything together and headed for the exit. "If you're worried about Marty, he's under armed guard. No one's going to mess with him."

"I'm just feeling off today. I'm going to pick up a new cell phone and go home. At least you'll be able to get in touch if something occurs."

Mark wasn't buying it, but he had work to do.

Sullivan stopped me before I made it to the door. "Parker," she said, "maybe you've forgotten how this works, but it's easier when we're all up to speed." She wasn't fond of the special treatment I was getting. I wouldn't have been fond of it either since there was a good chance I was acting like a prima donna.

"Fortunately for you, this is just an assignment. However, this is my life, so I might need some space in order to keep it together." Without waiting for her snarky response, I left, stopped at the store to get a replacement phone, and took the most convoluted route possible back to Martin's.

Since his business trip kept him away from the office for a week and I kept him away a few days before that, I didn't expect to see him until late. In the quiet of his home, the anger and resentment over my own actions ate away at me. After plugging in my new cell phone to charge, I changed into a sports bra and yoga pants and headed for the first floor home gym.

After recovering from shoulder surgery, Martin purchased a heavy bag, speed bag, and a boxing ring. The reason he needed all this equipment, particularly the ring itself, made no sense, but having an obscene amount of money led to some peculiar purchases.

After I stretched, I cranked up the music and wrapped my hands.

The sweat poured from my face and soaked through my clothes as I made the bag dance. Maneuvering around, I worked on a few combos of jabs, crosses, uppercuts, knees, elbows, and kicks. My heart pounded, and my muscles ached from the exertion. The bag ratcheted on the chain as I continued, ignoring my body's protest. This was my way of beating myself up. Dammit, Parker. You're trying to identify a group of corrupt cops by becoming tainted yourself. What is wrong with you? Hitting the bag with renewed frustration, I was surprised when the music suddenly stopped.

"Aren't you supposed to be taking it easy?" Martin asked from twenty feet away.

"This is easy. No one's hitting back." Stopping to catch my breath, I was certain I wouldn't be able to lift my arms to continue. After chugging a bottle of water, I pulled at the hand wraps with my teeth.

"Did you eat?" His gaze roamed over my body. "I sent Marcal to get take-out."

"Maybe I'll join you for a quick bite." With the music off, I no longer had an outlet to escape my internal rage, and the self-loathing returned. "I just need to get cleaned up first. I'm dripping sweat here."

"It's hot. Well, you're hot."

"You need to work on your A-game," I retorted, retreating to the guestroom. "Oh, I left a check to cover the loan you gave me. It's on the kitchen table. I'd be more than happy to reimburse you for staying here and using your car if you give me a figure."

"This is more than enough. Honestly, I don't—"

I cut off his response by shutting the bathroom door and turning on the shower.

When I returned, I already felt sore. Being laid up

for two weeks with an injury wasn't conducive to an insanely difficult workout.

Martin was in the living room with a couple of take-out containers sitting on the coffee table. He was on the phone with the R&D department, discussing the compatibility of a microchip with the functionality of a new product line. Tuning him out, I picked up a container of orange chicken and went to stare at the theory board I moved into his second floor office. Vito's name taunted me from the center.

"What do you want?" I asked it.

Chewing thoughtfully, I leaned against the desk and picked up the briefing notes but gained little useful information from them. A small group, consisting of two to four men, was responsible for the recent string of thefts, or so the theory went. Surveillance photos on Hoskins, Metz, and Fisher were included, but they were too good to be caught in the act.

Martin's home phone rang, and I went into the kitchen to see if it was for me. He was still on his cell phone, so I answered.

"What the fuck is wrong with you?" O'Connell growled.

"Plenty. Do you want a list?"

"Parker," his tone calmed slightly, "trying to get a cop to shoot you again isn't the best way to work a case." Obviously, he heard about my tactics with Hoskins earlier today.

"I told you I was going to do something. This is me doing something."

"Heathcliff's on administrative leave. Hoskins came down to major crimes, and they got into it." Since Heathcliff was the most by the book detective I knew, whatever Hoskins said must have been particularly offensive. Then again, with the way the men in major crimes acted sometimes, I could imagine what it was like to have brothers. Overly protective brothers. "On the bright side, Hoskins is suspended while it gets sorted out. Maybe something will shake loose. In the meantime, the LT wants you as far from the precinct as possible. This place is a powder keg, and your sparky personality is enough to set the place ablaze."

"I think you mean sparkling." My voice grew quiet. "Nick, I'm sorry." It felt like I was apologizing for things he didn't even know about. "If you talk to Derek, please tell him that."

After disconnecting, I slumped against the kitchen counter. I needed a new approach, a clear head, and calm rationality. Martin's call ended, and when I turned around, he was sitting sideways on the sofa, studying me. Going to the fridge, I pulled out a bottle of water and joined him on the couch.

"Are you okay?" he asked. He wasn't a huge fan of silence.

"Just wishing I could start today over and do it differently."

TWENTY-TWO

Saturday night raised the stakes. Even though Jones, aka Bruiser, remained on twenty-four hour bodyguard duty and two vans full of federal agents were stationed outside the house, I slept on the sofa with my nine millimeter only inches away on the end table. It never hurt to be prepared for the worst.

I was lying on my stomach, facing the backrest, when Martin came down the steps for his early morning workout. He didn't notice me, and I didn't have the energy to move. My muscles were stiff, sore, and uncooperative, just like most things in my life. Thirty minutes later, on his return trip, he paused on the stairs. I had been discovered. Forty-five minutes later, the outer edge of the cushion sunk in slightly.

"I wondered why you didn't come to bed. Should I be jealous you picked the couch over me?"

"I do really like this sofa," I muttered. "Plus, the heavy bag kicked my ass yesterday, and I didn't think I'd make it up the stairs or back down." My workout yesterday and the self-inflicted physical stress had aggravated my still healing side. Stupid doctors and their stupid medical advice. Why did they always have to be right?

"I thought you were taking it easy since the bag doesn't hit back."

"Bite me."

After Martin left for work, I dragged myself off the couch, dreading today. More than likely, I would dread all the days ahead until I was no longer indebted to the head of a crime family. However, depending on what the favor was, I might regret those actions for the rest of my life. Dumbass move, Parker.

My coffee cooled as I perused the information from yesterday's briefing. It was time I got my shit together. Compartmentalize and get to work. I couldn't do anything else. Maybe Vito wouldn't provide us with any evidence, and I was worried for nothing.

"We received a special delivery this morning," Sullivan said over the phone. "Is Her Highness planning to grace us with her presence or should we do this without you?"

"Sullivan," I sighed, "I'm not trying to win a popularity contest. I'm not much of a team player, and when I walked off the job, I planned to stay gone. Regardless, I'm sorry about yesterday."

"Then get your ass in here, Parker. We don't have all day."

I listened to the unfriendly click of the disconnect. Maybe I wouldn't win most popular, but Sullivan wouldn't win any congeniality awards either.

When I arrived at HQ, Cooper wasn't in the conference room. Webster and Sullivan were working on a project, and Mark and Darli were reviewing security cam footage. As soon as Mark spotted me, he excused himself and hauled me by the elbow out of the room.

"Good morning to you, too," I said.

"What did you do?"

"Nothing. I just got here."

He wasn't buying it. "How'd you get this other footage? None of the burglarized clubs had working cameras, but hidden surveillance recorded the heists."

"What footage? We received more footage from the shootout at Infinity?"

He narrowed his eyes. "Do I need to hook you to a polygraph?"

"What good would it do? You know I've been trained to pass those things."

"Goddammit." He stomped back to the conference room. We weren't talking about this anymore.

Taking a deep breath, I plastered an indifferent expression on my face and resolutely decided to maintain it for the rest of the day. Today, I needed to be the sole female equivalent of the famous monkey trio. See, hear, and speak no evil. Quietly slinking into the conference room, I got to work.

Vito's newly supplied footage provided images of two masked men involved in the commission of a heist. Their clothing and appearance wouldn't have seemed abnormal if it weren't for the ski masks pulled over their faces. Darli shifted the feed to the big screen, and we watched as the two men conducted a second robbery. They split up. One hit the bar while the other disappeared off camera. Money was taken from the register, and the second man returned with a hefty looking bag. The two exited without further incident.

"IT's working on getting stats," Sullivan supplied. "Hopefully, we'll have height, weight, race, and maybe even eye color."

"Is it the same team in all four robberies?" I asked

"IT will verify, but as far as we can tell, it is," Webster said. "How many guys did you see at

Infinity?"

"Only one." My mind was elsewhere, dwelling on the possibilities. So many theories had been thrown around, I wasn't sure which were outlandish. "Are there any other angles we can use to see what burglar number two is shoving in the bag?"

"It's the cash from the safe," Darli spouted without a moment's hesitation.

"How do you know?" Mark asked, jumping to my rescue, even though he was still suspicious of how the footage came to be in our possession.

"We know the clubs were cleaned out, and the safes were hit. It's how the burglaries were reported and a huge part of the investigation." Darli grew defensive, but his FBI teammates didn't rush to his aid.

"Jablonsky, what do you think is in the bag?" Webster asked.

"I don't know. Assumptions are clouding this investigation. They've been hurting us since the beginning."

"It doesn't matter what's in the bag." Although, I didn't believe my own conviction. "We're here to identify a corrupt team of police personnel. We need to find an angle or footage that will lead to a positive ID."

At least two corrupt cops were involved in knocking over mob-controlled clubs. My money was on Hoskins and one of his buddies from burglary. But we needed proof.

Before we could consider the identities of the masked men, Cooper entered the conference room, flanked by Heathcliff and Thompson. Heathcliff took a seat, and Thompson stood near Cooper. Something happened. We had a situation.

"People," Cooper flipped off the screen and stood in front of it, "earlier this morning, surveillance on Carl

Hoskins noted him entering a bank and leaving with a briefcase. We pulled his financials. He emptied his bank account. Currently, Detective Hoskins is on administrative leave. We believe he plans to run. His cut from the heists should be nearly half a million. He's probably too afraid to spend it now, so he'll need to use his own funds to get away from here. We've issued a warrant for his arrest, but after the bank, he slipped the surveillance team."

"IAD is up to speed, but the commissioner doesn't want to risk further internal incidents. We're hoping Hoskins can be brought in quickly and quietly," Thompson added.

"If we can bring him in and get him to talk, maybe he'll name his partner or whoever else is involved and end this," Cooper continued. "Right now, we have no idea where he might be. Agents are covering the airports, train stations, and bus depots. The toll booths have his photo and information on his vehicle, and we're monitoring his financials. If he uses a credit card or his EZ Pass to cross one of the bridges, we'll know."

"We're keeping tabs on his family, friends, and even his CIs," Thompson said. "With any luck, he'll be in custody by tonight."

"Go back to your place, Parker," Cooper ordered. "Detective Heathcliff has enlightened us on your less than professional antics yesterday, and I'm guessing if Hoskins can't get out of town, he'll come for you."

"Great."

Heathcliff nudged my thigh with his knee as a show of moral support. "I have some free time if you want backup."

"I'll give you two a ride, pick up your double, and bring her back here," Thompson offered.

"Keep radio silent since Hoskins knows our

frequencies and tactics. If you need help or have something to report, phone in," Cooper said as we left the conference room.

* * *

Heathcliff took a seat at my kitchen counter and began working his way through a crossword puzzle. Calm, cool, and collected, all the things I aspired to be. I, on the other hand, couldn't sit still. Even though I was sore from yesterday's workout, I scoured every surface. This was my home, and no one was going to stay here and impersonate me any longer. I was back on the job. By the time I sat down, Heathcliff had read the paper cover to cover, finished the crossword and Sudoku puzzles, and read the obits and comics twice.

"What did you do to get put on administrative leave?" I asked.

He folded the paper neatly and considered the question. "I didn't care for Hoskins' attitude."

"Is this another one of my blunders?" I got up and pulled down a stack of clean plates to rewash.

"I'm not blaming you for this." He remained silent for a few moments before asking, "Why are you rewashing the dishes?"

"How do I know they're clean? I wasn't here to see them get washed. Maybe they weren't even used. Who knows?"

He tilted his head in thought before abruptly standing up. "How do you know they're dirty then?" He wasn't talking about the dishes. Something clicked regarding the case, but I was too far gone to see any connection. "Do you mind if I borrow your computer?"

"Go for it." When I was done rewashing the dishes, I went to see what he was doing.

"The report on police corruption was sent anonymously. Prior to the information IA and the Bureau received, there wasn't even an inkling of impropriety."

"Inkling," I repeated to his chagrin.

"Normally, IA suspects dirty cops before allegations are made. They find something amiss in a police report, or they have to field a few civilian complaints. There's always something that tips them off but not this time."

"You think IA's involved?"

"No." Whatever he was thinking, I wasn't following. "What if something else is going on here?"

"I have a scar down my side and along my back to prove I didn't hallucinate getting shot by a cop. Harrigan can say the same." I wanted to see Sam instead of being stuck in my apartment, waiting for a vengeful asshole to come after me again. Same old tune, different lyrics.

"And you know it's a cop because of the badge and how he talked to the officers outside. What else?"

"A waitress spotted a dented cruiser parked outside when she left for the night. It probably belonged to the shooter, or he borrowed it from the motor pool without permission. At least that's what records indicate."

Heathcliff leaned back, looking smug. "So if you got a hold of a gold shield and wanted to rob a place, what would you do when the cops arrived? And let's pretend you aren't on the job."

"I'm not a cop." It was a statement of fact, not part of the scenario we were constructing, but he didn't see the difference. "But if my only options were to confront an armed former federal agent or go outside and face the police, impersonating a cop wouldn't be a bad idea."

"It would have to be someone who used to be on the job or familiar with our protocols and lingo," he deduced.

"Cop swagger," I added, and he grinned. "It still doesn't fit. How would the guy know I was working at Infinity? Officer Taylor got me the gig, and other than you guys in major crimes, the only other people who knew about Infinity were the guys in burglary. Plus, the police cruiser outside, Martin getting harassed Saturday night, and Hoskins' actions today, all add up to dirty cops."

"No, they don't. Drop everything recent and focus on the beginning. When did you first believe it was a dirty cop?" Heathcliff was certain he was on to something and wanted me to understand.

"When the responding officers treated him that way." Flashing back to the club, I remembered my initial belief was the thief had been impersonating a cop, but once he identified himself to the officers, I made the logical leap to dirty cop. Could we have it all wrong? I shook my head. When Vito picked me up at the park, he spoke of police corruption. He gave us footage of the two-man team in exchange for an unnamed favor. Those two men were probably the same men who beat the shit out of Ernie.

"Parker," Heathcliff shook my shoulder, "you zoned out. Where'd you go?"

"Derek," I swallowed, "I did something incredibly stupid." Picking up the phone, I dialed Cooper. When he answered, I asked him to have IT verify the dates and times the footage was taken in order to ensure it wasn't altered in any way.

After I hung up, Heathcliff raised an eyebrow. "Are you gonna tell me what the stupid thing is? Or how stupid it is?"

"Jury's still out, but we should have a verdict soon."

TWENTY-THREE

"Ah, fuck." I hung up the phone and paced the room. In the interim, I had filled Heathcliff in on the entire situation, top to bottom, everything related to the shooting, my evasion tactics, and my run-ins with Antonio Vincenzo. Right now, he was the only one aware of the situation and my unimaginable idiocy.

"Parker." He was in full-on interrogation mode. Thankfully, we weren't at the precinct, or he'd chain me to the table. "We have to fix this."

"No kidding. Cooper just confirmed the new footage wasn't from the dates and times in question. They were doctored. The techs believe the data was created four days ago. That means Vito's been lying this entire time. The clubs are in his pocket. Stoltz Bros. is in his pocket. And now it looks like half the police department is in his pocket too."

"It was filmed Friday night." Heathcliff exhaled. I had been played like a well-worn violin. "Call James and find out exactly when he decided to make the trip home. We need to know when he filed the flight plan, and who knew of his departure. It might be a coincidence, but dollars to donuts, Vincenzo pulled out all the stops to ensure you played right into his hand."

"What about Hoskins?" Our entire investigation was unraveling.

"I don't know. Is there anything else you aren't telling me?"

I circled the kitchen to get away from his pointed glare. "I told you everything. If you want to arrest me for known criminal affiliations, go ahead, but there's nothing more to tell."

"You know you screwed up." If this was a pep talk, he needed to spend more time watching television therapists. "But I can't say any of us is perfect. Make the call and get your head on straight because we need to stop this before the entire precinct goes down in a sea of paranoia. I'm guessing the shooter isn't a cop, and based on what you've said, I bet he's one of Vincenzo's guys. But if cops are on the take, we need to flush them out."

Reluctantly, I dialed Martin's cell phone. When he answered, I asked the relevant questions, relayed the answers to Heathcliff, and said I was working so I'd see him at some point in the distant future.

Heathcliff's expression turned to one of confused curiosity. "I'll see you when I see you? No offense, but I'm glad we never dated."

"Don't be bitter. You've probably spent more time with me in the last three months than Martin has. It's like we're dating but without the perks," I joked.

"So what? With all the time you and O'Connell spend together, does that mean the two of you are married and Jen is just a figment of his imagination?"

"Nick's a polygamist, but don't spread it around." Our brief kidding quickly turned to serious as he searched for the flight information Martin provided. The flight plan had been filed Friday morning and was cleared by the FFA sixteen hours before landing, thus giving Vincenzo plenty of time to gain awareness of the situation. Since the phony surveillance tapes had been created Friday, it made the whole situation that much more questionable.

"Do you think the cops who stopped Martin work for Vincenzo? Or did they just happen to get some information on who to hassle and when?"

"I don't know, but all this speculation is driving me crazy." I slumped onto the couch. "Can you get Moretti to question them?"

"Let me make a call."

We sat in my apartment for an eternity, waiting on answers from Moretti. It was slow going to bring in an officer and detective, both of whom had already been questioned in relation to Martin's harassment. The FBI teams were still working on locating Hoskins, but they had even less going for them than Moretti did.

"Do you want to order in?" I stared at my almost empty fridge. "Or are you going home since it's getting kind of late."

"I have nowhere else to be, and since Thompson dropped us both off, you're stuck with me until he returns."

I handed him a stack of take-out menus and went in search of my car keys. My double had driven my car back to my place, so I could offer it to Heathcliff as a means of escape. "You don't have to stick around if you don't want to." I held up the keys. "It's not much, but it'll get you from point A to point B."

"Nah, I'll hang around and keep you company. You have a bad track record as of late. Plus, this way, it doesn't feel like I'm on administrative leave."

"C'mon, tell me what happened."

"You aren't the only one cornering the market on stupid." He winked. "I'm thinking Thai. Any complaints?"

"None."

*   *   *

After dinner, I took the garbage out since I didn't want my apartment to smell like Thai food for the rest of the week. Heathcliff was on the phone with Moretti, discussing the interrogations from earlier this afternoon, and as far as I could tell, he hadn't divulged my involvement with Vito. After tossing the bag into the dumpster, I turned around and was shoved against the brick wall.

"I'm not going to hurt you," Hoskins said, "but I need your help."

"Great way to ask for it." I struggled against his grip, but he held me firmly against the building, removing my holstered weapon and performing a quick pat down before letting go. "What do you want?"

"I'm being framed."

"Join the club." As far as I was concerned, he was too late to jump onto that bandwagon. "The thing is you look a hell of a lot guiltier than I ever did because you emptied out your bank account, slipped your surveillance detail, and dropped off the grid."

"None of those things are actual crimes. I thought since you've already dealt with whoever is pulling these strings, you might be willing to lend a helping hand."

"You assault me in a dark alley, take my weapon, and ask for my assistance. Need I remind you that yesterday in the precinct you were ready to throw me through the wall?"

"Because you started tossing around accusations."

"Give me back my gun. Then you may come upstairs, and we'll talk things out. If I don't like what I hear, I will turn you in."

"I'm holding the gun, and you're making demands?" he asked.

"If you're not guilty and you want my help and trust, then you'll play by my rules." I held out my hand, and he reluctantly handed back my weapon. "What a gentleman. Now let's go upstairs." He remained in the dim light, not moving. "After you," I insisted.

When we made it inside, I announced a guest was joining us. As I predicted, Heathcliff's hand rested on the butt of his revolver as he assessed Hoskins with such intensity I thought he might have an aneurysm.

"Look what the cat's dragged in," Heathcliff muttered, not so gently frisking Hoskins. "I'm surprised you don't have one hell of a shiner."

"Derek," Hoskins was uneasy, maybe even rigid, "I might have been out of line."

Heathcliff tensed and before the two could go another round, I stepped in between the men. "Play nice, boys," I warned. "Hoskins, take a seat." Heathcliff stared daggers, but I shrugged it off. What was I supposed to do? I didn't invite Hoskins here. "You have five minutes to explain your predicament, and then we're calling it in."

"Start talking," Heathcliff said.

"Two months ago, burglary got a report of a break-in at the Odessa, it's the bar inside a swanky hotel," Hoskins began.

"We know. Cut to the chase." Heathcliff tapped his watch.

"Anyway, someone ransacked the bar, smashed the bottles, took the register, and emptied the safe."

"Similar MO to the latest string of heists," I said, and Hoskins nodded.

"Two days after we got the call and did the initial walkthrough, the case was closed."

"Who closed it?" Heathcliff got up from his chair and leaned against my counter. My apartment was cozier than the precinct's interrogation rooms, but the difference was lost on my police counterpart.

Hoskins shook his head. "I don't know. It was shut by the upstairs brass. You know how things are. Cases pile up, and it's a relief to have one less to worry about. Frankly, I didn't even think about it until the second club got hit. When I began digging through my notes, I realized the Odessa case file was missing. The photos, evidence, and reports were all gone."

"Why didn't you say something sooner?" I stared at Hoskins, trying to determine his sincerity. "I came to you and asked for help on the clubs."

"I don't know you. You're not a cop, and I had no reason to trust you."

"Then why are you here now?" I asked, exasperated.

"Where else am I going to go?"

"You expect me to believe, after the shit you were spewing yesterday, that you didn't come here to silence the only person who can positively identify you as the shooter from Infinity?" Heathcliff baited the hook.

"It wasn't me." Hoskins looked for help, his eyes pleading. "Tell him it wasn't me."

Pressing my lips together, I remained silent. I had no idea if it was Hoskins or not, but letting a suspect sweat was interrogation 101. Right now, it was all the leverage we had on the guy.

"Frankly, your invidious comments yesterday ought to be construed as a threat," Heathcliff continued, his voice acidic, and I had to resist the urge to glance at him.

"Like I said, I might have been out of line." Hoskins sounded contrite. "I didn't need to bring up old wounds."

"Old wounds?" Heathcliff's tone lowered to something lethal. "Accusing major crimes of not being able to protect its women reads like a threat to me."

I flashed back to Heathcliff's former partner, who had committed suicide, and Jen's threats. No wonder Heathcliff lost it. As it stood, I was livid by the gender-biased attitude of this asshole.

"Sounds threatening to me." I glanced at Heathcliff to make sure he had himself under control. It took a lot to fire up Detective Stoic, and I doubted I'd be able to physically pull him off Hoskins if it came down to it.

"I'm confused," Heathcliff's stone-like demeanor returned, "what exactly are you even saying happened or is happening, and why should we believe you, let alone help you?"

Hoskins cleared his throat. "After the second club heist, I began digging around and asking questions. A couple of uniformed cops remembered the scene, but no one had any clue how the case was closed. It was all hush-hush. I began my own investigation, and just when I made some headway, I hear about the IA investigation. Fingers are getting pointed in my direction, and yesterday, a stack of photos was sent to IAD, positively placing me at the scene of the shooting." Hoskins focused on me. "I wasn't there."

"Where were you?" I asked. He was hiding something, but I didn't know what it was.

"Elsewhere."

"Convenient," Heathcliff said. "You need an alibi and someone to verify it. If not." He tilted his head and shrugged.

Hoskins sat quietly, not talking. Maybe we wouldn't be able to break him, but we also didn't have to put up with him anymore.

"I'm calling it in," I declared, heading for the phone. "Do you have a preference? I'm thinking of giving him to Cooper, but if Moretti would rather have him back, I'm game."

"Give him to Cooper first. Moretti can request a prisoner transfer if he wants."

"Wait," Hoskins interrupted, "you can't do this. Whoever tried to frame me for shooting you is probably the same person who tried to frame and kill you. What do you think is going to happen to me?"

"Probably the same thing that happens to most cops who get sent to prison." I picked up the phone and began to dial.

By the fourth digit, Hoskins sang like a lark.

TWENTY-FOUR

"Hoskins' alibi checks out." Heathcliff hung up the phone. "Cooper wants him in protective custody."

"Damn, it's catching." I tossed a forgiving smile to Hoskins. "They'll keep you safe until everything gets straightened out. In the meantime, you need to give us everything you have, whatever you remember, all of it."

"You're on to something." Hoskins looked at the two of us suspiciously. "I'm such a fool to think you ever believed it was me."

"Actually, we didn't know," I offered. "And believe me when I say, 'damn, you're paranoid'. No one gives a shit who you were banging in the back of a patrol car on Saturday night."

"Moretti might," Heathcliff deadpanned, "but that's more a regulations thing."

"Promise you'll keep it quiet if you can," Hoskins begged. His sexual preferences and orientation were of no interest to me, and Heathcliff felt the same way.

In the time it took Mark and a team of agents to

procure our latest asset, Hoskins had spilled his guts on the matter at hand. His personal investigation into the hotel bar burglary, the connections he found to Antonio Vincenzo's crime syndicate, and the dirt being swept under the rug by the upstairs brass stunk to high heaven. Heathcliff ran names and data on my computer faster than I believed my outdated hardware was capable of processing.

I mulled over the information while Hoskins babbled on, relieved to be able to trust someone. "What were you going to do?" I asked once the information turned into nothing more than obscure theorizing.

"Get the hell out of Dodge while the getting was good." He had decided on the more feasible route toward self-preservation – escape.

"One last question, Carl," Heathcliff turned to him from behind a sea of numbers and letters, "any idea how far this thing goes?"

Before Hoskins could answer, Mark and Cooper entered my apartment with a team of agents. My living room looked like a bowl of alphabet soup.

"Parker," Cooper sighed, "you don't follow orders very well, do you?"

"Now what?" As far as I knew, only Heathcliff was aware of my current predicament with Vito.

"You were supposed to be bait, not bring someone else in from the cold."

"The groundhog must not have gotten the memo because winter's still kicking our asses," I retorted. "Hoskins has relevant information to provide in exchange for his ensured protection. Some discretion may also be necessary to properly maintain his well-being."

Cooper nodded to a couple of federal agents, and they escorted Carl Hoskins out of my apartment. "I have paperwork to process concerning all of this. Apparently, I have to explain the unnecessary reason for allocating resources to keep a tail on an asset instead of our prime suspect." Cooper didn't sound pleased as he and the marshals left my apartment, slamming the door behind them.

"Detective," Mark growled, "would you mind giving us a few minutes?"

Heathcliff glanced at me, probably to make sure I wasn't in fear of my life, before he went into the hallway, muttering something about going to the lobby to talk to the remaining agents. I took a seat. Pissing Mark off at this moment would not have been a good plan of action by any stretch of the imagination.

"What have you gotten involved in?" He uttered each word with such force it sounded like a string of single statements.

"Are you sure you wouldn't prefer plausible deniability?"

"Parker," he snapped.

"Antonio Vincenzo." I bit the inside of my lip and waited. He turned scarlet before slamming his hand on my kitchen table hard enough to shake the floor. "He approached me when I was working on getting evidence to clear my name."

"And you didn't think it was important to mention?" He was livid, his tone and posture controlled to such a degree I was afraid he'd internally snap in half from the stress.

"He found me. Gretchen is the au pair for one of his guys. She must have called her boss who called his boss. At the time, none of this made any sense. Vito turned in the original security cam footage from Infinity the same day we met, and he made it clear our business was concluded. It was a favor for a favor."

"Vito." Mark's death glare could kill those with weaker constitutions. I'd seen it done in interrogation. It only had me quaking in my boots; well, if I were wearing boots, there would have been 7.5 magnitude quakes. "You're on the run and decide to get in bed with a mobster. Great. Just fucking great."

"No." Taking a breath, I forced myself to continue. "I thought that was the end of it."

"You thought that was the end of it? What do you mean you thought that was the end of it?"

"If you think this is bad, you're not going to like what comes next." Sarcasm and jokes aside, I didn't like what came next either. Mark visibly braced himself with his hands digging indentions in my countertop. "Saturday night, after Saturday night, y'know, with everything going on, I felt it might be important to have this thing resolved sooner rather than later. So Monday morning, I went to Vito and asked him to be civically minded and surrender anything he had from the other four heists."

"The bogus security footage. Did you know they were fakes?"

"No," I said, and he could see I wasn't lying. "I wanted evidence to catch the crooked cop and be done with this."

"What'd you agree to do for Vito in return?"

Shrugging my shoulders, I swallowed uneasily. "I don't know yet."

"Where did any of this get us?"

"Vito's involved in the thefts. They're his clubs. The liquor supplier, Stoltz Bros., is his too. Hoskins confirmed a fifth burglary as the original burglary, but it was swept under the rug by the upstairs brass. Heathcliff and I have been running through ex-cops. I'd say Vito has some high-ranking officer on the take and a former cop or two conducting the heists."

"If that's true, why did he tell you about the police corruption? Was it to frame Hoskins since he was getting close to uncovering the truth? Why would Vito knock over his own establishments?"

"Insurance?"

"Perhaps, but what better way to come off clean, or as clean as one can, when you have a federal agent indebted to you?"

"I screwed up."

"That doesn't even begin to describe what you did." Mark's anger abated, but I preferred it to the disappointment etched on his haggard features. "What were you thinking, Alex?"

My gaze dropped to the floor. I wasn't thinking. I was reacting to bad intel, a horrible couple of weeks, no leads, and mostly letting personal feelings and demons from my past wreak havoc on my rational thoughts. Finally, I pulled my gaze from the floor. "What are you going to do now?"

He rubbed his hands over his face a few times before meeting my eyes. "I'm turning this over to Cooper. You don't deserve it, but I'll put a nice PR spin on things so you'll come out on top. This entire investigation just got flipped on its head. We're now gunning for former cops and police brass in the mafia's pocket. It's a hell of a leap to justify from chasing after a couple of crooks in burglary division."

"If anyone can do it," I offered.

"Don't. Just don't." He strode to my front door. "Stay put. Keep someone around for backup because you've messed with the wrong people this time. I'll pick you up in the morning."

"Mark," I said as he opened the door, "I'm sorry."

He snorted. "Funny. I can count the number of times you've said those words without an excuse or explanation on one hand."

The self-loathing had fully kicked in by the time Heathcliff re-entered my apartment. He locked the deadbolts behind him and met my eyes. Choosing to remain silent, he went to the computer and resumed scouring the local and federal databases for whatever leads he was working on.

After enough time passed, I regrouped and went to the computer. He pulled a chair over without a word, and I sat down as he continued running the data. "Glad you can still sit." He smirked slightly. "I figured with the ass-chewing you received, you might slide right out of the chair." I graced him with a brief chuckle. "The prognosis looks good," he continued. "Your sense of humor remains intact."

"Might be the only thing I have left once everything is said and done."

*   *   *

Mark decided the silent treatment was part of my penance. He picked me up at six a.m. the next morning. Heathcliff and I had pulled an all-nighter as we dug through what felt like hundreds of incident reports, old news stories, and whatever IAD records he could access. The situation was grim. Civilian complaints ranged in the hundreds; the majority unsubstantiated. After trying and failing to instill this newly gained knowledge to a completely silent Mark, I gave up and sipped my coffee from the passenger seat. On the bright side, Heathcliff got to go home and enjoy some well-deserved rest. The wicked weren't so lucky.

The too-familiar conference room seemed particularly cramped today as agents from organized crime sat in to discuss ongoing investigations and surveillance regarding Antonio Vincenzo. While suspected of having his hands in drugs, guns, and girls, no solid evidence ever surfaced. After the briefing, Cooper updated the remaining agents on our most recent discoveries. Det. Hoskins' statement regarding the first burglary caused all police records and evidence to be reevaluated, this time by a crew of federal agents. Moretti must love having his precinct invaded by the Feds. It was another hex mark to add to my current tally.

By lunchtime, boxes of files and evidence flooded the building. O'Connell and Thompson stopped by to check on our progress. The rumor circulating through the precinct discouraged the fires of distrust among the cops. The scoundrel was believed to be caught, and life was set to return to normal. The good guys had badges to go along with their guns. However, the few lucky enough to be in the know were keeping a close watch on their commanding officers to make sure no one acted particularly squirrely or interested in locking down the whereabouts of the detained Det. Hoskins.

Too many cups of coffee later, I found myself dazing off into the ink covered fibers of the paper in front of me. "Parker," someone said my name, and I snapped my gaze up. A quick sweep of the room failed to produce the speaker, and I drew into question my own sanity. After a few moments of observation, I returned my focus to the page.

The report was from the night of the original heist at The Odessa, currently dubbed heist zero. While the report was supposed to be about a mugging that occurred two blocks from the hotel, something seemed off. Scanning the pages two more times, I finally pinpointed the oddity. Captain Stephens, the man in charge of the entire precinct, signed off on the report. Since when did a captain concern himself with a petty mugging? Maybe it had been a slow night, or the victim was a personal friend. But something didn't sit right.

"Parker." The conference room door opened, and SAC Cooper and Director Kendall stood in the hallway. "My office. Now." Kendall didn't give me a chance to argue.

Making a quick note, I headed out the door. Was this the long procession to my execution? After all, my head was on the chopping block for the guillotine. Mark made my lapse in judgment seem like treason, and that's an offense punishable by death.

"Yes, sir?" I stammered. Mark was already in Kendall's office, and Cooper blocked the door and any getaway attempt I might make.

"Agent Jablonsky has informed me of your extracurricular activities. Apparently, your time away from this office has done nothing to dull those instincts of yours." Kendall gave me a focused and knowing look. "How you managed to uncover crime family connections to current and former law enforcement officials is astounding." None of this sounded like the torture I expected. "The information Hoskins provided has given us enough impetus to squeeze the shit out of Papadakis."

"Sir?" I wasn't sure what I wanted to say at this particular juncture, but I felt compelled to utter something.

Kendall held up a hand for silence. "You requested an interview with Harrigan, and now seems as good a time as any. Between the descriptions and connections Papadakis has affirmed, thanks in large part to the dedication of Detective Hoskins' strong-willed work ethic, maybe you can cajole something solid out of Harrigan. He might be able to recognize the shooter from a list of former officers we've compiled."

"There's a suspect list?" I shouldn't have been surprised, but I was.

Cooper produced a USB drive. "It contains pictures of everyone who could be in Vincenzo's back pocket. You're a friendly face, and Harrigan may be more willing to open up to you than one of us. These are their rookie photos, so maybe the uniform will help refresh Harrigan's memory."

I glanced uncertainly at Mark, who intentionally avoided my gaze as if I were Medusa. "I don't understand." I couldn't wrap my mind around why I was still working the case and hadn't been thrown in holding for violating the penal code prohibiting dumbassery.

"Parker," Mark spoke without looking at me, "these are your leads. You run them down."

"The marshals are downstairs, waiting to escort you to the safe house. When you're finished, they'll bring you back here. Anything you find out, bring to us immediately. If you don't believe you can handle that, I'll assign a babysitter to keep you on track," Kendall added.

Obviously, Mark's spin on things painted me in a positive light with my only flaw being my go it alone attitude. If Mark ever wanted to go private sector, he should work as a political campaign manager. With his silver tongue, he could probably get the antichrist elected.

"No babysitter necessary, sir."

"Good. Now get back to work."

Cooper opened the door, and I stepped into the hallway. Mark and Kendall were in the midst of discussing things, maybe me, so I gave Cooper the pertinent file number and informed him of the gnawing feeling Captain Stephens' name on the report had triggered. By the time the elevator dinged, Cooper was well-versed in my theory and had formulated an attack strategy for the rest of the files and evidence stuck in review.

We parted ways as the elevator doors opened, and he went back to the conference room. I continued down to the garage and met the marshals, who stuck me in the back of an SUV with darkly tinted windows to help protect the location of their safe house. It was late in the afternoon by the time we pulled to a stop in front of a nondescript building, and I was allowed to see Sam Harrigan, bartender extraordinaire.

TWENTY-FIVE

"Mr. Harrigan," I called, knocking gently against the partially open door. "Sam?"

The safe house was a small, secluded, single dwelling with a few marshals stationed inside. The bedroom occupied by Sam Harrigan was converted into something strongly resembling a hospital room. The only furniture present was a dresser with a television, a chair, a tray, and a hospital bed. Harrigan was in bed, and despite the couple of weeks he'd already spent recovering, he didn't look so good.

"Alexis?" He hit mute on the television remote and stared as if trying to determine if I was a wraith coming to claim him or simply a figment of his imagination. "Did they bring you here for questioning?"

I wondered if his mind was jumbled from painkillers, the entire ordeal, or if no one bothered to fill him in on what was going on. "Can I come in?" I asked, trying to be respectful of his personal space. The marshals briefed me on his prognosis and recovery. As of yet, there was no feeling in his lower extremities. The doctors weren't positive if his spinal cord was compromised or if it was a reaction due to the extreme trauma. Either way, they weren't sure when or if he'd walk again.

"Sure." He offered a brief smile. "But don't be offended if I can't get up." In the short time span in which I had gotten to know Sam, he wasn't one to complain, but there was a forlorn sourness to his tone.

I walked into the room and leaned against the nearest wall. "Mr. Harrigan, words cannot begin to express how sorry I am."

"Alexis," he studied my clothing, perhaps seeing the real me for the first time, "you're one of them?"

"Sort of." I swallowed the lump in my throat, but it remained lodged in my chest. "Mr. Papadakis hired me to assess the possibility of Infinity being robbed. Unfortunately, things spiraled out of control. Now I'm working for the FBI to track down the shooter."

"But you're a waitress."

"Actually, I'm not. Former federal agent, reinstated," I said. His eyes filled with resentment. "Mr. Harrigan, I know you've been through a lot and have answered so many questions already."

"You knew this would happen?" The heart monitor beeped as his pulse and pressure spiked. "You let some asshole cop bust into the bar and shoot me in the back. Where the hell were you when that was happening? Aren't you supposed to protect the public?"

"Sam," my voice faltered, and I reminded myself this wasn't about me, "we need your help identifying the shooter."

"What really happened?" He grabbed the metal bar dangling above the bed and hoisted himself into a seated position. "You were there. All I remember is the door opening and a man walking in and saying he's a cop. I turned around to grab my wallet off the bar to show him my identification, and everything went black."

Tossing a nervous glance toward the door, I wasn't sure what the marshals would think if I clued in their star witness, but Sam deserved to know what happened that night. "Nice guys finish last." I stared into the empty space above the bed. "You were trying to be a gentleman and waited to walk me to my car. I was in the storeroom, getting my purse, when the double doors opened. I heard talking and then the gunshot."

"So you left me to die?"

My mind screamed yes, and I shut my eyes to bury the answer far away. He didn't need to be revictimized by the admittance of my guilt.

"The man in question came around the bar. He fired a few shots into the door. I caught a ricochet. As I attempted pursuit, he burst out the double doors and told the group of police officers I was the shooter. I shouldn't have left you there. It was a mistake to run."

His angry expression abated slightly as he considered my words. "Why'd it take you so long to come here?"

A bitter chuckle escaped my throat. "Between being on the run, getting released from the hospital, and sorting through evidence and filing the proper paperwork, bureaucratic red-tape can be a bitch." He didn't necessarily warm to my presence, but at the moment, his resentment was under control. "We've made progress and have some solid leads. I know it's an inconvenience, but would you mind looking at some photos to see if you recognize anyone?"

Three hours and numerous breaks later, he

positively identified two former police detectives as being at the bar Saturday night. They were regulars, and he spotted them easily enough. However, he was blank on the shooter. "It's just a blur. It was some guy, but everything about him is foggy."

"Do you remember what he was wearing? If he was white, black, Hispanic, Asian? His hair or eye color?" Although I already knew our suspect was a white male with dark hair, I didn't want to lead his answers. He tried to replay the night over again. "Try to focus on something small and insignificant," I suggested. "Did he have a jacket?" Maybe my guided questions would lead to something concrete. Although eyewitness testimony was always the least reliable, I just hoped mine wasn't included in that umbrella statement.

"Yes," his eyes lit up, "a police jacket. It was blue with an emblem on the sleeve."

"Good." I nodded at him encouragingly. "What else? Focus on the parts you remember."

"His jacket was open, and he wore a baseball cap." He frowned in contemplation. "Dark pants, no," he shut his eyes, "jeans with tennis shoes. They were white and silver and squeaked on the floor." Not particularly helpful, but at least he was engaging more than one of his senses. "There was a badge around his neck." He looked startled.

"What is it?"

"Four," he paused, "seven, one." Sam's stare was intense. "Two nine four seven one."

"Are you positive?"

"It was the first five digits of my ex-girlfriend's phone number. I forgot about it." He looked sheepish. "I've had Dawn stuck in my head this whole time, and I thought it was just because of the near-death experience."

After concluding my visit and wishing him a full

recovery as quickly as possible, I was whisked back to the FBI offices to help track down our three new leads. It was about damn time.

*   *   *

We worked through the evening, checking records on the two former detectives Sam recognized from the bar. After re-watching the surveillance footage for the umpteenth time, Webster spotted them sitting at the bar early in the evening and leaving with two young ladies. Cooper would bring them in for questioning in the morning. Hopefully, between now and then, facial recognition would find a match to the two young women in case our ex-detectives needed to have their stories corroborated.

The detective's badge, which I partially recalled in my dreamlike state and Sam completely remembered by happenstance, led to a dead end. We had all five digits, but they belonged to no one. It made zero sense. I tried rearranging the numbers, but this tactic led to too many possibilities. How could we have a badge number that doesn't exist?

"Try running it through the databases," Mark suggested as I slammed my palm on the desk and contemplated doing the same to my skull. "Maybe it's from a different city. Some of the emblems look the same, and neither you nor Harrigan got a good look."

"Fine." I entered the information into the search box and waited for results. Given the sheer number of law enforcement agencies in the country, from small towns to big cities, this was going to take a while.

"Are you sure Harrigan's not full of shit?" Mark asked from his desk.

The two of us moved upstairs to the OIO offices since Cooper sent his team home for the night to recharge their batteries in preparation for the morning's interviews. I was still trying to make up for each of my numerous screw-ups, and Mark was multitasking other cases that had piled up on his desk.

"He's not full of shit." I sighed and went to get a cup of coffee. It tasted like mud and was about as thick.

"What kind of coincidence is it that the badge number matches his girlfriend's phone number? You remember what I taught you about coincidences?" His tone was accusatory and smug. He was still punishing me for this entire mess.

"They don't exist," I repeated his constant mantra from when he was my supervisor. "But explain how I remembered three of the same numbers."

"Maybe he's wrong about the last few digits. His mind could have filled in familiar details. You said he didn't remember much of what happened, and you had to coax the memories out of him."

"I'll figure it out," I growled and turned back to the computer screen.

On a sheet of paper, I listed other possibilities and cross-referenced my new compilations with the local precinct's database. At some point, Mark must have said good night because when I looked up, he was gone. The entire floor was empty, except for a couple of unlucky agents covering the night shift. Settling further into my chair, I stared at the computer screen, waiting for something to ping.

* * *

"Parker?" I lifted my head off the desk, but my neck was stuck at a forty-five degree angle. "Have you been here all night?" Director Kendall asked.

"Sir." I carefully straightened up. "Working on a

lead."

"Your dedication is admirable, but don't let me catch you sleeping on the job again." He winked and continued to his office.

I wasn't used to the director being quite so chummy, and honestly, I didn't know how to respond to it. Rolling my neck carefully and listening to the pops and cracks of my vertebrae, I noticed the blinking message on the computer monitor. One match found.

Printing out the results, I stopped at the ladies' locker room and splashed some water on my face, wiped off the remnants of yesterday's makeup, and pulled my hair into a tight bun. Good as new. Hurrying upstairs, I found everyone assembled in the conference room from hell.

"We got a hit on the badge," I offered without being asked. "It was reported missing over a decade ago. Captain Stephens might be interested to know his old partner's shield was recently used in the commission of a crime."

"Where's his partner now?" Cooper asked, fully alert. "Maybe we found our guy."

"Records indicate he died, a victim of a hit-and-run. When his body was discovered, he was without identification. According to the report, that's when his badge went missing."

"Shit," Mark cursed. "Who found the body?"

"A couple of street kids. Stephens happened to catch the call and identified Detective Roberto Ramirez's body on scene."

"Hell of a way to get the news," Darli intoned sadly.

"Okay, focus people." Cooper reined us in. "Sullivan and Webster go talk to the men we brought in this morning. Darli, watch from the booth and verify every single word they say. Jablonsky, give Moretti a call and have him break the news to the Cap and pass it along to IAD. Everyone clear?" There was a round of ayes as the room emptied out.

"What do you want me to do?" I asked.

"Go home." Cooper was all business. "You were here all night. I tried sending you home yesterday, but you couldn't follow orders. Don't make me tell you again."

"But, sir," I began.

"Agent," he said the word sharply, "go home." I trudged slowly to the door, unhappy with my orders. Cooper should realize I wouldn't be able to get any rest when things were finally happening, and we had real, tangible leads. Before I made it out of the room, he added, "Nicely done."

TWENTY-SIX

I called a cab to take me home. Luckily, it was late enough in the morning to avoid rush hour traffic since all the commuters were already at work. Letting myself into my apartment, I was in the middle of an internal struggle to decide if I should eat, take a power nap, or indulge in a nice hot shower. Before any of these wonderful ideas could win out over the others, my phone rang.

"Parker," I answered before the first ring even finished.

"Ms. Parker, please hold for Mr. Guillot," the Martin Technologies assistant said before the piped in sound of elevator music filled my ears. Martin's office was violating the Geneva Convention's sanction against torture.

Eventually, the infernal sound was replaced by Luc's French accent. "Mademoiselle," he practically cooed, "I've been trying to reach you for the last two days."

"Sorry, I've had other obligations." Didn't Guillot

hear about my wanted status and arrest?

"That is the nature of having a consultant and not a full-time security analyst employed by the company," he sounded annoyed. "As we discussed last time, the finer points are collating, and another meeting to discuss uniform protocols and procedures is on the books for a week from this Monday."

"I'll be there."

"Miss Parker," he dropped the French colloquialisms, "there are important plans you need to approve, procedures in need of revision, and a final equipment check."

"What's the deadline?"

"Please complete them before the meeting. They need to be on my desk by that Monday morning, at the very latest."

"Very good." I wasn't sure where my current reinstatement was going to lead by tomorrow, let alone in a week and a half, so I asked for the information to be sent via e-mail in order to save myself a trip to the MT building. Guillot agreed and hung up without further comment.

Normally, he was overly friendly, but today, he sounded stressed. Maybe he heard the news of my arrest and was afraid of the ramifications the company might suffer because of it. Chalking it up to an additional oversight, if not a downright blunder on my part, I made myself a quick sandwich, took a five minute shower, and let the idea of a powernap fade into the background of lost dreams.

"Heathcliff, are you still suspended?" I asked when he answered his phone.

"Two more days." While he didn't actually sigh, I pictured his shoulders slumped in defeat. "What's up?"

"They forced me to go home. All-nighters are

frowned upon by the federal government. And since we're both unwanted, do you want to come over and run some scenarios with me? We can be pariahs together."

"I might be busy."

"Are you busy?"

"No. I'll be there in an hour. It's your turn to supply the beers."

"It's eleven in the morning." He wasn't usually this forward, and I suspected he wasn't happy being relegated to sitting at home, watching daytime television.

"And neither of us is working today, so there's no reason not to imbibe."

When Heathcliff arrived, I dutifully went to the fridge, removed a beer, and handed it to him. He looked at it as if to say 'didn't I bring these over' but refrained from saying as much. The beers he bought were at Martin's, but I happened to have a six pack of the same brand in my fridge. He placed it, unopened, on the table and took a seat. After I filled him in on the now identified badge number, we began conducting our own thorough investigation into Ramirez's hit-and-run. Heathcliff brought his laptop today, so we were making progress twice as fast.

"It must have been tough on the Cap," he said out of the blue. Meeting his eyes, I knew where his mind had gone. After his partner committed suicide, he found her body, wrists slit, in the bathtub. "The driver responsible for Ramirez's death was never found. There were no leads on the vehicle. Surveillance wasn't nearly as prevalent as it is today. Back then, the DOT didn't have traffic cams on every street corner."

"How long did the investigation continue?"

"It doesn't say. Captain Stephens was promoted from detective to a command position a month later."

"And there were no hits on the badge until the shooting at Infinity?" Getting the ping in the database should have provided usable intel, not chasing more ghosts down dead ends.

"I'm running a search on police impersonation reports, but unless someone got a badge number, I don't think it'll lead anywhere," he admitted.

By four, I was dragging, but Heathcliff was still going strong as he read through ten year old police records, making notations, and coming up with a list of people to question. My contribution was less obvious, seeing as how I was stretched out on the couch, struggling to hold my eyes open, and failing miserably. My phone beeped, signifying an incoming e-mail, and I got off the couch and went to the desktop computer.

"Now what's going on?" he asked, not bothering to look up from his notepad.

"Corporate security review." I printed copies of the attached documents. After skimming them quickly, stapling together the forms, and sticking them into a blank manila envelope for later consideration, I turned to his half-filled legal pad. "Are you working on the next great American novel?"

"You ask for my help, and then you bust my balls for working. Didn't anyone ever teach you how to properly communicate with others?" Giving him a petulant look, I waited for him to expound on his current discoveries. "Okay," he closed the window on the screen, scribbled a final thought onto his sheet of paper, and flipped to the beginning, "Ramirez's murder was never solved. No leads in the case, and nothing to indicate whatever became of his badge. So says the official report."

"Unofficially?"

"Hard to say what really happened. At the time of

his death, the deceased detective and Captain Stephens were working for the gangs unit. Vice and narcotics also had a large-scale joint investigation in the works. Girls, drugs, and guns."

"Sounds like it all ties back to gangs. Maybe even our organized crime friends."

Heathcliff touched the side of his nose and smirked in response. "A few small arrests were made. No one big was pinched, and no one from Vincenzo's family was brought in which seems strange since Ramirez was killed on Vito's turf."

"You don't think the hit-and-run was accidental?"

"I don't know. Could be bad luck, bad timing, and purely a coincidence, but I found the names of both current and former responding officers. I've read their files, and the majority were busted seven years ago by internal affairs for being on the take."

"How long has this been going on?" The knowledge of such corruption floored me.

"This is the first I've heard about it. Whenever IA cleaned house, no one heard a word. The guys were given early retirement, some portion of their pensions, and disappeared into the shadows."

"Politics," I fumed. "Do you want to give Thompson a call and see if he and Moretti have made any progress? Maybe we should update them."

He flipped through the pages again and picked up the phone. "I'll have Thompson see what he can dig up. Maybe he can have a chat with the captain and gain some insight into Ramirez's death."

*　　*　　*

By that evening, my apartment could have been its own precinct with the number of police personnel standing around my counter. O'Connell, Thompson, and Heathcliff hunkered around the notepad, spit-balling ideas. I was on the phone with Mark, filling him in on our progress and listening as he told me the proper uses for a day off. When everyone was up to speed, I took a spot next to Heathcliff so I could read over his shoulder as he concluded the rundown.

"What'd Moretti say?" I asked Thompson. I missed the earlier conversation thanks to Mark.

"He scheduled a meeting with the captain for tomorrow morning. Hopefully, we won't be kicked down the ladder to traffic because of this."

"Thompson and I will talk with the IA investigators tomorrow and see if they can provide further insight into what really occurred with the dearly departed Detective Ramirez," O'Connell added. "You wanna take a run at the retirees?"

"Might as well," Heathcliff agreed. "I'm suspended, so at least we'll have some common ground." The three detectives all turned to face me.

"Mo, Larry, Curly," my eyes darted from one to the other, "did you practice that little routine to music?" I got three pairs of confused looks. "Fine," I blew out a breath, "I gave Mark an update over the phone, and tomorrow, I'll bring all of it to Cooper and let him decide what he wants to do with it. They are working a few angles based on Sam Harrigan's eyewitness account. Two former detectives were at the bar that night. They might be involved."

"Did you ever hear anything else from the enemy you climbed in bed with?" Heathcliff asked, much to my chagrin.

"Vito sent over the bogus surveillance footage and dropped off the radar afterward. Mark's keeping me on a tight leash," I said. O'Connell and Heathcliff exchanged a meaningful look. "I'm behaving, all right? Jeez."

"Maybe we should send some units to ruffle his feathers," Thompson suggested. "If the investigation leads us there anyway, then there's no harm in rattling his chain."

Shrugging, I went to the fridge and retrieved the remaining beers and passed them around the counter. "Here's to some actual progress." I raised my bottle.

Heathcliff leaned in close and added, "Told you to buy beer."

TWENTY-SEVEN

Sam's insight resulted in a dead end. Sullivan, Webster, and Darli had taken a crack at the former detectives, who were now running their own pizza place, but they were clean. They just happened to be out looking for some tail on a Saturday night.

The police department's internal affairs division sent a liaison to help fill in the blanks concerning the resurfaced badge. Why they didn't provide the Bureau with a go-between earlier made no sense, but my guess was the proper paperwork wasn't filed correctly to make it happen sooner. Each day I reported to HQ my disdain for bureaucracy grew exponentially.

O'Connell phoned and said Moretti was dropping by to personally give us the lowdown on Detective Ramirez. With the IAD liaison, Lt. Moretti, and too many outdated police files to count, it was just another long day at the office. The hours dragged as each file, suspect, and piece of information was analyzed. Throughout the day, calls were made to and from the boys in major crimes, each of whom had some new tidbit to add either exonerating a suspect or moving them higher on our list of potential dirty cops.

When Heathcliff called, it was to my cell phone. Immediately, my brain flashed neon lights and the warning bells blared. Excusing myself from the room, I went into the hallway and down the corridor.

"I have news." He got straight to the point. "Are you alone?"

"Yes."

"All right, here's the thing, the guys I spoke to all had the same story. They were following orders when they responded to Ramirez's crime scene. The reports they filed were altered and re-filed. That order came from their commanding officer."

"Did you get a name?"

"Lt. Benjamin Rapier, but he's dead. Died five years ago from liver cancer. I'm standing in front of his tombstone right now. I considered digging him up to make sure he was there but thought that might be overkill. What do you think?"

"Let the dead rest in peace, Derek." Swallowing, I made sure no one emerged from the conference room. "Why'd you call me and not a more official number?"

"Something's not sitting right." A car door slammed in the background. "A bunch of uniforms are told by their lieutenant to falsify their reports, then the guy's partner gets a promotion so he can't investigate, and when IA cleans house, everyone gets an early retirement, and it's all swept neatly under the rug."

"What are you saying?" My gut knew what he was saying, but I wanted someone else to say the words besides me.

"It's proof Vincenzo's got police brass in his pocket. Worst case, it could be someone from IA."

"Goddamn."

"Exactly. I'm on my way to you now. Pull Cooper aside, and I'll fill him in. There's no reason for you to get into deeper shit than you're already swimming through."

By the time Heathcliff arrived, Moretti had shown up and briefed us on Captain Stephens' recollection of his partner's murder. It was basic, preliminary, and sounded rehearsed. Then again, I was suspicious of everyone right now, including Moretti. My paranoia knew no bounds, and everyone looked like the enemy. Heathcliff entered the conference room and took a seat. After Moretti finished, I pulled Cooper aside. We went down the hall to his office. Heathcliff, Mark, and Moretti joined us. Casting a curious look at Heathcliff, I waited for him to share his discoveries.

"You're on administrative leave. What the hell were you thinking?" Moretti scolded.

"Thought I'd throw back a few with some good 'ol boys." Heathcliff had spent way too much time with me. He used to be strait-laced, not flippant.

"Nice work," Cooper commended. "Obviously, we need a new strategy. I bet we're getting closer and that's why we've been assigned an IA liaison to keep tabs on our progress." He turned to Moretti. "Can you find out who assigned him?"

"I'll do some digging." Moretti glared at Heathcliff. "In the meantime, you get your ass out of here and away from everything, unless you want your suspension to turn into something more permanent."

"Yes, sir."

"Parker," Mark had a similar glare, "I hate to say it, but let's get you wired. You're going to pay your new best pal a little visit."

"When?" The last thing I wanted was to go back to Vito's.

"Now." Mark threw a look to Cooper who nodded. "Come on, we'll get you outfitted properly, and I'll have Darli and Webster keep you in their crosshairs."

Heathcliff caught my eye and mouthed good luck. *Game, set, match, douchebag,* I thought as I mentally prepared for another showdown with a crime boss.

*   *   *

Darli and Webster remained in a surveillance van parked down the street from Vito's bar. They just finished sound check and gave the go-ahead. Mark was in the van, looking anxious.

"Do you want me to go in with you?" he asked.

"It's my mess to clean up, Jablonsky." I checked the clip in my gun, holstered my weapon, and hung my credentials from my front pocket. "If you have to come in, then something has gone horribly wrong." Opening the rear door of the van, I took a slow, deep breath and hopped onto the pavement.

"Alex, don't do anything stupid." He was worried, probably more than I was.

"It'd be a shame if I stopped now."

I shut the door and stared down the street. The goal was to get Antonio Vincenzo's cooperation, and if that wasn't possible, then something incriminating would have to suffice. He had cops on the take, and we needed names. Crossing the street, I turned and walked up the opposite side toward Vito's, palming my cell phone in my jacket pocket. Mark's number was already punched in. I just had to hit send. It was my secondary plan in case something happened with the wire.

"Ms. Parker," Vito cooed from a back booth, "did you come to thank me in person?" The muscle from last time sat on a barstool.

"Thank you? You want gratitude for providing falsified evidence?"

"I don't know what you're talking about." Vito had

been playing this game far too long to slip up. "You can tell the agents outside in the van the same thing." Damn, he must have security cams outside. "Or are they listening now?" He cocked his head to one side. "Hello, federal agents, care to join us for a drink?"

I took a step forward, and Muscle stood up, blocking my path. "Step aside," I growled.

He didn't even acknowledge my presence. Instead, he continued imitating a brick wall.

"It's okay, Tony. She won't shoot me. There are too many witnesses out front."

Tony the Muscle extended his hand for my weapon, and I glowered at him. "This time, I'm holding on to my gun." Tony cast a look to Vito who imperceptibly gave an okay signal because he stepped out of my way. Taking a seat on the opposite side of the booth, I asked, "Would you care to explain your reasoning behind sending faked footage?"

"Would you care for a drink?" Although his tone was friendly, his eyes were not. "I'd say you're a red wine type of woman. I'm certain in your line of work you've seen a lot of blood. Maybe you've shed your fair share or caused others to do the same." We stared at one another like two predators preparing to battle over a rotting carcass. "Frankie, bring Ms. Parker a nice glass of red."

"Are you going to answer my question?"

"Hmm," he lolled his head against the cushioned backrest, "I thought we had an understanding. I'm a businessman. It's not in your best interest to renege on a verbal contract."

"You broke our deal when you supplied phony surveillance footage. Was that to send us in the wrong direction? Or did you do it to make sure the guys you have in your pocket stay in your pocket?"

"Honey, if you want something from me, I suggest

you call off the hounds and lose the wire."

There was no point in arguing. He had done this his entire life, and he was good. He had never been caught, and there was never enough circumstantial evidence or eyewitnesses to make any charges stick to him. I reached inside my jacket, and Tony practically pounced.

"Stay cool," I warned. Vito showed the vaguest sign of interest in what I was doing as Frankie set a glass on the table. With any luck, Mark would stay cool too. Unbuttoning my blouse, I untaped the wire and yanked it free before dropping it, to Vito's satisfaction, in the wine glass. "Happy now?" I asked, surreptitiously reaching into my pocket and hitting the call button before anyone could be the wiser. "Mind if I button up? There's a draft in here."

"This is a much more civilized way of having a conversation, don't you agree?" He focused on my cleavage. "I take it you're not going to leave well enough alone."

"Is that supposed to be a threat?"

"No, on the contrary, I'm intrigued that an investigator would bother to look a gift-horse in the mouth. I could have made your case a slam dunk, but instead, you poked around at the footage. Maybe you've talked to some people, asked a few too many questions, but then you come back here. You're either confident or crazy. Which is it?" He was poised to strike. His tone was pure malice.

My heart started to race, and chills made the hair on the back of my neck stand at attention. But I remained outwardly calm and disinterested. "Hell, I'm both." Body language was a great way to nonverbally communicate, and I stretched out on my side of the booth, opening my body in a confident, relaxed manner, and smirked. It was fucking stupid, but it was the only way I could think to rattle his chain. "Deal's off. I'm not returning any favors since you haven't given me anything I want. Tonight, I stopped by to tell you we're through. You have your inside guys protecting your interests, and that's great. But you probably shouldn't count on them much longer. It's like shooting fish in a barrel. We're just lining 'em up now and bam." I slammed my palm down for emphasis and hoped Tony wouldn't turn trigger happy and blow a hole through my brain.

Vito remained unperturbed and motionless. My theatrics didn't even make him blink. He wasn't going to flinch.

I stood, sipped the wine, and fished out the wire. "Eh, not that great." I turned and headed for the door.

Two steps in, he cleared his throat. "You shouldn't play poker, Agent. The truth is written all over your face." He was talking which meant I had him by the short and curlies, even if he wasn't willing to admit it.

Slowly spinning around to face him, I leaned against an empty booth. "Hey, whatever you have to tell yourself. It doesn't make it true though."

"I have a soft spot for you. You've got tenacity and spunk. I'm not too fond of the tenacity, but I'm a playful guy. Spunk's acceptable in small doses." He was doing his *Godfather* impression again. "I have a feeling if you keep this up, something unimaginable might happen, if you catch my drift. You've got a pretty face and some great tits. It'd be such a waste." Since he veiled the threat in a sexist compliment, I must be on a roll. "How's about we come to a mutual agreement?"

"Tried and failed. Fool me once, shame on me, but fool me twice," I scrunched my nose and shook my head emphatically, "nah, I don't think so."

"Let bygones be bygones. You and your friends stay

away from me and my business, and I'll give you a name."

"Whose name?"

He looked past me to a spot on the wall, taking his time to contemplate matters. "The cop that shot you."

"You're a smart man, so you know one name won't end this. It's just a stepping stone in a large-scale investigation." *Parker, shut your mouth*, my internal voice berated.

"You really want to push boundaries?" His voice was back to deadly. I was royally pissing him off. Maybe if he made a move, Mark could ride in and arrest him for assault, attempted murder, or murder, depending on how long it took to get inside the bar.

"What can I say? I'm all kinds of crazy."

"You back off of me, my clubs, and everything non-police related, and I'll give you the shooter. Wherever he leads, that's their problem, not mine."

"And I'm supposed to take this on good faith?"

"No," his eyes narrowed, "it's this or the alternative. Keep in mind, there's a lot about you on record. It'd be easy to track your friends, family, that rich boss of yours you're fucking." My blood boiled, and the image of pulling my piece and piercing Vito's skull with a bullet was tempting, but not today. "Think about the consequences before you decide to take this investigation beyond the scope I laid out for you."

"I can't control where the investigation goes once I conclude my role and lose my reinstated status." It was unlikely the Bureau would drop its investigation into Vito, especially if something tangible surfaced.

"I'll bear that in mind before doling out consequences." We were in another standoff. It didn't matter if I walked out now, or if he said his own father was the shooter. If he wanted to silence me, he would.

"Give me the name."

TWENTY-EIGHT

"What the hell?" Mark gaped in disbelief as I entered the back of the van.

"I know." I climbed in and pulled the doors shut. "He compliments my face and tits and doesn't say a word about my ass. I have a fantastic ass. Darli, Webster, either one of you want to weigh in on this?" The two male agents looked away, embarrassed, as Mark continued his dead-eye stare.

"Smart thinking to phone in. Luckily, we recorded the entire exchange."

Oh goody, I could listen to Vito's threats again as if they weren't already replaying themselves in my brain. My bravado was fading quickly, and my pathetic attempt at joking wasn't working since Mark was taking this too seriously.

"Mark," I said quietly. My hands shook, and I rubbed my face so he wouldn't notice.

"We'll monitor Vito and his movements. Our ear's to the ground in case there's any chatter about a hit. It'll be okay. You spooked him, and he reacted. But he's too smart to make a move on you."

"Not if it'd be less trouble to remove me from the equation."

"Then we'll just have to make sure you're not too much trouble."

*   *   *

I spent the night at the office. Maybe it was to work leads, or maybe it was because I was afraid there would be a horse's head in my bed when I got home. Although, I doubted Vito could find a horse on such short notice. The next morning, I got out of the small cramped chair behind Mark's desk that I attempted to sleep in, went down to the locker rooms, took a shower, and tried my best to look as if I was well rested.

"Any word on Eli Gates?" I asked, entering the almost empty conference room. Gates was the name Vito had given us.

Darli and Webster had the morning off. Sullivan was tracking everything she could find on Ramirez, his badge, his cohorts, and Captain Stephens' recollection. Cooper and Mark were the only two people in the conference room. Cooper was on the phone, listening intently to someone on the other end.

"We've compiled a list of his aliases. His description's gone out over the wire. We have employment history and financials, but he might as well be a ghost."

"Is he on the job?" I asked.

"No," Mark said.

Narrowing my eyes, I thought about Vito's words. He said he would give up the cop who shot me. Lying son of a bitch.

Cooper held up a finger and hung up the phone.

"Actually, he was when he was using the alias John Rodgers. Moretti's sending over the files now."

How deep down the rabbit hole would this take us? There was just too much to process. Before anything more could be said, an assistant knocked on the door and requested Agent Jablonsky report upstairs.

"And then there were two," I said to Cooper as he took a seat at the head of the table.

"I listened to the recording from your conversation yesterday. Are you doing okay?"

"Peachy."

"Look, I might be able to swing something if you think your family or friends need protection."

"Cooper, regardless of what Il Douchebag might threaten, I'm pretty much a solo act. My friends have badges and guns, and the only one who doesn't has an armed bodyguard. It's all good, all the time."

He bit his thumbnail and observed me silently for a few moments. "Vincenzo was wrong about one thing."

"Yeah?"

"You are a convincing liar. It's probably why he gave you what he did. You have him running scared, so he's cutting his losses and moving on." I sighed, still not willing to drop my poker face. "There's a loveseat in my office if you don't go home tonight. It's probably more comfortable than Jablonsky's chair," Cooper offered.

"Thanks."

"But if you change your mind on the detail, let me know. We'll work something out."

"We'll see. I'm hoping this will be done before it comes down to that."

*   *   *

An hour later, O'Connell was escorted into the

conference room by a probationary agent. Nick looked confused by the escort but let it slide without comment as he handed a stack of files to Cooper.

"Have you been briefed?" Cooper asked, flipping through the pages before closing the file and passing it to me.

"On what?" O'Connell was behind, and Cooper filled him in as I read through Officer John Rodgers' personnel file.

Rodgers aka Eli Gates had been in the same class in the academy as Detective Ramirez and Captain Stephens. Rodgers was still a rookie when he was fired for inappropriate conduct. Rodgers and two fellow rookies had been seen brutally assaulting a man in a back alley of a questionable neighborhood. Why the three were in an alley in that particular neighborhood had never been resolved. Although, years later, it was the same neighborhood and same street corner where Detective Ramirez had been the victim of a hit-and-run.

As I continued perusing the folder, it was apparent the two other rookies had never been positively identified since Gates/Rodgers didn't snitch on his cohorts. If my suspicions held any credence, then one of the other two rookies must have been Ramirez. Maybe Gates turned resentful, called Ramirez for a stroll down memory lane, and stole his badge from his cold, dead hand. It would have been the career he never had. Or maybe Ramirez was investigating the cold case and got caught at the wrong end of a speeding car.

"I need a board. A whiteboard, corkboard, glass on wheels with some markers, hell, cardboard even. Frankly, I don't care what it is, but it needs to be a decent size that I can either write on or pin things to. Maybe both." Lack of sleep made me demanding.

"There's too much here to keep straight. For any of us to keep straight."

"Agent Parker," Cooper looked utterly amused, the first crack in his monotone, serious exterior, "I shall go find a board for you, milady."

"Thank you, sir." It seemed possible I overstepped my position, but Cooper was letting it slide. Maybe my badass attitude and wicked bluffing made him malleable to my requests.

The door shut, and O'Connell stared, fascinated. "Look at you, all dominatrix-like, ordering the men around. Do you want some leather boots and a whip to go with that feisty exterior?"

"Don't start."

He chuckled and rested his hips against the tabletop. "Here's the thing, Heathcliff's benched for the day. Moretti's been chewing on something. It's big, and he isn't talking. My gut says one of his bosses is a dirtbag, and he's trying to gain enough evidence before he calls it in. And Thompson's apparently a secretary because all he's doing is running errands and making calls."

"What about you?"

"Solved the metro murder yesterday. Jen's gone out of town to visit her folks, so I'm back to business. Unofficially," he leaned in closer, "I've read the reports." He jerked his chin at the files. "Three rookies mean the same class in the academy."

"That could be hundreds of guys."

"Yeah, but you can narrow it down by precinct assignments since Rodgers or Gates, whatever the fuck you want to call him, knew the other two guys which would explain his lack of ratting them out."

"Get to the point." I was tired of extraneous details.

"Heathcliff has a list of guys who were pulled off duty, a list of guys who are no longer kicking, and a list still on the job. The thing is the ones no longer on the job have moved on. Some have moved away, and others are in different lines of work. The majority don't have a dog in this fight, if you catch my drift."

"You're saying the two unidentified rookies are still on the job?"

"I'd bet my badge. Hell, I'd bet Thompson's and Heathcliff's too."

"Damn, I hope you're right because you're the only three cops still talking to me. And with my current predicament, I might need some gun-toting, badge-carrying backup."

"Trust me, I'm right about this." He looked like the cat that swallowed the canary. "So do you want the short list of names or am I supposed to wait for you to beg before I give them to you?"

"Names now would be nice."

"Fair enough." He reached into his breast pocket and pulled out a folded sheet of paper. "Obviously, the captain's on the list, along with Sergeant Smolders, Lieutenant Winston, and some detectives."

Looking through the seven names, I had my suspicions. "You said Moretti's mulling something over concerning one of his superiors?"

"Same conclusion I came to." He swallowed. "But if we're wrong," his voice dropped, letting the negative job ramifications float in the space between us.

"The more serious question is what if we're not. The precinct's captain could be in a mobster's pocket." Pushing away from the table, I stood and kicked my chair underneath, hearing the clang reverberate through the empty conference room. "Dammit."

"Every case, every arrest, convictions, evidence, internal affairs investigations, everything is going to be reconsidered. How many criminals will get released because of this? How many good, clean cops will get their names dragged through the mud? Even if we all transfer out, no one will want to work with any of us. And the community," Nick shut his eyes and slammed his fist against the table, "they don't trust us now, just imagine what it'll be like after this gets out."

"Who assigned the IA liaison?"

"Stephens. IA's supposed to be separate, but it's his house. They still report to him."

"All right, look, we're going to wait until Moretti gives us something solid or Sullivan finds an undeniable connection. There's no reason to jump to worst case scenarios just yet. We could be wrong."

"I hope we are." He left the comment hanging in the air until Mark came into the room, looking as if someone just shot his dog.

TWENTY-NINE

By the conclusion of yet another endless workday, all the evidence pointed to Captain Stephens being the remaining unidentified rookie. Moretti had gone through the evidence room and located the original paperwork. We had proof the documents had been altered, and with present technology, the original text on two typewritten reports had been recovered. The report stated Officer Stephens left the precinct with Officers Rodgers and Ramirez. The same report also specified Stephens and Ramirez returned together that night from a tour with bruised knuckles and bloodied uniforms.

Additionally, the investigation into Detective Ramirez's death linked Stephens to another cover-up. Stephens wasn't called to the scene to identify the body. He arrived first on the scene and told the responding officers he had no idea who the victim was. A note had been placed in a long lost file from Lt. Benjamin Rapier to resubmit the case file with the corrected information. Rapier was also responsible for

Stephens' promotion to a command position.

"Rapier was one of the original dirty cops," Sullivan concluded from the front of the room. "Unfortunately, he's not able to testify against any of his accomplices. But he groomed Stephens to take over."

"I'm sure it was Vincenzo's idea." The disdain dripped from my words.

"Look," Moretti sat at the conference table, along with the three detectives who had been assisting the FBI's investigation all along, "I have a meeting with the commissioner first thing in the morning. His press secretary said to keep a lid on it until then. If word gets out that the head of the precinct is working for a mobster, we're all going to hell."

"The Bureau is letting the commissioner take the lead. Stephens is key, and anyone else working for him is going down. In the meantime, we have to find Gates. He might not be a cop anymore, but he is our shooter. To simplify things, let's refer to him as Gates until further notice, just to assist in keeping a tight seal on current matters," Cooper said. "For official purposes, the name Gates won't trace back to the police department like Rodgers will."

"Any leads on his whereabouts?" Thompson meticulously straightened the stacks of files in front of him. Thompson was a note taker, and since we were off book, he didn't know what to do with himself.

"Nothing yet," Webster said, clicking the mouse on his laptop a few times. "Everyone has a description, so it's just a matter of time."

"Yeah, because it's not like it took us over a decade to find Osama bin Laden," Heathcliff mumbled under his breath.

"Parker." I turned at the sound of my name. Sullivan stared at me. "If Antonio Vincenzo's been following your movements this entire time, someone must be filling him in."

"It was probably the waitress who moonlights as an au pair for one of his higher-ups," I replied.

"What about Ernie Papadakis?" she asked. "He runs Infinity, but Vincenzo pulls the strings."

"Dammit." I forgot about Ernie. Losing sight of the forest because of all the damn trees was happening far too frequently.

"Get a team over there now," Cooper ordered. Apparently, I wasn't the only one suffering from nearsightedness. "After last night, Vito's cutting ties for his own protection."

*   *   *

From the doorway, I stared into Ernie's apartment, feeling responsible. The marshals had been stationed outside all day. No one entered or left, and there was no indication anything was amiss, except for the corpse lying on the bathroom floor next to the broken metal shower rod. The marshals sent in their own team of investigators to work alongside the Bureau's coroner and forensics unit.

"COD?" I asked one of the guys in the dark blue jumpsuits as he pushed a gurney past me through the open door.

"Dr. Jeffries has ruled out the hanging as the cause of death. Preliminary evaluation indicates blunt force trauma to the skull."

"The guy's brains are all over the corner of the vanity and the floor," Mark so eloquently stated. "I'd say he tried to hang himself, and when the shower rod broke, he tumbled into the Formica. And it was lights out."

"Someone get phone records. Check the mail. I don't care what it is but figure out how Vito got to him," I barked.

Storming out of the apartment as if I were on a mission, I found myself standing outside in the pouring rain, doubled-over and doing my best to keep my stomach contents on the inside. *Another one bites the dust*, the inane lyrics played a macabre tune in my head, and I wanted nothing more than to crawl out of my own skin. An escape from my own sick, twisted subconscious mind and my lethally failing deductive reasoning and impaired decision-making abilities would have been a great relief at the moment. Too bad they didn't sell electroshock therapy from street vendors, at least not in this neighborhood.

"Parker?" Webster called, exiting the apartment building. "Hey," he stood next to me, uncomprehending, "what are you doing?"

"Having a picnic. What the hell does it look like?"

He seemed confused but had the foresight not to respond to my rhetorical question. "We found a throwaway in Ernie's apartment. He received a text message almost six hours ago. From the coroner's estimation, it looks like he spent a couple of hours working up the nerve before ending things."

My stomach twisted, and the bile rose in my throat. Swallowing the burning acid, I met Webster's eyes. "We should have stopped this. I should have realized it sooner. It didn't have to go this way."

"Parker," his tone was softer, "it's not..."

"My fault?" I cut in. "Right. Do you really believe that?" Scrutinizing him, I continued, "Yeah, I didn't think so." Standing up straight, I strode back to the building.

"Alex." Mark was in the living room. A couple of techs occupied the bathroom as they checked the body for evidence and photographed the scene. "We've upped the security at the safe house where Harrigan is, and we have teams keeping an eye on Infinity staff, particularly Gretchen and Mary, just to be on the safe side. Do you want an additional unit sent to Marty's?"

"There's no reason." My conviction was hollow. Mark would use his own judgment, so my response was pointless. "Vito's eliminating anyone who could be a danger to him, those who know of his club connections and maybe about the dirty cops. Martin doesn't know anything about any of this."

"Who does? Give me some names."

"Gretchen. Mary." I rubbed my face. "I don't know. Me."

"We'll keep a closer eye on Det. Hoskins. Even though he's in protective custody, he started looking into the connection in the first place, and with dirty cops, who knows who can be trusted." Mark watched as I exhaled uncomfortably. "Go downstairs and wait in the car. While you're there, give the office an update."

"I'm fine."

"That wasn't a request. Follow orders, Agent Parker."

"Yes, sir," I grumbled. Mark wasn't pushing. This time, he was just watching out for me.

Getting into the passenger's side, I knocked my head against the seatback. *Dammit*, I cursed and slammed my fist repeatedly on the dash. Hopefully, no one was around because it probably looked like I was having an awful seizure or mercilessly killing a swarm of bees. Only when the glove box popped open did I pause, kick it closed, and stop. The side of my hand throbbed.

"I'm sorry, Ernie." Biting my lip, I called Cooper.

Ten minutes later, Mark opened the driver's side door and glanced inside. "Are you okay?"

"No, but we have work to do. Moretti's meeting

with the commissioner now, and we don't have time to sit around and wait for more of the case to end itself. We've been ordered back to HQ, and if Moretti gets the go-ahead, we'll have a tac team on standby to assist in bringing in Captain Stephens."

THIRTY

I was in TacOps, tactical operations, watching the team prepare. The commissioner had given Moretti the go-ahead, and after informing the DA's office of the situation and locating a judge willing to sign an arrest warrant, we were set to move. The men suiting up were federal agents trained for crisis situations. With any luck, the warrant would be served, and Stephens would come along quietly.

Lt. Moretti and Thompson were the only two police personnel present. O'Connell had been ordered to stay away by Thompson's insistence to protect his partner from psychopaths involved in organized crime. Mark stood with the three of us, watching as everyone was briefed on the situation. SAC Cooper donned a tactical vest and lifted an assault rifle. Apparently, he transferred from hostage negotiation.

"Glad to know the monotone voice was put to good use in the past," I joked.

"Cooper's an expert marksman," Mark said, "but he isn't the greatest at leading the desk brigade."

"Takes time," Moretti chimed in. "Leadership is leadership, but it's different tactics to get these hardheads to listen."

"Don't I know it," Mark added as Thompson and I exchanged a look. Obviously, we were the lot who was difficult to corral. Before the conversation could continue further, Sullivan burst into the room, paper in hand.

"Warrant's signed," she announced. "Stephens is at home."

"Let's move," Cooper ordered, and the group assembled marched out the door.

*　　*　　*

Maybe it was professional courtesy or the hope Stephens would act more civil in front of his own men that sent Lt. Moretti knocking on the front door. The tactical team covered the perimeter, but they were pulled back pretty far. Cooper was the exception to the rule as he stood on the side of the doorway beside Mark. Thompson and I covered the only other exit, the back door.

"Captain," Moretti called after he rang the bell, "open up. We need to talk." Stephens' wife, Margaret, answered the door. Thompson and I heard the commotion from our side of the house, but we waited for a signal before moving in. "Ma'am," Moretti began, but the rest of his words were cut off as he entered the house.

Thompson signaled to check the windows, and we circled in opposite directions across the back before the radio squawked to life. Immediately, we returned to the door, and I counted us off. Thompson kicked the door in, and I entered first, staying low to the ground with my gun at the ready. Thompson was behind me, and we quickly located the cause of the radio call.

Stephens sat behind his desk, a glass of bourbon next to him and his service piece in his hand. Margaret stood in the corner of the room, screaming at him to stop. Moretti was in front of him, trying to talk him down while Mark and Cooper flanked him from either side, guns at the ready. I couldn't see someone else commit suicide, not today.

"I always knew the past would catch up with me." Stephens finished his drink and waved his gun around as if he were gesturing with a fork and not a loaded weapon. "Things were different then. The job was different. I tried to get out from under this mess, but I couldn't."

"Captain, please," Moretti tried again, "put down the gun. There's no reason for anyone to get hurt."

"C'mon, Dom, you and I both know what they do to cops in prison. And with the things I've done, there's no way I'd walk."

"Honey," Margaret pleaded from the corner of the room, "I don't understand. Stop this foolishness."

"Maggie," he focused on her, "I love you." He looked at me. "Get her out of here."

Cooper gave a slight nod, and I went to Margaret and spoke quietly, trying to encourage her to leave the room. She shrieked and lunged forward. I grabbed her around the waist and hauled her away, kicking and screaming.

"Mrs. Stephens, calm down. Please, ma'am, no one wants to see your husband get hurt. You need to contain yourself, and let us do our job." She continued to fight, so I dragged her into the nearest room and shut the door. Releasing her, I blocked the exit. "I'm sorry." She crumpled to the floor and sobbed. Having ovaries shouldn't mean I had to be the shoulder to cry on, even though part of me would have loved nothing more than to curl up on the floor and cry too. Today really was just one of those days.

The reverb from a single gunshot echoed through the house, and my blood ran cold. I spun around, cracked the door open, and listened. Someone over the radio asked for an update, and a few tactical guys breached the front door.

"Stand down," Moretti ordered, coming out of the room with Stephens in cuffs.

"It was a misfire. Stand down," Cooper repeated the order over the radio, and the tactical teams pulled back.

"Maggie, it'll be okay," Stephens insisted as I held her back while Moretti and Cooper escorted him outside.

"A little help here," I called to Mark and Thompson. Mark did his soothing, calm in a crisis situation thing while Thompson and I looked on unhelpfully. "What happened?" I whispered. The gunshot put us all on edge.

Thompson pulled me out of earshot and said, "Stephens was about to eat his gun when Cooper crossed the room and knocked it from his hand. Moretti lunged and cuffed him."

"Ma'am, we'll have some officers wait with you. Is there anyone you can stay with for a few days? Relatives or friends?" Mark reached for her cordless house phone.

Margaret had a sister an hour away, who was willing to pick her up, so Thompson and I were given sentry duty and instructed to wait and make sure she got out of here in one piece. Half the tactical team was still outside on standby to ensure she wasn't in any danger by an outside assailant.

Thompson and I sat in the living room, watching

Margaret as if she were an exotic animal. We were afraid to get too close, but at the same time, we didn't want to leave her unattended. During our wait, we took her statement and questioned her about Stephens, any recent changes to his behavior and anything else we could think to ask. She had little to offer as she finished a box of tissues. Finally, her sister arrived, and after recording the address, telephone number, and ensuring we could reach her at a moment's notice, we let her go. It had been a long day.

"It's all a day in the life," Thompson said as we turned Stephens' house over to the crime scene techs for evidence collection and drove Mark's SUV back to HQ.

When I arrived at the office, the members of the team were scattered throughout the building. Cooper, Moretti, and Jablonsky were conducting the interview, and the rest of us had paperwork to fill out and incident reports to file. Since I was in another room with Mrs. Stephens at the time, I completed my paperwork quickly.

I found myself hiding in Mark's office, rattled by Ernie's suicide and Stephens' attempt. Ernie's death was on me, but Stephens did this to himself. I didn't have any sympathy for him, but my mind kept wandering back to Ernie. Leaving the sanctity of the office, I went in search of the preliminary report on Ernesto Papadakis.

Ernie had received a text message from a throwaway cell phone that couldn't be traced. The message gave him two options. For bringing these problems upon himself, he could end it all in a comfortable manner or someone would end it for him in a slow, painful way before going after everyone he loved. What choice did he have? Ernie had been naïve, self-aggrandized, and a bit of an idiot, but despite his faults, he seemed kind, funny, and genuinely a good man. It wasn't fair. He hired me to protect his club, and instead, I brought nothing but pain to him.

"Parker," Thompson stood in the doorway of the file room, "I was on my way out and wondered if you wanted to grab a drink." Thompson and I were friendly, but we weren't friends. The offer was uncharacteristic. It must have been because of the shit day we had.

"Thanks, but I'm not leaving anytime soon."

"Okay." He turned to go but reconsidered. "Do you think Mrs. Stephens had any idea who she was married to?"

"Do you think Moretti had any idea who he was reporting to every day? Who all of you were reporting to every day?"

"Touché."

After Thompson left and I reread the Papadakis folder half a dozen times, I left the file room and hid in Mark's office. The men would be working throughout the night to get answers from Stephens. No one was around to tell me what to do, so I stared into nothingness while being plagued by guilt.

Picking up Mark's desk phone, I dialed a number I knew by heart. On the third ring, Martin answered. "Hey, stranger. I'm glad you called." He sounded pleased by the turn of events. If he knew what transpired, he wouldn't be so cheery.

I couldn't think of anything to say since I just wanted to hear his voice, so I listened to the awkward silence fill the void. After a time, I managed to come up with something. "Is Bruiser still earning overtime?"

"Yes, but I don't really," he began, but I interjected.

"The vans outside are still keeping you constant company too, right?"

"Alex, what's going on?"

"Nothing. You know how paranoid I can be sometimes. It helps when everyone else is just as coo-coo for Cocoa Puffs."

"Alex?"

"I'm fine. Are my things still taking up space at your house? Whenever I get a chance, I should probably come by and pick them up. It wasn't my best plan to just run out and not come back to clean up."

"Alex," he tried again.

I was in rambling mode and needed to hang up soon or else the prattling could go on indefinitely. "Okay, well, I should go. Nose to the grindstone and all. If anything," I swallowed, "just be safe. If you see or hear anything strange, call for help, okay?"

"Of course, but–" He was still trying to get a word in edgewise. Honestly, the man needed to learn how to accept defeat gracefully.

"Good night." I hung up and found Mark standing in the doorway. There was no way to determine how long he had been there or what he had witnessed.

His facial expression looked grim, and I got out of his chair, intending to brush past him and go back to the conference room where we had been sequestered for the duration of this case. Instead, he shut his door and took me hostage.

"Do you need to take some time?" he asked.

"I'm fine. What'd you get from Stephens? Did he have anything on Vito? What about Gates?"

"I'm not worried about Stephens at the moment. I'm worried about you."

"I'm fine minus the fact I keep fucking up every single time I turn around."

He looked like he was about to say something, but before he got a chance, Darli knocked on the door and summoned him to the interrogation room. "Go home, get some sleep, get a change of clothes, and I'll see you back here in the morning."

Begrudgingly, I agreed, even though the last thing I wanted was to be alone with my thoughts. The drive to my apartment was uneventful, and I stopped at a fast food place on the way. *Might as well sublimate some of the guilt with fatty fries and greasy burgers,* I reasoned. Unlocking my apartment, I did a quick check for signs of intruders, ate my dinner, and took a shower. I had just changed into sweats when my phone rang. Sullivan informed me the commissioner called, and we were working through the night on Stephens' information.

Throwing on a different outfit, I packed my overnight bag with a couple of days' worth of clothes, some basic toiletries, and makeup. It didn't matter what Mark ordered because I wasn't in the right mindset to be relegated to the solitude of my apartment just to drive myself crazier than I already was.

THIRTY-ONE

"Coffees all around." I entered the conference room with two full drink carriers of espresso-infused beverages. "Thought we could use a boost." There was a round of thanks as everyone took a cup and went back to work. Sullivan handed me a list of names and dates which linked to police corruption cover-ups under Stephens' reign. By the time I finished running names and compiling the facts needed for each of the incidents, it was almost three a.m.

"Why are we doing this?" Webster whined from across the table. "I finished researching my list of names, and they're all dead or long gone. Why does the DA's office even care? Are they planning on serving warrants on people who haven't even stepped foot inside the state for the last decade?"

"It's just more busy work for us," Darli said bitterly. "It's so they can call witnesses and have tons of evidence to use against Stephens in court."

"Anyone find any connection to Antonio Vincenzo?" I asked. No one replied in the affirmative.

"Then why is Stephens singing like a caged bird about everything else? He can't expect to get a plea-bargain with the useless shit he's giving us." Stopping, I had a feeling I knew what he was hoping to accomplish.

"His lawyer's been present all night." Sullivan eased away from the table. "Jablonsky and Cooper have been going at him, trying to determine how he originally got involved, who his partners were, how far back this goes, but he just keeps spouting out more incident reports with either dead, retired, or removed cops."

Stephens figured the best way to stay breathing was to keep his mouth shut on things that really mattered. It was a good plan. Maybe he also surmised, by providing names and events so far in the past, the case would be dismissed due to statute of limitation issues or because it was too difficult to compile the evidence. As it was, the DA was hard-pressed to prosecute the head of a police precinct for fear all closed cases might be reopened.

"I'm getting coffee. Anyone else?" No one took me up on the offer, probably believing they were just minutes away from being sent home to bed. Down the corridor, I measured the coffee and added water to brew a fresh pot. Mark was having a conversation with Agent Cooper when he spotted me standing near the interrogation room.

"You're still here? I told you to go home hours ago."

"Sullivan called. Are you still taking a stab at him?" I gestured at the closed door.

"DA's office wants him at the courthouse first thing in the morning for an arraignment. They want a head start before the media gets wind. Thank god, it's Sunday and no one will be the wiser when Monday morning rolls around."

"You do realize everything he's given us has been

total bullshit, right?"

"Oh yeah. He had a private conference with his attorney and then started listing dozens of names and dates. It's an information overload, so anything important or injurious gets overlooked. It's fucking brilliant."

After pouring the coffee into my mug, I leaned against the wall. "How did some stupid dance clubs getting knocked over turn into a decade long mafia-orchestrated police corruption scandal?"

"Face it, Parker, you're just that good," Mark teased, eyeing me suspiciously again. "Did you talk to the shrink before they reinstated you?"

"Don't start. I'm fine."

"You're just as full of shit as Stephens. This thing is coming to a close. We're federal agents, not the local PD. Vito's off your ass, and whatever's going to happen to the 'ol Cap is going to happen. Not much left for you to concern yourself with. You can relax."

"We still haven't located Gates, and Vito might be gunning for me. So don't start planning my going away party this early."

"Go tell everyone to call it a night and take Cooper up on his offer to sleep in his office. You're ruining the fluffiness of my chair cushion."

*   *   *

A few hours later or what some might consider the next morning, depending on perspective, I was hard at work in the conference room. No one had shown up yet, probably since it had only been four hours since they were sent home. Stephens just left HQ and was being escorted to the courthouse under armed guard. It looked like a parade with the number of agents and police involved in his departure.

Apparently, the light of day didn't scare away the demons lurking in the shadows and instead reinforced the possibility any of the dozens of people Stephens could rat on, Vito included, may think silencing him permanently would be a good idea. With the tranquility in the office, I read the original reports related to the club heists, reviewed my notes on Ernie, and tried to figure out when it all went sideways.

Gates was the missing piece that connected one half of the puzzle to the other. He alone could explain the connection between police corruption and Vito's crime syndicate. Someone, maybe Ernie, Mary, or Gretchen, narced on me to Vito, who in turn called his friends in uniform to solve the pest problem. Since Det. Carl Hoskins had been exploring a similar angle, they probably believed the easiest way to nip the problem in the bud was to kill me and pin the murder on Hoskins, thus solving the police corruption issue while keeping Vito's name out of it. That's probably when Vito called Gates to do some wet work.

Given what a brain trust I was, evidence could have been planted implicating me as the burglar because of the knowledge I possessed. After all, my own office was full of notes on how to break-in and commit the robberies. With twenty-twenty hindsight, choreographing ways to conduct the crimes was a bad idea. Maybe Hoskins and I would have gone down for all of it since a dead woman can't talk, except I escaped Gates and to everyone's surprise didn't immediately surrender to the authorities.

Now, with the failed plan, Ernie was dead. Harrigan had been shot. Hoskins was whisked away to protective custody, maybe to never be heard from again, and I was sitting alone in the conference room from hell. Jen, Nick's wife, had been threatened, Martin had been threatened, and Gates was still out there somewhere. How could Mark be so confident this was over?

My phone rang, and I jumped. Too much caffeine and not enough sleep made me edgy. Answering, I wasn't surprised Martin was calling with a follow-up to yesterday's phone conversation.

"Since I initiated the call today, does that mean I actually get to say more than two words?"

"You just said more than two words."

"Luc wants to know when you plan to analyze some security devices. You've failed to put anything on the books with him."

"It'll get done before deadline."

"Great," he sounded passive-aggressive. "On a similar note, I was wondering when you were planning to see me. We haven't put anything on the books either."

"I'm busy."

"Alex, I know you. You called last night because something was wrong. Something is wrong." He must be psychic because, as soon as he said those three words, the office went abuzz in activity. The few agents in attendance rushed to turn on the television.

"I can't talk about this right now. Pencil me in for Friday night, okay?" I disconnected before he could say another word.

On the screen, a live news feed aired in regards to the murder of a police captain on the steps of the courthouse. As the news reporter droned on, phone calls were made. No one else was injured, but a sniper killed Stephens. So much for testifying. Assistants and secretaries called in Darli, Webster, and Sullivan. I remained frozen, trying to figure out which way was up. I grabbed a hold of one of the assistants and learned Jablonsky was on his way back. At least he'd be here to fill me in.

While I waited for Mark and the other agents to return to HQ, I fielded calls from the boys in major crimes. Heathcliff's suspension was over, and he just reported to work when the news broke over the wire. I gave him a summary of yesterday since Thompson and O'Connell were otherwise occupied and Moretti was at the courthouse with Stephens.

"Just stay there unless you hear something official. I have no idea what's going on. We're federal agents. We don't usually deal with local crimes, and protecting prisoners and witnesses is a job for the Marshal Service." Biting my top lip, I felt like an outsider for the first time since being back in the OIO/FBI building.

"If you need something from us, let me know." Heathcliff hung up as Mark exited the elevator, striding purposefully in my direction.

"ESU's on scene. The locals are canvassing the area for witnesses. Moretti's coordinating the investigation. We're done," Mark declared as I fell into step beside him. He continued toward Director Kendall's office. "The commissioner is cleaning up this mess. Stephens, dirty or not, was one of theirs."

"Any idea who the shooter is?"

"Flip a coin. Maybe it was one of Vito's guys or even Gates."

"But there has to be something more for us to do." I grabbed his shoulder, halting his procession.

"What? The only reason we were asked to investigate this case was because of the police corruption. Last night, Stephens gave us every tidbit of information on the scandal he could muster, or at least that's what we have to believe. The precinct's been cleaned up. Our only solid connection is dead. Sure, Gates, or whatever the hell he's calling himself, is still out there, but he's not a cop. So it's not our problem."

"But–" I didn't know when to step away.

"Back off, Parker. Unless the director says otherwise, everyone else has said to back off. Cooper just got word from the governor. The police commissioner agreed. If we keep on this, more harm than good will be done. You already feel responsible for Papadakis' death, so are you gonna take responsibility for every single crime these lowlifes commit if solid cases start getting overturned because they could have been tainted?"

"No, sir." This wasn't an argument I was going to win, nor one I should be making. The problem was the guy who shot me and Harrigan was still out there somewhere.

THIRTY-TWO

Stephens' murder was being investigated by the locals. Over the course of the next three days, the case was closed or relinquished, whatever the proper terminology was, and Director Kendall wasn't going to intercede. This was out of our hands and beyond our jurisdictional line. It was over. With Stephens gone, the only thing connecting any of the police corruption to Antonio Vincenzo was unsubstantiated claims and hearsay supposition. Of course, I embodied the only living, breathing reminder that not all the loose ends had been cut.

The precinct was back in normal working order, and homicide was knee-deep in evidence and tracking leads. The sniper had been careful to take his shell casings with him. There was nary a hair or print to be found. He was good. My money was on a professional hitman or someone who had a lot of experience being a ghost, namely Gates.

"There's nothing left for you to do here," Cooper said as we boxed up the last of the files. "The bartender is being released from protective custody since there is no case."

"Can you keep some guys on him for a couple more days, just to be on the safe side?"

He analyzed me for a few minutes before acquiescing. "Do you still want a team on Martin? And maybe one to cover you? I can give you through next week if you want."

"Can I dismiss Martin's team myself? My move from the hospital back to my apartment somehow resulted in his place turning into storage."

"Sure, I'll radio them to follow your instructions."

"Good. And I'll be fine. I have my own team, Smith and Wesson."

"Parker, you need to get some sleep and lose the cheesy lines."

Signing the chain of custody form, I picked up the box and went to my car. For all the schlepping back and forth the major crimes boys had done, I thought it was the least I could do to deliver the files to them personally.

Back at the precinct, I received quite a few dirty looks. The loathing and disdain were at the surface for most of the officers I encountered, but luckily, the aggression was well hidden. Dropping the box on Lt. Moretti's desk, I handed him the evidence form to sign. Everything was in triplicate, and I folded my copy to return to Cooper.

Taking a detour, I stopped in the ladies' room to freshen up. Staring at myself in the mirror, I could see the weeks had taken their toll. Dark circles ringed my eyes from lack of sleep. My skin was uncharacteristically pale, and if I took the time to smear blood red lipstick over my mouth, I could be cast in the next big zombie flick as a brain-eating extra. Everyone insisted it was done, but it didn't feel done. Maybe it never would. Sometimes, there wasn't any closure.

I just unlocked my car door and pulled out of the parking lot, heading for HQ, when my phone rang. Glancing at the number, I answered the call to find Cooper on the other end.

"Did I forget something?" I asked.

"We found another box. It was the files IA delivered. Moretti just called and wanted to make sure you didn't leave them in your car. I told him I'd bring them by myself, so if you want to wait, I can collect the custody form and save you from coming all the way back here."

"That's okay. I'm already on my way." Flashing lights were in my rearview mirror. "Dammit, can you believe I'm getting pulled over?" My rhetorical question remained unanswered. "I'll call you back."

Disconnecting, I clicked on my four-ways and slowly pulled onto the shoulder. It shouldn't be dark yet, but the impending thunderstorm had turned the sky black. Any minute, torrential rain would fall. Sighing, I rolled down my window and pulled my credentials from my jacket pocket.

"Ma'am," the officer said. His uniform hat covered most of his face, and his collar was turned up in preparation for the downpour. "Do you know why I stopped you?"

"Not really." Maybe it was for talking on a cell phone while driving, or speeding, failing to signal, or because, right now, the police despised my existence.

"Your taillight is out."

"Damn."

He took my credentials and analyzed them as if they might be fake. "Maybe it's just a loose wire or something. Do you want to step out of the car and take a look?"

Not particularly, but instead, I responded with, "Okay." I opened my car door, and the officer held it as I stepped out.

"Stop right there." His voice changed to something eerily familiar. "Are you carrying a weapon?"

"Of course. I'm on the job," I snapped. He should know the gun was secondary to the badge, and that was when I realized there was something off about this guy. When I turned to get a better look at him, he shoved me against the rear door and confiscated my gun. "What the hell?"

Getting arrested wasn't on my list of things to do, so I resisted the urge to fight back as he frisked me. His hand came to rest on my side where the bullet had been lodged, and he pressed his weight into that tender spot. I jerked in pain, but he held me against the car so I couldn't turn around. The sky opened up, and instantly, I was drenched. Tilting my face toward the ground to keep the rain out of my eyes, I saw white and silver sneakers.

"Why couldn't you have made it this easy back at the club?" He slammed his knee into my side. Instantly, I went down. The pavement was already covered in a layer of water, and stonewalling myself against the pain, I kicked into his shin, causing him to slip and fall to the ground. A gun clattered out of sight.

"Gates," I scurried around the vehicle and narrowly dodged the bullet he fired, "tell me something," I yelled over the roar of the thunder, "did you kill Stephens?"

Moving around the car in search of my fallen gun, I considered the possibility of getting my backup from the glove box, but bullets ripped through the door beside me. I hunkered next to the tire well as he fired a few more shots that tore through the recycled plastic cola bottles auto manufacturers use for the body of cars, but he didn't respond. Instead, he used the lack of traction from the rain to slide over the hood. Now we were facing off, and I was outgunned.

"Did you decide to come after me on your own, or did Vincenzo send you?" I asked, slowly easing myself into a standing position, arms raised in surrender as I back-stepped away from him.

My eyes tried to focus on his trigger finger, but with the nonstop sheets of rain and the dark from the storm, I couldn't see. He remained silent as he approached, preparing to fire again. My shoes lost traction, and I slid off the asphalt and down an embankment.

He skidded down the hill after me, but the flooded, soppy ground was something he didn't expect. He landed face first in the mud and lost hold of his gun. Lunging in the direction it traveled, I scrambled to find it in the puddles. He yanked my leg from behind. Turning, I kicked him in the chest and got to my feet. Where the gun went, I didn't know. But if he knew where it was, he'd have made a move for it by now.

Carefully, we circled one another like two cage fighters, waiting for the other to screw up. The ground was squishy under my feet, and it was challenging to remain upright. He rushed forward, and I sidestepped. Unfortunately, he didn't lose his footing this time.

"I can go all night." His voice was venom. "Why don't you make it easy on yourself? I can make this almost painless."

"Why don't you go fuck yourself?"

"The only thing standing in the way of resuming my life, maybe starting over somewhere new, is you." He pulled something from his belt, and when the lightning lit up the sky, I saw the reflection on the blade. "Mr. Vincenzo's been trying to remove you from the beginning. Then when you proved too difficult to kill, he thought he could turn you. But once again, you just couldn't leave well enough alone. That's why I've been given a second chance to eliminate you. If I fail this time, there will be no peace. Now give up." He lunged, and I jumped backward. On his second approach, his blade caught in my shirt but missed making contact with flesh. The momentum behind the swing was enough to throw my balance off, and we both ended up on the ground.

I landed a few good jabs before he got his hand around my throat and slammed my head into the ground. Mud flew up, temporarily blinding him, and I kicked him in the sternum, sending him sprawling onto his back. Lightning flashed again, and the knife was no longer in his hand. He was up, and I got to my feet, elbowing him in the jaw. On his way down, he grabbed my hair and spun. He landed on top, pinning me below him. Headlights flashed above us from the passing cars, but no one seemed to pay any heed.

I struggled against his bulk. My fingers clawed through the mud for something I could use against him. The knife, the gun, anything. As my hand wrapped around the knife handle, he reached to the left and picked up the gun.

"Federal agent. Drop your weapon." Cooper's voice came from above. Casting a brief look upward, I spotted his car stopped next to mine. He had a flashlight steadied under his gun, pointed directly at Gates. Gates didn't even react; it was as if he didn't hear Cooper. "Drop it." Lightning flashed again, and the echo of the gunshot was drowned out by the roll of thunder.

Lying in the mud, I had to remind myself to breathe. For a moment, I didn't know if I had been shot or if Gates had been shot. Then Gates slumped to the side, and I frantically scurried away.

"No," I screamed. I knocked the gun away and immediately assessed the damage. Cooper was an expert marksman, even in the dark with torrential rain. The side of Gates' skull blew apart where the bullet exited. "He was all we had to get Vito. Goddamn it." I rocked slightly on the ground, unsuccessfully attempting to wipe the mud from my face.

"Parker," Cooper made it down the embankment, "are you okay?"

"He's dead. The only way we could connect Vito to the corruption scandal is dead. We needed him alive. He had the answers. Everything we needed. He had it."

"It wasn't worth the cost."

Cooper watched warily as I got off the ground. I was a little shaky with a few cuts and bruises, but overall, I was okay. The hit to my side would probably require another round of stitches, but it was better than having half my skull blown apart.

Making my way up the embankment, I found my gun underneath the car. Picking it up, I checked the safety and slid it into my holster. "The bastard killed my car." Anger replaced the regret, anxiety, or whatever it was I experienced in the muddy ditch. The side of my car was riddled with bullet holes, and I was pissed off.

"Better it than you." He went to his SUV and returned with a towel. As I attempted to clean up, regular uniformed officers arrived on the scene. The call had gone out over the radio. Cooper talked to the officers and then sat next to me as they assessed the scene and body. "Hey, if you don't get a chance to take a shower, at least the rain will wash off the mud."

"How'd you know?" I fished out the wet and muddy

custody form and attempted to hand it to him as it wilted further in the rain.

"Like I said, I was on my way to the precinct with evidence when I spotted your car. The door was open, and no one was around. It's my job to be observant."

"That was one hell of a shot."

"Sniper training in the Marine Corps. Oorah."

"Semper Fi, Agent Cooper."

*   *   *

The problem with shootings is not only does someone typically end up dead or maimed, but also, there is an astronomical amount of paperwork to go along with it. Thankfully, I hadn't done the shooting. Unfortunately, I had to recount the event numerous times and fill out an incident report regarding my involvement and Cooper's marksmanship.

Luckily, the precinct has an excellent women's locker room, and even though my car was taken away for some purpose unbeknownst to me, my overnight bag was relinquished to my custody. Freshly showered and changed, I swiveled in O'Connell's chair. Mark drove over, probably to make sure I was competent enough to fill out the forms correctly, and the night turned into morning.

Finally dismissed, Mark gave me a ride back to HQ where I had to go through a similar rigmarole, this time solely focused on Gates and the information I obtained prior to his demise. At the moment, everyone was being tight-lipped about divulging any information regarding his identity, who hired him, or if the Vito angle was still sealed tight.

While I waited in the conference room for the I's to be dotted, my phone rang. The fact it even worked after being drenched in mud and rain made me consider sending the manufacturer a thank you note. It was Martin. Somehow, it was already Friday. I wasn't sure where Tuesday or Wednesday went, but my endless work week could probably explain the linear discrepancy. He had a working dinner tonight but insisted I come to his place and make myself comfortable, and he'd get there as soon as he could. Last night's details weren't important to discuss, so I agreed and disconnected.

When Mark and Cooper came back to the conference room to collect me, I was relieved to have a break. It had been a long week, and no one wanted to be in the office for a minute longer.

"We'll hash this out on Monday." Cooper handed back my badge. "Until then, hang on to this."

"Whatever you say." My debt to him had turned me into something resembling civil, perhaps even downright appeasing.

"I'll give you a lift to Marty's," Mark offered as we stepped into the elevator. "Unless you want to stop somewhere on the way, grab a pint, and talk about some things." I let out a sigh, and he caught the tired look on my face. "Another time, then. You look like you could use some R&R."

THIRTY-THREE

After dismissing the surveillance van from Martin's front driveway and sending Mark on his way, I let myself into the house. The place was empty. Walking down the hallway to the second floor guestroom, I found my belongings neatly folded, hung up, or hidden away in drawers. My notes remained on the whiteboard, pressed inconspicuously against the wall. Rosemarie, Martin's cleaning lady, was a godsend. She even got some old stains out of my shirts. I'd have to do something special for her whenever I got the chance.

Packing up the majority of my crap, I considered changing out of my work clothes but didn't have the energy. Instead, I took off my shoes and socks, brushed my hair, untucked my shirt before finding a rag and cleaning supplies in one of my bags, and took my gun into the living room. Sitting on the floor in front of the coffee table, I disassembled my handgun and meticulously cleaned every individual piece. The mud and rain weren't good for the metal.

I heard footsteps downstairs, and Martin's voice. From the sound of things, he was on the phone. He opened the door to the second floor, stopped in the kitchen to drop off a take-out box, and went up the stairs, not noticing my presence. When he came back, he had changed into jeans and a t-shirt. Obviously, his working dinner turned into a working conference call. Getting up, I went straight to him.

He smiled. "Hold on," he said before pressing mute on his phone and putting it on the table. "Sorry, I didn't expect to get back this late." Failing to say a single word, I collapsed into him, and we kissed with more passion than either of us expected. "I'll try to make this quick," he continued as I released him. "I picked up those spicy crab rolls you like in case you didn't eat yet."

"Not hungry, but get back to work. I'm not going anywhere." I returned to the living room to continue cleaning and reassembling my gun.

An hour later, I was sitting on the sofa. My nine millimeter and backup were both clean and reassembled, and I flipped on the television and stared into the abyss of the moving picture box. Martin was still working out details on something involving his R&D department.

"Go find out and call me back," he sounded business polite, but I could tell he was annoyed as he put the phone down and grumbled to himself. He was at the wet bar, probably pouring a scotch, but I couldn't be bothered to turn around. That would require movement, and I had no energy to waste on such trifling matters. The phone rang, and he set a martini glass on the end table beside me. "Gin martini for whatever ails you," he offered, before going back to talk shop.

Picking up the glass, I held it for a few moments

before taking the first tentative sip. Cold, crisp, and just the right amount of bite. Before I knew it, the glass was empty, and I was sprawled out on the couch, lying on my good side. My body propped against the backrest. When his phone calls were concluded for the night, he stood in front of me. I hit mute on the remote and looked up at him.

"Care for another?" he asked.

"No."

"Are you sure? There's plenty of gin, unless you want vodka, tequila, scotch, rum. You name it, I can probably make it."

"One's enough." I hadn't moved from my spot.

"Alex, do you want to go to bed?"

"Not right now. I'm too tired to move."

He stretched out next to me on the couch. His hand went to my hair, and he smoothed it away from my face. "How are you?" His voice was quiet, maybe even cautious.

"Ask me tomorrow."

He let out an uneasy breath, and I knew there were too many unanswered questions for tonight.

"What's going on at work?" I asked.

He launched into a long-winded explanation about how a headhunter stole one of his marketing directors who was lead on some new R&D project. I tried to listen and follow along, but all I got out of the conversation was the basic gist and something about sharks and blood in the water. I must have been dazing off because he nudged me ever so slightly, causing my eyes to focus on his green irises.

"You should get some sleep."

"Maybe in a bit. Right now, I'm too exhausted to sleep. I have to save up some energy first."

"When was the last time you slept?" He ran his thumb across my cheek, close to the black, puffy circles under my eyes. Before I could answer, he clarified his question, "For more than a couple of hours."

"It's been a busy week. A busy couple of weeks."

He remained tight-lipped, even though I knew he would have loved nothing more than to play twenty questions about what was going on with me and the case. We remained facing each other in complete silence for an unknown amount of time. My gaze penetrated the dark green cloth of his t-shirt as he absently played with the bottom buttons of my untucked blouse.

He buttoned and unbuttoned the last three repeatedly until he grew tired of the silence and spoke. "Want to know what my favorite part of your body is?" He sounded far too serious for the question.

"Don't be crass." I smirked and caught his eye.

"Right here."

With the bottom half of my shirt unbuttoned, he flipped the material out of his way as his hand traced a line along my abdomen and came to rest on my side, the pads of his fingers brushing against my newly re-bandaged back. His thumb rested against my ribcage and his pinky and ring finger on the ridge of my pelvic bone.

"Right here, you're all sharp angles. You have this hard, impenetrable shell to keep you safe. Your ribcage guards your heart and well," he tapped his pinky and ring finger against my hipbone and smirked, "even here," he ran his fingers across my obliques and down to my navel, causing my stomach muscles to flex automatically, "you're just this rippling, intimidating, daunting powerhouse." I cocked my eyebrow up in a 'yeah, right' look. "But for anyone you let get this close," he leaned in closer, so the space between us no longer existed, "your skin," his hand rubbed along my side, "is so soft and pure. It's the perfect physical representation of you."

I met his eyes, surprised by the tender sentiment. "I'm going to say something now, but I don't want you to react. Don't say a word." Swallowing, I gave him a content smile. "I love you." It was the first time either of us had said as much, and he brightened and opened his mouth to respond. Cutting him off, I kissed him. "Don't say anything. Please. Not now. Not tonight." I buried my face against his chest, and he wrapped his arms around me. The light from the television faded away as I drifted off to sleep.

When I opened my eyes, the room was bathed in a warm, golden glow which had replaced the harsh flickering from the television. Martin lay on his stomach, facing away, his arm hanging off the couch. Taking a deep breath, I assessed my own mental faculties. Even though it was a tired saying, sleep really did make everything better. But all was not right with Alexis Parker. I knew it'd be a long time before I could move past all the imbecilic things I had done that culminated in the bodies piling up. Right now, it would be best to focus on making it through today.

Time passed, and Martin stirred. Carefully, he sat up. Stretching and shaking some feeling back into his arm. Raising an eyebrow, I watched him for a few minutes.

"It's a strange turn of events for you to be awake before me." He made an exaggerated stretch. "Last night, I thought it would be a romantic gesture to sleep on the couch with you." His shoulder made a popping sound, and he winced. "Clearly, in practice, not such a good idea."

"And people wonder why chivalry is dead."

"How are you doing today?"

"That is the twenty million dollar question, isn't it?"

It wasn't an answer, but I couldn't provide one. Frankly, I didn't have one.

He stood up and turned off the television. As I sat up, a chorus of pops and cracks sounded as every vertebrae decided to elicit its own protest to last night's sleeping arrangement.

"I'm putting my foot down," he sounded serious, but his eyes were mocking. "We are not sleeping on the couch again. I have more bedrooms in this house than are necessary, and they all have beds. Sleeping on couches is what one does in their twenties after getting wasted at a friend's party. We're both a decade too old for this."

"But," I began to protest.

And he whispered in my ear, "Sweetheart, I hate to point this out, but you're thirty." I growled at him as he went to the stairs. "Now, I'm going for a nice long jog to work these kinks and aches out."

Realizing I sent the surveillance van home last night, I decided it best to keep an eye out. Being cautious couldn't hurt. "Would you mind some company?"

"I'd love it." He was determined to use the L-word as often as possible just to annoy me. So far, he was off to a good start.

Changing into some running gear, I met him in the kitchen a half hour later, and we set out for a leisurely jog. Unfortunately, I was determined to beat some sense into myself, and since he could be just as competitive, it didn't take long until we were both panting. Completing a two mile course, we rounded the corner of the house and spotted Mark leaning against his SUV.

"Marty," Mark greeted as we approached.

"Jabber," Martin gave him a cursory glance, "are you coming inside?"

"No. I just wanted to talk to Alex for a minute."

Martin nodded and left us alone.

"You're up bright and early."

"Why are you here?" I asked since Mark normally didn't just show up.

"Look, I know you. The fact that you're here and not at home and out running, instead of lying in bed in the dark, is a good thing."

"Did you want to slap me in the face with any more veiled compliments, or is that just a new interrogation technique you're working on?"

"Normally, I'm the first one to tell you to return to work. You know how often I try to get you to come back full-time at the OIO or throw consulting work your way." He looked away. "Kendall's going to offer you a new case on Monday. He thinks everything you've done has been stellar, but you shouldn't take it."

It felt as if I had just been punched in the stomach. The possibility I would take a job after everything was minuscule, but being instructed not to do so was painful. It made my failures obvious, and I didn't handle failure well. "Fine, I won't."

"Alex, hear me out."

"Why? I know what happened. Every cause has an effect, and I caused a lot of things to go horribly wrong." I blinked, refusing to cry in front of him. "It's fine. I shouldn't be anywhere near this."

"Goddammit. You always twist my words. Yes, you screwed up, but who's to say how things would have played out if you turned yourself in or didn't go farther into the Vincenzo black hole. The reason I'm telling you to stay away is because you need time to make peace with this. How many times have you been shot, not counting when you've had a vest on? This makes once. You've been afraid to go home. And to top it off, Thursday night you were almost killed. You need some space away from the job to get your perspective back. If you were a full-time agent, there would be mandated counseling sessions and desk duty or leave, but since you aren't, I'm telling you to take it."

"Are you done?"

"Are you?"

"For now." Staring at the ground, I waited a few seconds before asking, "Do you want to come in for breakfast?" It was a peace offering, even though I didn't want to make peace. Then again, I didn't know what I wanted.

"That's okay. But if you need someone to listen, give me a call. If not, I'll see you Monday to finalize everything."

"Yep." I opened the door and went inside, locking it behind me. I took a moment to regroup and listened to the sound of the speed bag being pummeled. The constant tap, tap, tapping. With my nerves solidified, and my emotions in check, I went deeper into the first floor and watched as Martin made the bag dance. "You're getting good at that."

He stopped and smiled, completely ruining his timing. I put on the extra set of hand wraps as he got back in the groove on the speed bag. Since he made hitting things seem like so much fun, how could I resist? I was taking out my aggression on the heavy bag when he grew tired of his routine.

"I'll steady the bag for you if you promise not to kick me in the head." He smirked. "Either head."

"I'll do my best." He got behind the bag as I ran different combinations.

"What did Mark want?" he asked, and I delivered a particularly strong kick to the bag. "Maybe I shouldn't ask."

"It's fine," I huffed, finding new vehemence. "He doesn't want me back at the OIO. I need to walk away, gain perspective."

"Alex," he interjected as I whaled on the bag, "is he out of line?"

Delivering a final roundhouse kick, I stepped back and began unwrapping my hands. "No. This last case," I tugged on the wrap with my teeth to get it loose, "I've lost myself, and I'm not sure how to find my way back."

THIRTY-FOUR

Dressed for a casual Friday, even if it was Saturday, I sat in my MT office, working on a report for Guillot. Martin provided a ride to the building since he needed to work out some R&D issues, and I was behind on my job. When we arrived, I performed a visual check of the equipment, ran a few tests and drills, and made the weekend security personnel utterly miserable. The report I was drafting was expected to be in Guillot's hands Monday morning so we could go over it and fine tune before the afternoon meeting.

At least my corporate job was less emotionally taxing. Completing the first draft, I remembered I didn't assess any of the technological security implementations or protocols. "Dammit," I swore, saving the file. Picking up the phone, I dialed IT's extension and waited for an answer. After speaking to the tech for a few hours and running numerous diagnostic checks, I concluded the second part of my assignment.

"Are you almost ready to leave?" Martin asked from

the doorway.

"I have to finish this report, but if you're in a rush, I can hail a cab home."

He tossed a look down the hallway to make sure we were alone. "I'll wait. After sleeping on the couch last night, I'm not letting you get away that easily." He returned to his office.

After typing the rest of the report, e-mailing it to Guillot, and printing a couple of copies, I knocked on his door.

*　　*　　*

Although Martin offered the option for a pleasant evening out, I wanted nothing more than to be in seclusion. While he cooked dinner, I went into the guestroom and boxed up everything I had on Vito and copied the information from the whiteboard before erasing it. These were my records and the only leverage or insurance I had against him. There was no way I was going to shred it until I knew the threat was removed.

When Martin announced dinner was ready, I dutifully reported to the kitchen, and we ate in almost total silence. "Thanks for giving me space," I said, clearing the table. "There are probably a lot of things you want to know, but I appreciate that you aren't pushing. This stupid robbery got blown so far out of proportion I can't even be sure what happened."

He shut off the sink and waited for me to continue. Instead, I stared at the different colored specks on the granite countertop. "Help me out," he said gently, "am I supposed to ask a question now or keep my mouth shut?"

"Someone died, and it's my fault. How do I come back from something like that again? The last time," I sighed and shook my head, "I lost who I was and who I wanted to be. I tried to forge a new path and start over to avoid the destruction, and here I am in the exact same place. None of it mattered because it keeps happening."

"Alexis, even if you're not sure where you are or how to get back, I know where you are. You're right here." Before he could continue, the phone rang. He hit ignore and studied me. His voicemail dinged.

Letting out a sigh, I turned to the half-cleared table. "Go ahead, it's important."

"So is this," he insisted, but I brushed past him to wash the plates. He gave up and went to his office, phone in hand.

After I finished cleaning the kitchen, I found myself lying atop the guestroom bed. My mind had given up, and I stared at the wall. There were no thoughts, only a numbing stillness. The creak of the floorboards sounded through the room, but I couldn't be bothered to turn around. All I could do was stare at the wall. An outside presence invaded the nothingness I had managed to achieve as Martin spoke from the doorway.

"Alex," he said cautiously.

"What?"

"I've never seen you like this before. Correction, the last time I saw you this still was when you were under heavy sedation." He paused uncertainly. "Do you want to talk about it? We were interrupted earlier." As I turned to face the door, he entered the room and sat on the bed.

"No. Maybe thanking you was premature."

"So you don't want to talk?"

"No."

"Fine. I asked politely, so now it's my turn to talk. You can listen." Before I could open my mouth in protest, he started on his list of rehearsed talking points. "First, I love you too. It wasn't fair you got to say it last night and then forced me to remain silent. It's not every day monumental occasions like this happen. I would like to participate instead of being told to hold my tongue."

"Martin," I tried to cut in, but he shushed me.

"Second, I don't want to beat a dead horse, so I'll spare you the reiteration. We don't have to talk about what happened. It's fine. You can stick it inside a neat little box in the corner of your psyche and add it to the source of your nightmares. By the way, I hate waking up to the sound of your screams, or gasping for breath, or trembling." He smirked. "There are much better reasons for screaming, gasping, and trembling to take place in the bedroom, but there hasn't been very much of that going on recently. Right now, the bad is definitely outweighing the good."

"Martin," I attempted to interrupt.

"No, sorry. You declined on talking, so it's still my turn. Where was I? Let's see, second, screaming in bed, right. Just so you know, I like waking up to you in the morning, preferably without the nightmares and drama, but I'll take what I can get." He nodded to himself. "You spend a lot of time worrying about me. About something happening to me. I mean, my god, the double teaming on the surveillance vans, a little ridiculous, wouldn't you agree? Especially when there's security at the office and Bruiser here all the time. But somehow, you fail to see the reality of the situation." I waited for him to go on since attempting to derail the conversation wasn't getting me anywhere. "More than likely, something will happen to you before it happens to me."

"Stop."

"Hmm, no." He looked defiant. "You're not

bulletproof. You aren't invincible, and sometimes, things get out of control. People are nutso."

"You would know."

He smiled, amused by my assessment. "Yes, actually I do know. Even though I make my own enemies, most of the time, they aren't taking shots at me. Knock on wood."

"What do you want?"

"Nothing." He brushed his fingers through my hair. "I just wanted you to have a more accurate perspective on the way things are. You said you lost yourself and couldn't find your way back. It's important you know that I have no intention of letting you stay lost. You keep me grounded, and even though you're a hell of a lot of work, I need you here."

"But," I began again, but he still wouldn't shut up.

"Look, stay here and wallow or be depressed or whatever it is you're doing that involves staring holes through the wall. You walk around with the weight of the world on your shoulders, and it probably gets too heavy every now and again. But tomorrow, I plan on being an even bigger pain in the ass than today. Leaving you alone too long with your thoughts tends to have detrimental effects on our relationship, and since you just took things to the next level without so much as consulting me," he grinned, "then I'm not letting you sabotage this progress completely on your own. That should involve all-out warfare, and you know I love a fight."

I reached for his hand. "Make sure you keep your left elbow up. If it's a fight you want, you have to work on your technique. When you were hitting the bag earlier, you dropped your elbow."

He lifted my hand and kissed my knuckles. "You know where I'll be if you decide you don't want to be alone any longer."

Spending some quality time in the darkened room, staring into empty space and slowly processing and turning things over and over again in my mind, I had my fill of the pity party. Someone much wiser once made the point that claiming someone's death as your own fault was robbing them of their final act. It was the last thing they could claim. Ernesto Papadakis killed himself, and it was his. The dominos were set to fall, and eventually, they would have toppled, even if I didn't blunder into the first one, knocking it over. The same could be said for Captain Stephens and Gates, or whatever the assailant's headstone would read.

I found myself outside Martin's bedroom, and I knocked on the doorjamb. He glanced up. The lamp on his nightstand was on, and he was reading expense reports.

"It's about damn time." His voice was husky as he got out of bed and met me in the middle of the room. "I was beginning to think you wanted to be alone all night."

"So you just enjoy reading in nothing but your boxer briefs?" I inquired as his hands ran gently along my back, and he pulled me close for a kiss.

"Depends on what I'm reading." His lips traveled downward, and I pressed myself against him. That night there was plenty of screaming and gasping, but it wasn't because of any nightmares.

THIRTY-FIVE

Rubbing my eyes, I flipped back two pages in my notes and created a new bullet point on my presentation. Martin's kitchen table had turned into my current workspace as I reviewed the procedures in place versus the updated version I planned to suggest to Guillot. Perhaps I had been guilty of procrastinating in the past but never to such an extreme.

"I thought you finished your report yesterday." Martin entered the kitchen and put my cell phone on the table. "Nick called this morning while you were in the shower. He said your car is DOA."

"What?"

"You tell me. I'm just the messenger boy."

"You answered my phone?"

"The proper response is thanks. To which I shall respond, you're welcome." He pulled up a chair and attempted to read the laptop screen from an angle. "Also, I've taken the liberty to invite him and Jenny out for dinner tonight. Try to be pleasant."

"Martin," stalling, I swallowed and leaned back, "thanks, but I don't feel like going out."

"Dear Atlas, the world will crush you if you let it." He commandeered the laptop and flipped my notes around, typing out the information in a more corporate appropriate fashion, complete with charts, graphs, and estimates. "Y'know," he continued to type, "it did occur to me that your car wasn't here, but for some reason, I didn't bother to ask where it was." He kept tinkering with the computer, not bothering to make eye contact. "Nick said the larger caliber bullets went through the shell, and a few ended up lodged in your engine block."

"I knew I should have splurged on a bulletproof vest for my car."

"Did you take it out for target practice and go a little crazy at the range?" His voice held a hint of an edge. "Or maybe you forgot to set the emergency brake when you parked on a hill and shooting it was the only way you could think to get it to stop. It gives new meaning to the phrase *stop or I'll shoot*."

"Is shooting you the only way to get you to stop?" I challenged. He finished a page of notes, hit save, and shut the lid, waiting expectantly for my elaboration. "Thursday night, the shooter from the club made an appearance. It's fine."

"All right." He squinted. "This is where I'm supposed to stop pushing and wait for you to come around, right?"

"Well, you didn't complain about it last night, now did you?"

"Your womanly wiles will always work against me, but I need to know if this particular assignment is finished. Alexis, I'm not going to sneak out of the office like a goddamn spy to come home and find you with a bullet in your back. I can't do it again."

"Neither can I." We sat in silence as a feeling of resolve settled around me. "I don't think I can do this anymore. This job. Before, I had nothing to lose, but now." I turned and studied the refrigerator door as if I had never seen one.

"That wasn't an ultimatum," he said softly. "I'm not asking you to walk away or choose. But I can't help you play fugitive again. That's all I'm trying to say."

Picking at the corner of my notepad, I continued. "Too many bridges were burned. Maybe they were already on fire before I got there, but I crossed them instead of finding a way to put them out. Mark wants me gone. The PD is licking its wounds, and no one there is going to hire a consultant anytime soon. A year and a half ago, I walked off the job because my team got killed." I looked at him. "And even though my reinstatement was only temporary, the body count is climbing again."

"It's a linchpin. One event leads to infinite more. You weren't even supposed to be working anything official. Face it, the universe won't let you stop, even if you want to." He attempted to be encouraging, but the possibility of no escape was disheartening.

"Then I'll have to find a way to make it stop." I slid the laptop over and opened the lid. "Would you mind asking the O'Connells to come here for dinner instead? We can order out, my treat."

"Okay." He rubbed my shoulders before leaving the kitchen, so I could review my notes and finalize my presentation.

* * *

"And then I said, Officer, I'd like to file a stalking complaint." Jen was in the middle of an anecdote involving one of her first dates with Nick.

Martin seemed enthralled. He was good at that. Listening to people, showing genuine interest, exuding joviality, it was impressive. Either that, or maybe he just liked having someone else to interact with who wasn't all doom and gloom.

"Excuse me." I pushed away from the table. "I'm getting a refill. Anyone else?" Martin shook his head as Jenny continued her story, and Nick offered to assist.

"Is it safe to leave the two of them alone?" Nick asked as we huddled together near the wet bar. "I mean, he is *really* charming. I'd be willing to let him in my pants, and I'm a proud heterosexual male."

"Easy, tiger." Pouring a glass of sparkling water, I spun a few liquor bottles around, but nothing struck my fancy. "I have a bone to pick with you. Where the hell do you come off telling him about my car? Don't you have to keep your mouth shut about ongoing investigations?"

"What's to investigate? We know how your car got decommissioned. Oh," his voice dropped, "you didn't tell him."

Rolling my eyes, I turned my back to the dining room. "Is everything straightened out now?"

"The LT has stacks of paperwork to file and review, and the commissioner's been to the precinct more times than I can recall, but it looks like it's resolved. The jackasses who were busy posturing themselves as superior for not ratting on their own have fallen back in line. We were right. They were wrong. Sometimes, it's just that simple."

"Nick, here's the thing." I glanced into the dining room. Martin and Jen were still lost in conversation as Martin fidgeted with a bottle of champagne he apparently pulled from the fridge. "Antonio Vincenzo."

"I heard."

"There's nothing solid, and I don't think I should pursue. He's too well-connected. Too many guys, too much shit. But if he decides I'm a loose end, I want to make sure there's some insurance in play."

He considered my options for a few seconds. "Okay, I'd say your best bet is a safe deposit box and instructions to a lawyer. If shit happens, have the files released to me, or Jablonsky, or both. You know we'd..." The rest of his words were drowned out as the champagne cork loudly popped, and I found myself on the floor. "Shit, Parker." He grabbed my arm, yelled something about wanting to see the patio, and pushed me out the back door. "It was a champagne bottle."

"I know." I trembled and gulped down air. The open space was exactly what I needed because inside was suffocating. "I've lost my edge."

"Once bit, twice shy." We sat on the ground. "Most of us don't get shot on the job. It's obviously a possibility, but statistically, it doesn't happen that frequently. On top of that, you normally don't face off against the same asshole a second time. You just need to take some time."

"So I've been told." My adrenal glands were confused as fuck, but at least I was reasonably calm again, even if my hands had yet to stop shaking.

He chuckled at a memory. "Picture me as a rookie. I was on foot patrol, and my partner and I were walking through an unsavory area. There was a drive-by. No one was seriously injured, but I was grazed. It was maybe six stitches. Nothing really, but two days later, I'm at a pizzeria, sitting at a table with my buddies. Car backfires, and I dove under the table, flipped the whole thing on its side. Owner kicked us out. But the worst part was I ruined a perfectly good pizza."

I let out a snort. "At least I didn't ruin our dinner."

"Exactly." He stood and offered his hand. "You're going to be fine. Accept it and move on."

As we came back inside, Martin and Jen watched us through the window. "Don't let us interrupt your romantic interlude," she teased. "We did come here to switch partners for an evening, right?"

"Don't even," Nick warned, "especially with the way you've been flirting all night, missy."

Martin was uncharacteristically quiet as his two guests playfully bickered. Instead, his eyes were on me, asking the unspoken question if I was okay. Nodding slightly, I went to get a glass of water from the kitchen. Martin followed and wrapped his arms around my waist.

"I thought you might have been planning an escape, and Nick was your getaway driver."

"Your cars are faster, so you're my first choice for getaway driver, but he was helping me work through some things."

"Then let's give the man a medal."

Turning around in his arms, I placed a chaste kiss on his lips and put my palms against his chest to make sure the tremors abated.

"See, I told you they make a cute couple," Jen's voice traveled into the kitchen, and my face flushed. Nick looked embarrassed for me, but I caught Martin's beaming, satisfied smile.

"It takes one to know one," I quipped. Nick was too manly to blush, but underneath that masculine exterior, I was positive he was beet red.

The rest of the evening was uneventful. Just a pair of couples having dinner and drinks while socializing. It was normal. Maybe normal was exactly what I needed. After they left, I snuggled with Martin on the couch.

"You were right," I murmured.

"What? Sorry, I couldn't hear you. Would you mind speaking up?"

"Jerk." Elbowing him in the ribs, I asked, "Is this how most of the world manages to stay sane?"

"Wow. First, I was right, and now I'm sane. Today must be my lucky day." I stretched out, considering everything I had to do tomorrow. "Just so you know, there is no amount of flattery that will convince me to sleep on this sofa again," he said.

"Your loss."

"Actually, it's not." He laughed and got up to clean the kitchen. By the time he was done, I was buried in documents for the debrief at the Bureau and the updated security protocols for Guillot. Tomorrow would be another tiresome day.

THIRTY-SIX

"I am thoroughly amazed." Guillot smiled. "Now all that's left is to pass the specs on to the Board and see if we get approval." He clicked a few keys on his computer, and copies of my presentation notes were sent to the printer in the assistant's office to be properly collated and stapled. "You're giving the presentation this afternoon, Ms. Parker."

"Sir," public speaking was not my thing, "I'm not sure I'm qualified. I can devise protocol and review schematics, but this isn't what I do." I gestured around the office as if to explain I wasn't a corporate bigwig.

"Nonsense," he picked up his copy of my presentation, "this is precisely what you're capable of doing. You set this in motion. This is you." He tossed the hefty stack of papers on his desk between us. "Did you write the report, run the diagnostics listed, approve cost-efficient equipment changes, and devise a uniform method for countless emergency situations?"

"Yes."

"Then you will be fine. Explain the benefits of these recommendations, how the uniform protocols will work, the timetable for implementing the training and transformation needed, and after that, I will handle the more corporate side of things."

"Yes, sir." There was no point in arguing with my supervisor. He had a point, and presentations were a natural part of corporate work. "What time is the meeting?"

"Four." It was only eleven. "Things have been busier than normal with the new R&D line and our short staff issues. Everyone's agreed to stay late so we can finalize phase one of our new security initiative."

"I will be back in time," I promised. "There's an unrelated matter I need to resolve."

He seemed curious, perhaps wanting some elaboration. But his phone rang, and he waved me away.

In the next five hours, I needed to attend the debriefing and close the door on my OIO job, get back to the MT building, and prepare to explain the dozens of security changes intended to take place. Too bad Agent Navate couldn't pretend to be my clone again today.

Rushing through lunchtime traffic, Marcal dropped me off in front of the OIO building before presumably taking the car to the bottom level to park. Having no car, I was getting spoiled by Martin's town car and driver. At least having a chauffeur allowed extra time to review and practice my presentation on the way back to the MT building.

"Parker," Cooper called as I exited the elevator, "we're meeting in my office."

"Agent Parker," Director Kendall sat behind Cooper's desk, "I wasn't sure you were going to make it today. Although this case is out of our hands and the commissioner and the PD have closed the file, there are still quite a few things to discuss."

Only Cooper and I encountered Eli Gates, and Kendall wanted every detail dissected. Unfortunately, our connection between the police corruption scandal and our organized crime boss blew apart at the same moment as Gates' skull. Shutting my eyes and pressing my lips together, I heard the shot, the moment of disbelief, and then Gates falling to the side. When I opened my eyes again, Kendall was observing me with a mix of fascination and worry.

"There was nothing else Agent Cooper could have done, and nothing would have saved Gates. He was dead before he hit the ground." I readjusted in the chair, wanting to pace the room since the cramped office was making me claustrophobic.

"Before he died, did he say anything?" Kendall asked.

The things Gates said weren't going to lead anywhere, and going after Vincenzo would lead to a bloodbath. This case was already littered with too many bodies. There was no reason blood needed to paint the streets.

"I didn't hear anything," Cooper said. "I identified myself, told him to drop the weapon, but he failed to comply. He didn't say a word." Cooper looked at me. From his vantage point and the torrent, he wouldn't have been able to hear anything.

"All he admitted to was trying to kill me at the club. I can't remember his exact words." It was enough of the truth.

Kendall closed the folder and picked up a pen, spinning it between his two fingers. "The corruption case is closed thanks to the information Captain Stephens provided, but he's gone now. The shooter,

Eli Gates, is dead. There's nothing left for the FBI to investigate."

"Yes, sir," Cooper and I responded in unison.

"Good job, Agent Cooper." Kendall shook Cooper's hand as he relinquished the desk chair. "Agent Parker, walk me upstairs. We have other matters to discuss." Kendall strode out of the office, and I nodded my thanks to Cooper before following the director down the hallway.

"I'm not in the business of sticking my nose where it doesn't belong, especially when it'll get my men into hot water," Kendall said as the elevator ascended. "However," the word hung in the air with substantial magnitude, "nothing has been resolved."

"Gates is dead."

"What did he say?" The floor numbers illuminated as we approached the OIO level.

"Officially, he identified himself as the man who impersonated a police detective in the club, the man who put a bullet in me."

"And unofficially?"

"Sir," my tone had an edge, "you declared the case closed. The only thing that matters is the official version."

"Bullshit, Parker. Bull fucking shit." The doors opened, and Kendall led the way to his office. Mark was waiting inside, and the three of us stood in an awkward silence for a time. "Nothing leaves this room."

"Okay," I forced air into my lungs, "Gates was working for Antonio Vincenzo. Vincenzo pulled him out of retirement to clean up the mess. Gates said he couldn't disappear again until it was resolved."

"You were the last mess to clean up?" Mark asked.

"Maybe Gates was the mess to clean up. He was the only connection. Even if he killed me, the investigation wouldn't have stopped there. Vito must have planned to end Gates somewhere down the line," I rationalized.

"Do you think he'll come after you, Parker?" Kendall inquired.

"What for?" The silence in the room was deafening. "The case is closed. The corrupt cops were stopped."

"Except they weren't," Mark added grimly. "Yeah, the trail of breadcrumbs led to Stephens, and Stephens connected us to a shitload of former corrupt officers and to Gates. But the two-man team on the phony surveillance tapes from the clubs, the two guys who bludgeoned Ernie Papadakis, the police cruiser outside, and the calls to the FBI and IAD about the corruption scandal have never been explained."

"It's because none of it has to do with police corruption," I said quietly. "Every single one of those things has to do with Vincenzo. It must be the same two guys, and they're probably his enforcers." I thought about his muscle, Tony and Carmine, and felt certain they were the two unidentified men. I slammed my palm on top of the desk in frustration. "And we can't fucking touch him because the only person who could corroborate any of it got his skull blasted into the mud." I turned away from the two men, and stood by the wall, hitting it with the side of my fist.

"Parker," Kendall implored, "do you want to keep digging into this?"

I spun around and saw the look in Mark's eyes, screaming at me to walk away. "My reinstatement was to last for the duration of the police corruption scandal. The case is closed, sir." I pulled out my credentials and shoved them across his desk. "I'm a civilian now." Out of the corner of my eye, I saw Mark nodding.

"If he comes at you, get your ass back in this office first thing. You hear me?" Kendall warned.

"Yes." Intentionally leaving out the sir, I opened the door. "Director, I hope our paths never cross again."

"Parker," he began, but I shook my head.

"I've said it before, but I won't do this again. The stakes are too high now."

He watched as I walked out of the office and down the hall. As I waited for the elevator doors to close, Mark left Kendall's office. His smile was bittersweet. It was just another day at the OIO.

*   *   *

My presentation had gone swimmingly. Guillot took over when my portion of the meeting concluded, and by seven, the Board agreed to all of the implementations. MT was set to move on to phase two of unifying security measures throughout its branches. Sitting in my MT office, I looked at the calendar, devising a workable timetable of events.

"Would you care to go out for drinks?" Guillot asked from my doorway. "It is customary. Because of you, Mademoiselle, everything was approved and is moving forward."

"Thank you, but no." I looked up from the pages. The bottom of a bottle wouldn't solve my problems, and tomorrow, I'd just have a hangover to add to the list.

Luc's tone shifted to something less familiar. "The next phase will require a more substantial advisory influence. I was hoping you could help locate a permanent, full-time consultant to assist in streamlining the process. HR is compiling a list of applicants, and they should be ready for review by Wednesday afternoon. If you could shortlist them by

Friday, I'd greatly appreciate it."

"As you wish, Mr. Guillot." He bid me good night and headed for the elevator. After the characteristic ding and the sound of the doors closing, my cell phone rang. It was Martin. I answered and stared out the door as his wall of windows changed from opaque to clear.

"Are you finished for the day? I'd like to go home, but since we're riding together, we need to devise a plan to sneak out of the office so no one will suspect a thing. Maybe I should go down to the twelfth floor and take the freight elevator to the back door. What do you think?" he asked.

"Why don't you leave first, and I'll meet you in the garage in a couple of minutes?"

He raised an eyebrow questioningly, assessing my expression before agreeing and hanging up. He got out of his chair, turned off his computer, and threw the file from his desk into the locked cabinet before picking up his jacket and leaving his office.

"Good night, Ms. Parker."

"Night, Mr. Martin," I responded automatically. The floor was empty, and I let out a sigh. Nothing was settled, and yet people who were living ordinary lives could be overjoyed when a business meeting went well. Why wasn't I one of those people? Could I be one of those people?

Meeting Martin in the garage, I waited for Marcal to open the back door, and I slid into the car. Martin put up the privacy screen and turned to me. "Excellent presentation. If I didn't know you better, I would have thought you were actually focused and committed to the concepts you were expounding. What happened at the OIO today?"

"It's too soon to tell." I had no way of knowing what was still to come.

He didn't like my answer, but he didn't have any desire to pick a fight. "You look like you need a hug."

"I think you're right."

THIRTY-SEVEN

My life was in shambles. At least that's what it felt like as I stared at the textured ceiling in Martin's bedroom. He left for work hours ago, and I still felt lost. Ever since getting shot at Infinity, I was emotionally compromised. It's what led to running scared, getting in bed with Vito, and making all the other blunders. Even now, with Gates dead and my reinstatement revoked, nothing was resolved. O'Connell was right. I needed to establish an insurance policy. My cell phone buzzed across the nightstand, and I answered for lack of anything better to do.

"We need to talk," Mark said without so much as a greeting. "Are you still at Marty's or have you decided you're a big girl who can stay by herself?"

"Martin's." I didn't have any fight left.

"Okay, I'll be there in an hour." After we disconnected, I got out of bed and made myself presentable. Mark arrived with a box of files, a bag of donuts, and a couple of lattes. "Peace offering," he said.

"Right." I picked up a cup and found a chocolate crème in the bag. "What'd you want to talk about?"

"What really happened over the past month." He popped the lid off the other coffee and shoved a donut in his mouth as he emptied the contents of the box. "This is off the books. Kendall doesn't know about any of this. Neither does Cooper or Moretti."

"I know what off the books means." Going into the guestroom, I returned with my own file box full of information, and we got to work.

A couple of hours later, our theory was reasonably sound, backed by as much evidence and coincidence as possible, and there weren't many unanswered questions left. "Obviously, there's a certain degree of supposition," I said, "but do you want to hear how the whole thing played out?"

"Go ahead. I've been waiting for your rendition for a few weeks."

"Antonio Vincenzo planned the heists in his clubs, probably for the insurance money. He was using one set of funds to bankroll another, and the two ends failed to meet in the middle. The clubs and liquor supplier were supposed to be cleaning his money, not bankrupting him, but staging a few burglaries would get him back in the black."

"The financial information from the first two club heists corroborates this theory," Mark pointed out, holding up a few sheets of paper.

"Heist zero, the one at the Odessa, was a practice run. My guess is Stephens was in Vincenzo's pocket, probably had been ever since he and his two rookie pals started moonlighting as enforcers for the mob. So the Odessa heist was swept under the rug by the captain, but because Detective Hoskins is actually good at his job, he didn't let it go. Vincenzo must have believed burglary division would discover his money laundering and feared that would lead them to the corrupt cops he was paying off, so he calls in a tip to IAD and the FBI as distraction tactics. If the investigation pointed to a crooked cop, no one would look too closely at the seemingly unconnected club owners. Vito must have planned to set up a cop all along."

"Why do you think Papadakis hired you if they wanted this to be kept quiet?" Mark loved blowing holes in my theories.

"Ernie didn't know. For all intents and purposes, he was an idiot. He honestly feared his club would be next, and his silent partners didn't tell him otherwise. I should have told him otherwise."

"Alexis." He tried to derail my pity party, but I was already back on track.

"Tuesday, the day after Ernie hired me, I showed up to the club unannounced and spotted him in the back room, talking to one of Vito's guys. That must have been when he told them who I was."

"Which would explain why the outside cameras were disconnected on Thursday."

"The day I began waitress training."

"Damn," Mark rubbed his chin, "that had to be when Vincenzo planned everything. What better way to distract from the actual crime and turn the situation into a bumbled burglary turned murder, especially when he could blame the burglary cops for it. Do you think it was Stephens or Vito who sent Gates after you?"

"I don't know. The police cruiser parked outside might have been supplied to Gates by Stephens. Stephens could have gotten it to him while bypassing the paperwork, and then when we tried to track it through precinct records, nothing substantial ever surfaced. So who knows?"

"Stephens was willing to eat his gun over this. That tells me one thing. He was in too deep. He must have been Vito's lapdog." We sat silently, letting the facts and theory sink in. "The photos the FBI got of Hoskins on scene were faked, and the missing shell casings and bullet from Harrigan could have disappeared because of Stephens."

"Mark, do you think there are more dirty cops out there? I mean we're talking forensic evidence being tampered with, photos faked, files altered. Do you honestly believe one guy could have done it alone?"

"Keep in mind, that one guy was in charge of telling everyone else what to do. I'm sure he didn't act alone, but there's a fine line between following orders and being an accomplice. But that pretty much concludes everything, doesn't it? It explains how Stephens and Vito were connected, why you were attacked, and how Vito found a way to manipulate you."

"The son of a bitch played me like a well-worn violin, and every move I made was exactly what he wanted." I circled the kitchen. "He tries to paint me as a murderer, and I run. He pops up after my meeting with Gretchen and offers to make my problems go away, and I cave."

"You were desperate. Desperate times and all."

"Except I didn't get desperate enough until Martin was threatened. He's my Achilles heel, and Vito had no problem taking advantage."

"I'm not sure that was Vito. The cops who threatened Marty were the same guys who went after O'Connell's wife. Spinelli and Perkins are overzealous cops who were mentored by some hardcore old-schoolers. But I'm sure Stephens encouraged the idea. Maybe he reported it to Vito."

"Either way, the first thing I did was run to that

motherfucker." I contemplated slamming my head into the table, but it would be too on the nose to try to knock some sense into my thick skull. "I wanted assurances, protection."

"And now you need protection from the slimeball." He sighed. "Why the hell didn't you come to me? How could you let this get blown so far out of proportion?" He had been harping on the same point since the moment I called him that eventful Sunday morning.

"It's me. Before this thing even started, I had this ominous feeling. I wasn't sleeping, barely eating. And then things just happened. Unexpected things."

"You have instincts. You always did." He looked glum. "So why did you throw rational thought out the window?"

"I didn't realize it until it was too late." His look of disappointment was back, and it made my stomach ache. "Before things get worse, I'm taking measures to stop them."

"What are you planning?"

"Mutually assured destruction."

He listened as I went over my idea to confront Vito, threaten him with evidence and blackmail, and guarantee if anything happened to me or anyone I knew, he would be destroyed. "You're insane," Mark watched as I separated my files into three piles, "but it might just be enough to keep the devil at bay."

"It's all I can do. If not," I swallowed, "well, it is just a matter of time, isn't it?"

"Alex," he touched my arm, "I won't let anything happen to you. Get the information together, get your safety deposit boxes, your lawyer's instructions, and whatever else you need in order. But this is preventative. It will never be used."

"You can't promise that. I got myself into this mess, and I'll get myself out, one way or another."

"Under no circumstances are you meeting Vincenzo alone. Do you understand?"

"Yes."

"Good." He turned at the sound of footsteps from the floor below. "Does Marty know any of this?"

"No, and he's not going to."

Mark nodded and lifted the two boxes from the table and took them back to the guestroom. Apparently, we were in agreement about something.

*　　*　　*

The next day, I rode with Martin to work, where I picked up the HR files, and hailed a cab. I needed to accomplish a lot of things. I opened two separate safe deposit boxes in two different banks, each containing exact copies of the evidence I had on Vincenzo. Honestly, it wasn't much, but it was better than nothing. A third set of files was delivered to the law offices of Ackerman, Baze, and Clancy. They were a high-powered firm which Martin used for his personal matters and which I had brief dealings. Handing off a sealed manila envelope with precise instructions to junior partner Jack Fletcher, I knew my instructions would be followed to the letter. They weren't to open or divulge any of the information unless they received proof of my demise.

My next stop was a rental car agency where I picked up a set of wheels. My insurance adjuster assessed my vehicle, but I didn't think bullet holes were covered in my policy. At some point, I'd have to go car shopping and move back into my apartment, but tonight didn't feel like the night to do it. By the time I made it back to Martin's, he was already home, preparing dinner.

"I'm glad you're still here." He uncorked a bottle of

wine. "There was the possibility you disappeared once again."

"If I did disappear, would you look for me?" It was a strange question to ask, and he put the wine down, puzzled.

"Wouldn't you be at your apartment or work?"

"It was just a question. Y'know, maybe I'll grow tired of this lavishness and disappear in the night, never to be heard from again."

"You wouldn't do that."

I looked away and rummaged in my bag for one of the two safety deposit box keys. "I might. You never know." It was meant to sound teasing, but it didn't. "In case that ever happens, I want you to have this." I handed him the key. "But only if I'm gone without a trace, don't open it otherwise. Do you understand?"

"Alex, what aren't you telling me?"

"Nothing." I examined the floor. "Everything's fine. It's just one of those stupid what ifs. If I remember correctly, you have your own doomsday scheme hatched too, and since I love you, it's about time I give you a heads-up in advance, unlike the emergency contact thing."

He didn't look convinced, but he picked up the key, opened his wall safe, and stuck it inside. "I never want to know what that key will unlock."

I didn't want to either. Plastering a grin on my face, I added, "Dammit, that's where the safe was this entire time. Crap."

"Sorry," he enveloped me in his arms, "I don't have any other trips planned." Before he released his grip, he whispered in my ear, "I don't want anything to happen to you. Alex, promise me everything will be okay."

"Nothing's going to happen. Not if I can help it." I clung to him a moment longer than I should, unable to come up with a joking remark. This were serious, and only time would tell what the future might hold.

THIRTY-EIGHT

The next day, I loaded the rental car with the majority of my belongings and set out for my apartment. The place had been abandoned for so long that everything was covered in a light layer of dust. After filling the washing machine, I did a quick once-over of all the surfaces, vacuumed at breakneck speed, and packed an overnight bag. I decided to stay at Martin's for the rest of the week. My apartment felt eerily quiet, as if someone would jump out of the closet at any moment.

Before I made it to my front door, my phone rang. It was Heathcliff, wanting to know where I was. After divulging the information, he asked that I sit tight and he and O'Connell would be over soon. What the boys in blue wanted, I didn't know, but I waited patiently in my apartment, beginning the preliminary assessment for a permanent MT security consultant to begin phase two.

"Jablonsky called yesterday," O'Connell said as he and Heathcliff entered my apartment. "Although we were going to draw straws to decide who was going with you to visit Vincenzo, we thought you might prefer having some say in the matter."

"You can't do this. You have Jen to think about. I'll be fine."

"Told you that's what she would say," Heathcliff piped up. "Which is why I'm going with you."

"Derek, you don't need to get involved. It'll be fine."

"If it's going to be fine, then there's no reason why you can't have some backup."

"But," I tried again, "this is my mess."

"And I would rather not have to worry about Hoskins being proven right, ever. Jablonsky said you needed some support, and since he'll be outside in case things sour, you need someone inside, preferably not a federal agent."

"But you're a cop."

"Don't worry, I remember a thing or two from my undercover days in narcotics. When do you want to do this?"

I chuckled at my own procrastination attempt. "I've been afraid if I do it, it'll be game over. But the longer I wait, same possible result, right?"

O'Connell caught my eye and gave me an encouraging look. "Is everything in place?"

"As of yesterday. Mark and Martin have the safety deposit keys, and the lawyers have the rest. It can be pieced together if it comes down to it."

"Then get it done tonight," Nick suggested. "Heathcliff, go home and make yourself hoodlum appropriate, and Parker, call Jablonsky and get him to meet us here. The two of us will sit outside and keep an eye out."

"Nick." I was prepared to argue.

"I'm staying outside. He'll never see me, and if he does, it'll be the last thing he ever sees," O'Connell said.

Heathcliff left, and we planned to reconvene at my place at seven before going to the bar where I had spoken twice to Vito. Third time's a charm, I hope.

* * *

The dive bar was busier tonight than it had been, but the drunks were too far gone to pay any attention. Vito's muscle was another story.

"I'm here to see your boss. And no, I'm not going to make an appointment."

Heathcliff stood a few steps behind me, dark glasses, tattered leather jacket, dark wash jeans with chains hanging from the pocket, and just enough scruff to pass for either a badass or a bum. With his outfit, I was leaning more toward badass.

"Tony," Vito called from the back booth, sounding bored, "let her through." He eyed me suspiciously. "Still wearing a wire?"

"I'm off the job." I wasn't in the mood for any of this.

"Who's your friend?" Tony approached Heathcliff, who barely moved, but somehow, Tony ended up on the ground, clutching his stomach.

"I'm her entourage," Heathcliff snarled.

I didn't know about Vito or his goons, but I wouldn't have wanted to mess with Heathcliff or run into him in a dark alley. Vito laughed and gestured to the other side of the booth, and Heathcliff sat at a stool, next to the seat Tony pulled himself onto.

"Ms. Parker, it's no longer agent?" Vito inquired.

"No, it isn't. I told you before, the corruption case was it. By the way, Gates is dead in case you wanted to send your condolences or maybe buy some flowers for his grave."

"It had to be done. He failed, and he became a

liability." Vito spoke with no remorse or emotion. "Maybe you did return that favor, after all."

"Mr. Vincenzo, I want to make one thing clear. As far as I'm concerned, you don't exist. I've never met you, spoken to you, or have otherwise encountered you. I'm not a federal agent, and any investigations into you and yours aren't on me." I leaned back in the booth. "That being said, I have what we're going to call assurances in place. Just because I'm not gunning for you doesn't mean I don't have enough to bury you." The words came out as a cold sneer.

"Ah, I see." He smiled, enjoying the dramatics. "Maybe you're afraid of me."

"The only thing I'm afraid of is the lineup at the courthouse to take you down. There could be a traffic jam, car accidents, pedestrians run over in the haste. It'd be a shame if any innocents got hurt because of you. So that's why I'm offering you the opportunity to avoid this." Placing my palms on the table, I leaned forward. "If anything happens to me, every shred of evidence I have on you, your clubs, your involvement with Gates and Stephens, drugs, guns, girls, it's all going to become public knowledge. Numerous copies will be sent to every high-ranking member of every alphabet soup agency you can think of. There will be no escape and no chance you'll get away, not again."

"Why haven't you already done it? Bluffing really isn't becoming on you."

"Quid pro quo," I responded, unfazed. "You gave me Gates. He was all I wanted, and he's dead. No reason for more bloodshed. As long as I stay breathing, you're protected. If I get hit by a bus while crossing the street, you go down. If you send Tony to put two in the back of my head, you go down. If anyone I've ever met or talked to gets killed, you go down. Do I make myself clear?"

"Crystal." His expression was unreadable.

Maybe I'd get up and he'd drop me, or I would walk out of here and never cross paths with him again. It was too soon to tell.

"Good." I stood up. "It was nice doing business with you. Our interaction is now concluded. If I see you or any of your guys around, well, you get my point." I narrowed my eyes at him, turned, and walked to the front door. Heathcliff followed, and we left the bar. Not wanting to tip off our mafia don of the backup outside, we walked a few blocks in the dark until Mark met us, and we climbed into the car.

"How'd it go?" Mark asked from the driver's seat as he meandered through traffic with no set destination in mind.

"Heathcliff's a total badass." I smiled. "What did you do to poor Tony?"

Heathcliff waggled his eyebrows and grinned.

"Will he leave you alone?" O'Connell asked, turning around in the seat to face me.

"I have no idea." Mark continued driving, ending up outside my apartment building. "Thanks for helping out, Nick," I said, getting out of the car.

O'Connell nodded. "Take it easy, Parker."

Mark and Heathcliff followed me upstairs, perhaps afraid Vito immediately sent someone to take care of the current problem.

"Here's the thing," Mark said once I unlocked my door, "you're getting out of here. Go back to Marty's and keep your head down."

"Mark, it's fine. I'm capable of taking care of myself."

"Is Marty?" he challenged. "Here's how I see it. Vito has three options, do as you say, come for you, or come for someone you care about. I'll stay here and make sure no one shows up."

"I'll hang around too," Heathcliff chimed in. Looking at the two of them, I knew they planned this out previously. "Plus, two's company and three's a crowd, so you should take off."

"I know you, Alexis." Mark took charge. "You can't relax unless you know he's safe, even though he has a full-time bodyguard, so go over there and keep an eye out. We'll keep an eye out here, and if nothing happens in the next few days, then you can come home. And we'll assume the whole thing with Vito is done."

"Actually, I'm pretty sure it's over," Heathcliff interjected. "He's not stupid. Plus, your entourage is a scary son of a bitch. He can't be sure you don't have hard evidence against him, and he won't risk it. Trust me, I know the type."

Having no basis for an argument, and in all actuality finding Mark and Heathcliff's points particularly compelling, I gave them each a hug, threw a few more days' worth of clothes into my overnight bag, and picked up the MT files.

"Y'know, you guys are the best."

"She says that to everyone," Mark mocked. "Take my car," he handed me the keys, "and stay out of trouble."

THIRTY-NINE

Friday afternoon, I was seated in Guillot's office with a small stack of the remaining applicant files. Guillot read the cover pages and asked questions about each potential new consultant's past experience. After spending over a dozen hours researching the applicants, I discovered no one had any real corporate know-how. Most were former military, former law enforcement, or pencil pushers with a degree in business management. Since I wasn't entirely sure what Guillot wanted, other than someone who could do my job full-time, I left a healthy mix in the pile. He flipped to the last applicant and looked surprised.

"Mademoiselle, you could have just asked to be considered for the job. But what about your other commitments?"

"Mr. Guillot," I took a deep breath, "my previous career is in the past. It's time I accept this and move on. My consulting with the police department and OIO is officially over."

"What about unofficially? Ever since I met you, Ms.

Parker, you have been working with law enforcement, first in Paris, then the police department here, and most recently, the FBI, if I'm not mistaken."

"If you're afraid I'm not qualified or too flighty, then by all means, please disregard my application. But I can assure you, I will work solely for Martin Technologies until the completion of the second phase of the security overhaul."

He swiveled his chair around and picked up the stack of applications and tossed them into the 'to be shredded' trashcan. "Let's inform HR, have the paperwork signed, and you will be made a full-time MT employee for a temporary duration."

"Thank you, sir. You will not regret this."

"I know I won't." He tilted his head to the side and appraised me. "I just hope you don't."

"No, I definitely won't. This is an incredible opportunity, and one that I would be insane to let slip away." At least, that's what I kept telling myself. Working full-time for MT was the excuse I needed to remain away from actual crime. My other consulting work was now too dangerous, and the risk wasn't worth it.

After signing the papers requiring a full-time six-month agreement and a non-compete clause, I was given a set of four, three-inch binders full of materials to begin reviewing. No rest for the wicked. Although I had the next two weeks to read it before the initial reports had to be turned in, it still seemed daunting. But it wasn't like I had anything else to do. This was my life now.

*　　*　　*

That night, I sat in Martin's living room, trying to find something worthwhile to watch on television while I waited for him to come home. He had a dinner meeting, and I was surprised he made it home before ten. He came up the stairs and gave me a curious glance before taking off his jacket and undoing his tie.

"I would open a bottle of champagne, but O'Connell's not here to whisk you outside when the cork pops," he joked, but it was too soon for that to be funny. "I found a new recipe for lemon drop martinis if you're game."

"Okay." I wasn't sure what prompted the champagne comment or why he was catering to me, but I was amenable.

He brought two drinks over and handed me one. "To you." He clinked his glass against mine before I could even comprehend what was going on. He took a sip. Following suit, I shut off the tv and focused on him. "You could have mentioned you were planning to work at my company full-time."

"I didn't want any preferential treatment. But perhaps I should have asked if it was okay, which it really isn't since we're involved."

"It doesn't bother me if it doesn't bother you. Guillot was overjoyed, but he didn't understand what would make you give up your other career, as he put it. Frankly, I don't understand that either."

"Yes, you do." I put the glass on the end table. "I told you I can't do it anymore. There's too much at stake."

"Is it because of me?" Maybe he had caught my paranoia.

"No," and it wasn't, "it's because of the mess I made. This is how it gets swept under the rug and how I can make sure it stays there."

*　　*　　*

That night, we were lying in bed. Martin had gotten a nightlight, which was a compromise but worked well. He didn't have to deal with the harsh glare from the bathroom light being left on, but I wasn't stuck in total darkness.

"I was thinking," he nudged me with his shoulder to make sure I was paying attention, "you should move in."

"What? Are you out of your mind?"

"No. We're practically living together now. You've been here for the last week, and you were here for a few weeks before that. Hell, when we first met, you moved in for a month."

"Okay, first of all, that was a job. Second, the couple weeks I was here, you weren't here for half of that. And third," he cut off my argument with a kiss, "that was a cheap tactic. But third, I'm going home Sunday. We've only been dating three months, and it's too soon. Honestly, I'm not sure I'm the cohabitation type. Plus, I'm an MT employee now. So there is no way I'm shacking up with the boss."

"Luc asked you to move in too?"

"Last time I checked, Guillot's name wasn't monogrammed on the door."

"At least think about it. I like having you here. It's nice coming home and knowing I'll get to see you or wake up in the morning to find you next to me."

"Martin."

"It's okay. You'll come around eventually. As soon as you figure out how to work the coffeemaker, you'll be begging to move in."

"And if I don't?"

"Sleepovers are fun too."

*　　*　　*

Sunday, I went home and kicked Mark and Heathcliff out of my apartment after making sure they hadn't raided my panty drawer or done any irreparable damage. It was nice to be home, and although it might have been premature to conclude Vito wasn't gunning for me, I felt certain of this fact. After I washed the sheets, it was time to get everything on track for my new job.

Monday, I showed up at the MT building, fielded calls and e-mails on the upcoming changes, and acted like the corporate security professional I aspired to be. During the course of the day, my insurance company called with the news that a check was in the mail. It wouldn't cover a new car, but it'd work as a nice down payment. In the meantime, my rental suited me just fine. My office space in the strip mall was put back together, courtesy of O'Connell and Thompson, and I was free to check in whenever I wanted.

Martin remained professional at work, and although our offices were twenty feet apart, I barely saw him during the day. He was busy, and so was I. It was a relief to know things could work out. Now all that was left was to convince myself this was for the best. This was a job I should have. It was something I was capable of handling, without risking my own neck or dealing with murderers or murder victims. Now, if only it could keep my mind busy.

By the end of the day, my thoughts drifted to Sam Harrigan and Carl Hoskins. O'Connell called to check up and offer his congratulations on the job promotion, even if it wasn't a promotion so much as an exit strategy. He said Hoskins was back at work and things in the precinct were completely back to normal. Until a new captain could be appointed, Moretti was acting as interim captain. Although he bitched and moaned every chance he got, O'Connell was certain he loved it.

Mark called my cell phone when I was on my way home to make sure nothing out of the ordinary happened. He was taking his promise to keep me safe very seriously, and I appreciated it more than he would ever know. When I asked about Harrigan, he said the Marshal Service remanded him from custody since there was no case left to be made. He was back in his apartment, and his prognosis, while not stellar, was better than being inside a box six feet under. Mark suggested I remain distant, but he'd check on him when he got a chance.

Two days later, Mark reported Dawn, Sam's ex-girlfriend, moved in and was taking care of him. Maybe tragedy could bring people closer together. It might have had that effect on my relationships.

By the weekend, my new life was well underway. The federal agent in me was still lost, and I didn't think she would ever return. It was okay. She didn't need to come back. People ended up dead when she was running the show, even though the small voice in the back of my mind insisted more people could end up dead without her. It was a thought that could be tabled and dealt with in six months.

For now, Vito was off my back, I had a full-time job, and the biggest dilemma was if Martin was spending the weekend at my place, or I was spending the weekend at his. To be on the safe side, I decided to stay with him for the next few weekends to come, which he took to be some great victory toward his goal of having me move in, but that wasn't happening until there was a cold day in hell. I was a commitment-phobe and having taken a semi-permanent full-time job was the most committed I could agree to be at any one time.

DON'T MISS RACING THROUGH DARKNESS, THE NEXT ACTION-PACKED ALEXIS PARKER NOVEL. NOW AVAILABLE IN PAPERBACK AND AS AN E-BOOK

Suspicion of Murder

ABOUT THE AUTHOR

G.K. Parks is the author of the Alexis Parker series. The first novel, *Likely Suspects,* tells the story of Alexis' first foray into the private sector.

G.K. Parks received a Bachelor of Arts in Political Science and History. After spending some time in law school, G.K. changed paths and earned a Master of Arts in Criminology/Criminal Justice. Now all that education is being put to use creating a fictional world based upon years of study and research.

You can find additional information on G.K. Parks and the Alexis Parker series by visiting our website at
www.alexisparkerseries.com

Made in the USA
Las Vegas, NV
26 October 2021

33108939R00194